# THE FIRE WALKERS

### A
### WALKER
NOVEL

## SHELLEY N. GREENE

## THIS BOOK, MY FIRST PUBLISHED WORK, IS DEDICATED TO THE FOLLOWING:

To my sister, Jen - In every time of challenge you've been there to hold my hand. There are no words to say how grateful I am for your love and encouragement.
*I would not be here if not for you.*

To my mother, my guiding light and spiritual compass.
*Your strength inspires me.*

To my dad, for the phone messages that touch my heart.
*I love you, too.*

To Sarah Allan, my critique partner, sounding board, co-conspirator, and trusted friend.
*Thank you for always being there. The Oxford Comma is for you.*

To the Maryland Romance Writers for their support and wisdom, with special thanks to Amy Villalba for showing me the indie ropes.
*I finally got published. Chocolate for EVERYONE.*

To the organizations and volunteers that care and provide for rescued animals.
*Many thanks for the unsung work that you do.*

And to K, for covering me in hay.
*The adventure began with you.*

# CHAPTER 1

Kelly felt like hell. Before she could rank being sick in a strange place on the *Life Sucks* scale, her body cut the thought off, curling her into a ball. No position quelled the nausea, so she tried *still*. Maybe *still* would work.

The idea was vetoed with a loud gurgle.

A panoramic view of the ceiling went by as her head lolled, her hot temple pressing into the chilly cement. The cool surface soothed her, but the shift in weight did little to ease her stomach.

*These are the moments people make promises to the universe.* And hers was that she was never going to drink again. *Ever.*

Kelly dragged in a breath, holding it as she felt the bile return.

Building a tolerance to alcohol had never landed her flat on her back before. She struggled to remember the last time she'd gotten drunk, her foggy brain moving slow.

*Grandma Patty's special eggnog. Christmas of last year.*

The only side effect then was that Kelly had fallen face-first into bed and slept like a rock. Not like now. Not light-headed and—her vision flickered like a bad light bulb, threatening to go out.

*Stay awake. Don't...sleep.*

She propped herself up and managed to roll into a hunched-up lump, her churning belly approving of the pose. With the help of the wall, Kelly got the first real look at her surroundings. Recessed lights shone blue from behind a grill of steel, bathing the room in the soft glow of projected squares. Painted cinder blocks framed a brightly colored fabric cot bolted to the wall. Next to it was a stainless steel toilet with no lid.

The bucket sitting next to her must have been left by the officer who'd carried her in.

The guy she'd gotten sick on.

Her cheeks flamed with embarrassment. She was thankful her mother couldn't see her now. She sniffed and wiped at her face, staring down at her once decorative party clothes. The nicest stuff that she owned, now the material looked morbid in the filtered light. Smeared with dirt and clingy with perspiration, the sight of it made her long for a wet washcloth. Her mind flashed back to when she'd put them on earlier, the progression of events stuck on replay in her spinning brain: a late night in the biology office, the party invitation, stark shadows cast by leaping flames...

She squeezed her eyes shut.

The recollections were out to haunt her, trees illuminated by the fire's glow. The faces—blurred, distorted faces—popped in and out of her vision, their features washed out by the white light. The dancing bonfire was branded into her brain along with its horrifying soundtrack, laughter morphing into screams of pain. She trailed her numb fingertips down her forearm, the skin puckering into gooseflesh at the contact.

She needed the touch, even if she hated the cold. Any feeling was an anchor to the present, a call away from the repulsive. Her head swayed on her spine, vertigo skirting the edges of her consciousness, ready to take over.

"Carson!"

Kelly's eyes peeled wide as she shot upright. The booming voice resounded from the hallway, a few doors—cells—down.

"It's my medication, Carson! God damn it..." The voice trailed off, the tone warped, as if the yeller were impaired in some way.

Heart thundering in her ears, Kelly sidled up to the far wall, coming as close as she dared to the bars. Concealing herself in the pocket of shadow next to the door, she listened.

"Medication. Uh-huh." The raspy male reply came from a distance, followed by the faint scrape of a chair moving across linoleum.

"What do you want us to do about the girl in ten?"

Kelly stretched her ears to catch all the words.

"She was at the scene, intoxicated. No ID, we couldn't tell if she was underage. There were over a hundred people there, all fleeing like rats when we pulled up," Raspy answered.

Kelly sent a hand south to pat her pockets.

*Nothing.* No car keys, no license. Her purse missing.

*Oh, no.*

"And the fire?"

"Took us two hours to get it under control," a new voice interjected, a bass voice.

Kelly went still.

"I heard that the kids you took to the hospital were in bad shape."

Kelly angled forward, the light from the hall spilling onto her face, blinding her. She waited, ears straining to hear him speak again.

"The doctors were planning skin grafts when I left," Deep Voice responded, granting her wish. "They also confirmed that cocaine was found in the boys' blood. They're working with us, but wanted to disclose the news to the parents in private." The man's timbre sounded troubled, worried.

The conversation hit a dead end. Kelly frowned.

"More than just a kegger?"

"Yeah," Deep Voice replied.

Her anxiety wound back up again as Kelly leaned her head against the bars, the rails parting her bangs.

"Given the hallucinations, I'd guess it was a concentrated dose—"

"Have you questioned the girl?" Deep Voice cut Raspy off, agitated.

Kelly's head popped back, the sudden movement making the nausea return and her upper body weave.

*They have to be talking about someone else.*

Her brain scrolled over everything, and came back with static.

*Drugs at the party?* She hadn't seen any—she wouldn't...

The horrible screams from the bonfire echoed in her head.

"Not yet. She was trashed when we brought her in and she's still pretty disoriented. At last rounds she was still puking in her cell. She got Eric good," Raspy said. Someone chuckled. Kelly heard a man grumble something incomprehensible in response.

"We have to wait for her to come around before we can talk to her," Raspy continued, his serious tone returning. "But from the look of her, I'd say she's going to have one helluva hangover."

Kelly knocked the bucket away and pushed off the floor, grabbing the bars for balance. She teetered on her feet and summoning what energy she had, called out into the hall.

"Officer... *Officer?*"

The murmur of conversation came to an immediate stop. A hushed exchange was followed by the sound of a metal gate rolling open. A tall uniformed figure appeared on the other side of the bars. A policeman emerged with a cool face, dark hair, and shadowed eyes. He stared down at Kelly with rigid concern, his deep features paired with a no-bullshit gaze that made Kelly feel transparent.

She gripped the bars with one hand, holding herself steady as she stared up at him. She didn't know what she was being held for but she was of age to drink, and she didn't commit a crime.

"I want to go home now." Kelly's words came out in a low gust, the truth her only defense. The cop's forehead wrinkled, his hardened expression unwavering, as if he were trying to read her mind.

"One minute," he replied roughly, walking away. Kelly matched the man to the second voice she'd heard as he disappeared down the hall.

When he was out of sight, she listened carefully to another low exchange, a hurried jumble of all three men. She struggled to isolate the deep voice, but the conversation occurred so quickly that she didn't hear it—or the verdict.

*Crap.*

Before she could fear the worst the officer reappeared, a large set of keys in his hand. The clang of metal on metal rang out as the door slid open.

"Hey! Why does *she* get to go?" the loud inmate started in.

The officer ignored the stream of objections as he escorted Kelly down the hall. The stark lights of the corridor were a painful change from the dimness of the cell, making spots appear in Kelly's vision.

At a second set of bars the officer stood like a shadow, keeping to one side as he unlocked the heavy metal grate. He led her down another short hall that funneled open into a wide space divided by partitions. Peppered with desks and bordered with bulletin-covered corkboards; paper notices, and alerts stared back at her from short-walled cubicles.

Warm in comparison to her meat locker of a holding cell, Kelly paused, relishing the change. Relocking the gate, the officer eyed her, seeming to affirm that she could operate without a bucket.

A rustling noise lured Kelly around the corner where an older uniformed officer sat behind a desk littered with papers. A second man dressed in civilian clothes anchored the corner, one hip propped against the edge of the desk, his back facing her.

The leaning man won the bid for Kelly's attention instantly, his masculine profile like that of a marble statue on display. A muscular torso flowed into long arms the man had crossed over his chest. The black, short-sleeved shirt he had on was a second skin across the width of his broad shoulders, the cotton hanging loosely over the valley between his shoulder blades and at the gather of his narrow waist. Kelly's stare traveled over his bare forearms, the tanned expanse of skin covering a load of taut, striated lines. Moving down, his lower half was a complimentary match to his lean upper body, his physique filling out the dark jeans that clothed him down to his black boots.

*Whoa. What department is this guy from?*

Kelly didn't immediately see a badge or the holster of a gun, but what looked like a lightweight, black jacket was draped over his propped up thigh. He must not have seen her come in because he hadn't moved.

Feeling her cheeks heat at the man-praisal she was performing on a complete stranger, Kelly tried to remember that for all she knew she was currently under arrest, and that didn't make it a good time to scope out a date.

Besides, men that gorgeous required seduction, along with a load of equal feminine appeal. Kelly had a deficit in both areas, which was the reason why she avoided the lady-killer types. Men who were stocked with looks more often than not lacked in brains, and she wanted more than just a chiseled face. Plus the players tended to live for the chase, ready to run after the conquest.

Kelly's head throbbed at the reminder.

"She's feeling better," her officer announced, ushering her into the office.

The leaning man stood up in a flash, and Kelly's brain got wiped clean of all rational thought as she caught sight of his face.

The man's features were stunningly symmetrical—from his bright eyes, the prominent line of his jaw; everything parallel right down to the masculine bow of his full, chapped mouth. His cobalt irises scanned her with enough consideration to rival airport security.

"She's requested to go," her officer said.

Blue Eyes stopped short, looking to the officer and then over to Raspy. The expressions on their faces hinted that sending her home wasn't what they had in mind.

Kelly picked up on the body language, her sense of rebellion kicking in. "I lost my license but I'm over twenty-one..."

Blue Eyes' head swiveled back to her, apprehension staining his face.

"We'd like to speak to you before we release you, if you don't mind," the officer responded, glancing tentatively between the other two men.

"We need to make a call first," Raspy barked, picking up the phone.

"Excuse me—what am I being held for?"

Three sets of eyes snapped to her, putting Kelly on the defense.

They couldn't keep her there if they weren't going to charge her with anything—she'd learned that much from the cop shows.

"Nothing," the officer answered as the seated officer punched out a phone number, and spoke in some kind of police jargon to the person on the other end of the line.

"Okay," Kelly murmured, unease flicking through her.

Why did they need her to stay?

Staring down at her un-cuffed wrists, she tried to focus. She had the right to ask questions, but kindergarten inquiries seemed the only thing she could channel through her clouded brain. She flipped her eyes up, honing in on the one thing that helped her concentrate.

Blue Eyes hovered next to the desk with his head bowed, closely monitoring the phone conversation. His short hair lay in tousled layers, a nest of brown like it hadn't seen a comb in a while. The kind of stuff a girlfriend would be eager to touch, complete with a matching five o'clock shadow trailing the square line of his jaw.

Kelly pulled her gaze away, searching for some distraction.

*Endorphins triggered by pretty face.*

Her eyes snuck back to the man.

She watched him, tracing his cheeks and the lines of his eyes, a warm tingle going through her. She couldn't pinpoint what made him so appealing; all of his parts together simply made an attractive whole. The word "handsome" pinged through her head right as the man's eyes shifted back to her, the orbs changing, hardening into dark blue hollows.

"We've got the go ahead," the desk cop announced, hanging up the phone.

"I'm going to go," Blue Eyes said. Kelly's head snapped his direction, the motion making her head pound. "Call me with the results, okay?"

The syllables washed through her, soothing her ears and setting off an unraveling sensation in the center of her chest. Kelly's thoughts shot off like fireworks.

*Blue Eyes is Deep Voice.*

He pushed off from the desk, rolling his spine to his full height. Shoving his arms through the sleeves of his jacket, flashing a patch of an insignia.

Arson Division.

He nodded to the officer at the desk.

"You heading out already?" her escorting officer asked, sounding perplexed.

"I'm going back to the hospital. Call me with a status," Blue Eyes instructed.

Kelly sank back on her heels, her escort leaning forward in response. Exhaling, she placed a firm hand on her stomach.

She didn't feel sick anymore, just crazy. She didn't need a bucket for crazy.

Blue Eyes zeroed in on the movement, face cast in a pained expression before turning to leave. Kelly watched him walk away; the irrational fear of never seeing him again throwing her into a strange panic.

Turning, the officer waited for her at the entrance to a small room. Kelly's gaze drifted past him into the compact space that awaited her before settling on the guy's uniform. The brass pin on his breast pocket spelled the name *Carson* in copperplate letters.

"When you're ready," Officer Carson said softly.

Kelly nodded, glancing back to the empty spot where Blue Eyes had stood.

She turned and walked into the room, a pair of footsteps following her. She jumped as the door clicked closed behind them.

Officer Carson's benevolent tone came through the void, the gentle lilt of words resounding in her ears. "We're just going to ask you a few questions, Miss Monroe. Then you're free to go."

# CHAPTER 2

Aidan opened the door of the farm's break room, the space bringing back images of hot summers and horseback rides. He passed the bank of cubbies used by the volunteers, the staff having assigned lockers inside another building, if memory served. New kitchen appliances sparkled in contrast to the aged countertops, old meeting new. The furniture seemed much smaller now, or maybe he was taller. A giant, circular center table took up a good portion of the place, the legend of King Arthur rekindling in Aidan's mind, making him smile. He'd imagined himself as one of Arthur's knights; guardians that wielded swords and rode horses. Back before they drove squad cars and wore badges.

He breathed in deeply.

Even the smell—that combination of leather, hay, and mud, transported him into an earlier time.

Aidan exhaled and stowed his nostalgia. He walked over to the corner door, his eyes meeting with a polished metal plate displaying the name *Sophia Hammond*.

*Not here to say hi.* He stuck the mantra on his frontal lobe like a Post-it, and knocked loudly.

"It's open," a familiar voice called back. Aidan let himself in.

Sophie's massive oak desk dominated the stretch of floor, the monster more like an antique from a British manor than furniture from a farmhouse. Paired with the tufted leather chair she was sitting in, any outsider could tell that she was a CEO regardless of the rustic setting. An equine queen.

"Aidan Wright!" she exclaimed. Her eyes crinkled, her face lighting up at the sight of him. In a flash of brown hair and blue jeans, she crossed the room in two steps, mouth stretched into her trademark, mega-watt smile. She hugged him tightly, wrapping Aidan in warmth and comfort.

"Hi, Sophie," he murmured into her hair, catching the natural perfume of her shampoo mixed with the aroma of horse feed. He had to smile.

Sophie had never been the typical grandmother type.

Even though Aidan stood a good head taller, it was clear who was doing the holding when Sophie hugged; her petite arms were firm, but never crushing, powerful for a woman who was almost sixty. Aidan figured there had to be something rejuvenating in forty years of working in a profession that she loved.

*The fountain of youth.*

"It is *so* good to see you," she said, taking a step back to lean against her desk, her shrewd gaze inspecting him for changes. "My Lord, it's been a while."

Pulling back, the woman's dark eyes captured his face, her warm hands reeling him down to plant a kiss on his cheek. The warmth of her lips lingered at the point of contact.

Aidan's cheeks burned like a schoolboy's. "A few *decades*. I'm not fourteen anymore."

"Me, either, darlin'," she quipped, her chuckle ringing.

"But still gorgeous," Aidan added before she could refute it.

"Still our sweet Aidan," she said, patting his arm with a strong hand. "I just spoke to your mom last week. She and your dad are having a grand time. Sounds like they love Florida," she said, the twang of her voice warm and neighborly.

"They're snowbirds. Gone down every September for years now," he replied, trying to recall exactly when his mother and Sophie had first met, but knowing it was well before he was born. Thumbing at the cell phone in his pocket, he wasn't even sure he had the phone number to the Florida house. "I think Mom is seriously considering moving when Dad retires."

"Well, I'll miss her but God knows, in this life, you gotta do what makes you happy." Sophie tucked herself back behind her desk, digging out a day planner from one of the miscellaneous stacks. "I'm surprised to see you. Hank said you were coming in tomorrow. He must have gotten the days mixed up."

"Sorry to show up unexpected," Aidan said, the levity draining from his tone. "I need to discuss something with you, if you've got a minute. It involves a new volunteer."

"Have a seat." Sophie motioned to the chair across from her, instantly switching into manager mode. She pulled a register from a file of papers. Flipping open the notebook, she rested her eyeglasses midway down her nose, scanning through the lenses. "What's the name?"

"Kelly Monroe," Aidan answered, his throat going dry. He sat down, getting as comfortable as he could while she perused the documents.

"I have her down for community service..." Sophie's forehead furrowed as she reviewed the file, flipping through another pile to find the information forms associated with the girl. "She's older for a first timer," she said, staring at notes, not appearing to find anything out of place with the paperwork.

"Yes." Aidan struggled to pick his words carefully, trying not to put her on guard.

Sophie ran her farm on the level and he knew that as much as Hammond's loved taking on new volunteers, safety always came first. If an applicant had a bad record, they weren't setting foot near Sophie's farm or her horses. And what Aidan had in mind walked an unorthodox line.

He needed to keep the girl at a remote location, with people he trusted, so getting Sophie on board would require some schmoozing. No favor to a friend would change the way she guarded her animals.

Looking up at him, Sophie's face morphed into a mask of concern, the expression a dark cloud over her bright features. Aidan shifted in his seat.

"The hundred hours is for public transgression," he told her. "A minor charge. She has no previous criminal record. I want to unofficially monitor her while she's serving, if you don't mind." He dealt the facts out like playing cards and waited for Sophie's response. He'd play hardball if he had to, although he didn't want to strong-arm her.

*Not that that would work.*

She watched him carefully as if she were picking up on his subterfuge. "We've had teenagers and college kids here for community service before, Aidan. Plenty of juvie cases—"

"The girl's not juvie. She was let go on a misdemeanor. I submitted the appeal for her to perform the service."

Her eyebrows knit together, making Aidan pause.

"I don't have grounds to report her hours, not legally."

"You need to monitor her but—not legally?" Sophie repeated slowly.

"Yes." He straightened in his seat, shoulders locking back.

"What's going on, Aidan?" she asked, calling him out.

Of course Sophie wasn't buying it. He should have known from the get-go that the most direct route was the only one with her. And he wasn't soft-spoken anyway.

Aidan met Sophie's stare head-on.

"Just say it," she prompted, gentleness melding with the steel in her voice.

"The girl was arrested at a field party where two college students walked through a bonfire." Aidan let the words fly, the subject matter leaving no room for delicacy. Sophie inhaled sharply. "The kids suffered second to third degree burns. I've been visiting them at the hospital for the last month. One nearly died. Blood tests from the night of the party show that the two had cocaine in their system. We obtained a sample of the drug from a bag found at the scene. Trace elements of the dust proved to be a specific brand."

"Oh, dear Lord—this has to do with *Paul?*"

The name made Aidan flinch. Few people knew, and even fewer dared to say his former partner's name out loud after what happened, which was stupid—like avoiding the subject helped. The very mention caught Aidan off guard, like having a Band-Aid ripped off and stuffed down this throat.

IIe wiped the anguish off his face, which required genuine effort.

Aidan had learned early on that putting your pain out on display didn't win you anything more than other people's pity—the carnival-sized, large stuffed animal kind that just got handed to him by Sophie. The split-second of grief he'd flashed her must have been enough, because she leaned forward like she was about to come after him with another hug.

A beat of tranquil silence followed, and Aidan felt a surge of gratitude. Sophie didn't assail him with the mothering, didn't pepper him questions like Capt. Reeves.

He sat up straight and tried to get himself together. He needed to get over it.

Three years hadn't diluted the guilt, hadn't buried the fact that it should've been him...

He started rubbing at his right shoulder.

*Three years.*

That was forever given the fact that he'd *never* been the emotional type. Aidan had taken every kind of hit over the course of his career; he'd been punched, shot, choked, but nothing had hurt him as bad as losing Paul. So all the promises that he'd get better with time, that his life would eventually get back to normal seemed like a load of greeting card crap.

He continued to work at his shoulder, the spot wearing raw.

"Is this girl involved?" Sophie asked, her voice tentative.

Aidan dropped his hand, shaking off the past. "Witnesses confirm that she was seen with a woman who meets...Rachel's description." Anger flickered the moment Aidan said her name, the image of the woman's face hitting his frontal lobe. Clear as day, he saw her holding a revolver up to killing level; her cold, unremorseful eyes seared into his memory. Aidan had taken a bullet to get a visual ID on Rachel Lancaster— and lost more than blood in the end.

He watched Sophie's face drain of color, the implications sinking in.

"Aidan—" She turned in her seat, the pads of her fingers resting on her mouth as if she'd been stricken speechless.

"I need to know if it's her, Sophie. There have been no leads on the Dove case in three years, not since the shooting. If the Dove group is responsible for these boys—" He had to get her to agree while the shock had her off-balance, his inner bastard chiding himself for not giving her time to re-coup.

Sophie's eyes darted to his, fear flashing in the chocolate brown, her thoughts written on her face. Aidan read between the lines easily.

She didn't want him meeting the same end as his partner.

A sudden billow of memory transported Aidan back to the day of the shooting. He'd lain in his hospital bed, surrounded by beeping machines and sterile walls. The doctor had walked up to him, clad in a white coat, the man's face drawn and solemn. A screaming silence followed the disclosure that his partner had died on the operating table. The words had stayed with Aidan every day since, numbing him. The very mention of Paul's name dragged him back to that hospital bed, to the pain.

And that was why everyone was on eggshells around him. Why Reeves didn't want him anywhere near to the woman known as Rachel Lancaster. Why Sophie feared his involvement. But Aidan couldn't let the lead go; it meant too much.

Vindication for Paul. For himself.

He watched as Sophie's hand drifted to her throat.

"Aidan, I trust you but, are you sure?" she spoke again. "Are you sure you can handle this?" Her face shrank into a wince after the words were out.

*Ouch.*

She was questioning his stability, which was a kick to the ego-balls, but with good reason. Aidan's jurisdiction over the case had ended when he was transferred to arson. His search for drug evidence was a conflict of interest, a covert way for him to link the Dove case to his investigation of the bonfire without anyone knowing. He could work the burn victim case on its own, avoiding the drug angle completely, he'd just have to turn the Dove lead over to the officer currently assigned to narcotics. He had a simple answer for that.

*Hell, no.*

The first break the department had had in three years and he'd be damned if he'd hand the information off to another NARC who'd just throw it in an evidence folder to collect dust. Whether his jacket read arson or not, the lead was his. No one else was going to touch it.

Sophie pivoted in her chair, staring out at the rolling hills through the window behind her desk.

Out of respect Aidan gave her a minute to decide. In the quiet his mind turned to Josh Moreland, the college student now lying in a hospital bed of his own, the same white walls doing little to soothe his blistering, open wounds. The operations to reconstruct the kid's skin were not slated out over months, but *years*. Decades of skin grafts and scars followed by a lifetime of slow mental healing. All that awaited a boy barely twenty-one years old. The injustice of it brought Aidan's voice back with a vengeance.

"Please let me do this, Sophie."

The *please* hung in the air, a strange sound coming from his lips.

With the dignity of an ambassador, Sophie turned to face him. "This girl's coming to orientation today?"

"Yes."

"Do you need us to monitor her?"

Aidan felt his chest open, his lungs release. For all Aidan knew Kelly Monroe could be a new member of the Dove group, but something in the girl's eyes that night at the station said otherwise.

"No, just let her work the service. I'll be here to keep tabs."

"Okay." Sophie's reply was soft, hesitant.

"Thank you."

She laid her hand on the desk, palm up. "Promise me. Promise me I won't regret this, Aidan."

Aidan angled forward and placed his warm hand firmly in hers. Squeezed.

"I swear to you, Sophie. You won't."

# CHAPTER 3

Kelly swung the Honda into the first available space at the back of the packed parking lot, the engine's high-pitched whine downgrading to a rough idle as she shifted into park. She glanced at the clock on the dash.

*Ten minutes late.* Story of her life.

Reaching into the passenger seat, she grabbed her purse and riffled through the worn sack of leather to be sure she had—*aha!* She had her audio recorder, a notepad, and something to write with. She looked up, her eye catching on the fuel gauge, the needle sagging at half-mast for having just filled up.

*A half tank of gas after going twenty miles? That can't be right.*

But she didn't have the time to fuss. After killing the engine she hopped out, locking up as hot popping sounds echoed up from the undercarriage. At almost eleven years old, the car had never been bad on gas before, but maybe it was the gauge that needed replacing.

*Or this is stage one of it getting ready to croak.*

She focused on the positive and made a mental note to stop using the cheapo gas station down the street. Paying a few cents more per gallon was better than frequent gas stops, or premature death leading to transportation rigor mortis.

Like the thing's days weren't already numbered.

The muggy summer air engulfed her as she briskly set off to find the meeting room, the name listed on her orientation letter. Kelly shielded her eyes from the late afternoon sun and scanned the outcrop of buildings. A large yellow country house sat opposite the parking area with various-sized barns guarding it on all sides, and a large piece of farm equipment peeked out from a gigantic barn directly ahead of her. She was already late and tempted to just run in any direction until she found the place, but ending up lost in a grazing field didn't strike her as a good way to start off her community service.

She made a slow circle to get her bearings.

"You here for orientation?" a male voice said from behind her, making Kelly wheel around. She nailed the man in the stomach with a wayward elbow and retracted her arm. "Oh— *sorry*. I didn't see you," she said.

The older man smiled down at her with creased eyes, his gray hair a match to his well-groomed beard. The white polo shirt he wore bore the farm's logo on one side and the embroidered name *Henry* on the other.

*Oh good, a staff member.*

Embarrassment squeezed at her as Henry subtly rubbed at the spot where she'd ribbed him.

"Sorry," Kelly repeated.

"No problem." He chuckled giving his belly a pat. "This is a tough old tire. Been working on it for years."

Kelly smiled at his grandfatherly manner, finding no fault with a man who appreciated a good meat and potatoes meal. If she could go out to eat more often, she would.

"I'm here for the orientation, but I don't know where—" Kelly started as the man pointed to the left of a red-roofed building.

"The meeting room is next to the main barn. Walk straight toward the red roof then hang a left—you can't miss it."

"Thanks," she replied, eager to get going. She paused to glance at his shirt again. "—Henry."

"Hank," he corrected and waved. "Hope to see you around."

"You, too."

Kelly started walking fast, passing the main barn on her way; the place was cavernous, with huge doors opening to rows of wooden clapboard gates topped with metal rails. Empty from what she could tell, as no horses poked their heads out from the stalls.

A soft hum of voices began to fill the air as she approached the large shed; one of its doors open with light and noise radiating out. Peeking in, lines of chairs faced a small, industrial-looking podium holding several people wearing the same polo shirt as Hank, but in different colors. A woman stood at the front podium, her strong voice belting out a speech about the farm's history.

Kelly was compelled to stop and listen, but spotted an empty chair near the back of the sea of heads. With a quick movie-theater maneuver past two seated women, Kelly grabbed a bench behind someone short, giving her a clear view of the front. Kelly could see that the seat's occupant was a younger girl, the woman stationed next to her appearing to be the girl's mother. The woman hovered but remained a close distance as if respecting the girl's personal space.

*A teenager.*

Kelly plopped down and whipped out her note-taking supplies. She placed her recorder on her thigh and pressed the little *on* button, the record light illuminating in a pinprick of red. The compact device had saved Kelly a hand cramp on many occasions, helping her log college lectures, helpful for those early-morning classes when the coffee hadn't quite kicked in.

A clipboard nudged her elbow along with a handout. Kelly printed her name on the list, passing it on to circulate the room. She settled in and glanced up at the speaker, the woman's voice resonating despite all the background activities going on around her. The woman's tan skin complimented her graying brown hair, and she spoke with the kind authority of a respected leader.

Kelly listened, jotting down notes, bullet points running down the length of the page.

*Hammond's Horse Farm and Rescue:*
*• A rescue facility for abandoned and mistreated horses.*

• *A non-profit that rehabilitates horses in need of care.*

• *Free training for volunteers.*

• *Staff with decades of professional equine experience.*

Kelly underlined the part about it being an equine care facility. The community service edict had said the place was horse farm, but Kelly expected trail rides and saddle soap, not the horse equivalent of a dog pound.

She'd be dealing with sick animals.

*Big*, sick animals.

Kelly had grown up with fish. When they started to float she'd scooped them out with a net, which was the extent of her caregiving expertise. Back in New York she had taken a few riding lessons when she was fifteen, the age when a lot of girls go horse-crazy. But vague memories of curry combs and sitting positions weren't going to help when she went face to muzzle with an animal eight times her size. Her knowledge of quadrupeds needed a serious refresher and it seemed like some of the horses at the rescue were bad off.

Kelly figured that she could springboard off her love of biology, but the farm still felt like a much bigger ballpark. The horses there were living creatures, not plant cells under a microscope. She couldn't just write them off like one of her failed experiments if she didn't care for them right.

Overwhelmed, the old-school *Star Trek* began to play in her head:

*Damn it, Jim. I'm a biologist, not a veterinarian.*

Forcing her attention span to behave, she flipped her attention up right as the speaker had finished.

"We welcome all of you to Hammond's and thank you for supporting the horses," the woman said as the audience began to applaud. The girl in front of Kelly shifted toward her mother, whispering something.

"Don't worry," her mother said over the din.

*Well, at least I'm not the only one with a case of the nerves.*

The crowd stirred and stretched, standing up to get refreshments laid out on tables around the room as the speaker exited the stage, and a younger woman prepared to take her place at the microphone. Kelly watched the older speaker descend the stairs, stopping at the side of the platform, a young staff member handing her the sign-in clipboard. Scanning the list, the woman's head paused and then popped up.

Shrewd eyes filtered through the mass of faces, locking in on Kelly; the woman's soft brown gaze a heavy veil over serious thoughts.

Kelly suppressed the urge to glance behind her.

*Is she looking for someone else?*

Maybe the woman disapproved of Kelly's late arrival. Punctuality was probably important when dealing with the organization of a large farm, Kelly guessed. She'd do her best to be on time from then on.

Kelly returned the woman's stare, the lady's attention suddenly drawn to something at the back of the room. Kelly twisted in her seat, searching for the source of her distraction.

Kelly's breath stopped in her throat.

A tall figure stood out in the crowd, hovering around the coffee station. A masculine tower of lean muscle and straightforward attitude.

*It can't be...*

Kelly did a blatant Pisa-lean, unable to tear her eyes away.

Her arson cop looked up, his eyes lighting up in a flash of blue before disappearing in between the throng of bodies.

*It's him. He's here. He's here, he's...Gone.*

Kelly craned her neck.

Glancing around where she'd spotted him, she scanned the crowd, performing an evaluation of each person who walked by. There were at least a hundred people moving around wearing a similar uniform of jeans topped with t-shirts, making it a struggle to find him again. Frustration burned as she skimmed, finding no match.

Gripping the back of her chair, Kelly sunk down as the young woman at the front tapped gently on the microphone, calling everyone to retake their seats. The idlers drifted back, the room going quiet. Kelly tried to keep calm, combing over the area where she'd last seen him, finding nothing but empty space.

So strange.

Did he have an affiliation with the farm? Or was he just a guy who looked like Blue Eyes?

He'd vanished. Again.

*Damn it.*

Her skin prickled as she pivoted around. The new speaker on the podium introduced herself as Philippa "Pippa" Franklin, one of the senior staff members. Wearing a cap with the farm's logo, the young woman managed to look feminine with her hair tucked up off her face. A farm professional, if there was such a thing. On the stage behind her, two teenagers carried a life-sized model of a horse onto the platform, setting the figure's synthetic legs down with a heavy *thunk*. With one last furtive glance behind her, Kelly forced herself to let it go.

She had to be seeing things—people.

*Hot arson cops.*

She blew out a breath.

For the next hour she tried not to break her neck looking around during the tutorial on horse care. Kelly caught herself wishing that she had the same left and right brain separation a horse did, able to use both spheres at the same time, the way Pippa described.

"Horses are unique creatures. Early in their evolution they learned that it was safest to move in packs, *herds*. The mentality is deeply ingrained because it helps them survive. You'll see a camaraderie develop in a group of horses; in each herd a male and female *alpha* will emerge. They're the ones voted the strongest—a leader for each gender—then a beta, and onward down the chain of command, so to speak..." Pippa continued, outlining pack instincts.

As the minutes passed, Kelly's recorder earned its keep, retaining the details of the lecture: how to approach a horse, how to groom.

Notes that she would have to replay later. Despite the engaging demonstration Kelly's mind kept drifting in and out, lingering.

Had she imagined him?

Not to chastise her brain for conjuring up a sexy man, but she had to be losing it.

A ripple rolled through the crowd, pulling Kelly from her thoughts as Pippa started directing the group outside.

Kelly quickly stowed her stuff, standing up, moving with the flock out the door opposite the entrance. Kelly filed out behind the young girl and her mother, watching the two stay together as they funneled past a table with volunteers passing out pink name tags and paperwork. A single-page consent form was given, the document covering the dangers involved with the handling of large animals and what to do in the event of injury. The risks ran through her mind.

Animals were unpredictable, but the chances of being kicked or bitten was contingent upon behavior, both the person's and the horse's. Kelly figured that her odds of getting hurt were average given her experience.

She scribbled her signature at the X and moved on to the nametag area. Once her first name stood out in bold Sharpie marker, the group dispersed into the open area outside, standing in little clusters of those who knew one another.

The lone one out, Kelly kept within eyesight of the mother-daughter team, feeling somewhat familiar with them. In the daylight she could see that the girl looked to be around thirteen, her pink nametag reading *Andrea;* her mother's, *Marie.*

The last of the assembly spread out over the space, filling the wide thoroughfare leading to barns and fenced-off areas in the distance. The sun hung low in the sky as Pippa stepped up on a box crate, her face and body cast in the golden hue of early summer afternoon.

"There are several *paddocks* for animals to exercise and graze. This quarter—" she toed at the wood chips covering the ground where they stood "—is called the Common Area. The main barn is behind us, and the tack room is next door. The two large fields on either side of us are the gelding and mare paddocks."

Andrea's eyes widened a little as Pippa pointed to the grassland bordering them. The fields stretching out, peppered with trees. In the distance Kelly could see dark specks moving, galloping over the hills. Andrea huddled closer to her mom.

"We're going to break you down into small groups. Each will be assigned a guide and every volunteer will be given a horse." Pippa stepped off the crate, beckoning for a team of leaders wearing farm shirts to come forward. Kelly recognized many of the faces from the presentation. The band converged on Pippa, who quickly dealt out orders of who was going where.

A loud whisper caught Kelly's attention as the girl, Andrea, started talking in a murmured torrent to her frowning mother. The conversation came to a halt when the staff members held up numbers with their fingers, instructing everyone to look at their nametags to see what to which group they'd been assigned. Kelly glanced at her sticker. A small, red number three stood out in the lower corner, sending her the direction of a teenager holding up three fingers near the main barn.

"I'm Jason," the guy said as the final stragglers stepped up. The kid couldn't have been older than twenty, but exuded authority as he rounded up the group of fifteen in a tight circle around him. Glancing back, Kelly didn't see which group Andrea and her mother had walked toward.

*My day for losing people in a crowd.*

"Today we're going to give you a little interaction with the horses by letting you place hay in their stalls. I understand that a few of you have previous handling experience. If that's the case, please let us know how comfortable you feel or if you'd like more time before jumping right in."

They turned toward the main barn as Jason walked and talked, the common area clearing out as each of the groups moved to other parts of the farm. The sun illuminated the dark matted floor of the huge red barn, the door broad enough to bring large pieces of equipment in and out.

"The horses here are all rescues," Jason said. "Many are in various stages of rehabilitation and require special care and diet. When a horse arrives at Hammond's, an evaluation is performed to determine the health and temperament of the animal. We've established a color-coding system to ensure that only trained staff members handle the horses in critical care.

The color system is a stoplight: Green is for horses that are deemed docile and well broken in; Yellow is for mid-range horses—those who have specific quirks or who are not fully evaluated; Red is for senior staff members only, meaning that the horse requires very special handling; Purple is specific, for horses who have rehab needs. As new volunteers we ask that you seek permission from a senior staff member before working with horses that are anything higher than a green code level."

Kelly's gaze drifted to the long line of stalls trailing behind the guy. Somewhere between the walls and rails a flicker of movement—a swish of a tail?—broke the stillness.

"The recovering horses spend a lot of time here in the main barn, but we brought in the greens to welcome you to Hammond's." Jason started walking again, a loose line forming behind him as, one by one, long muzzles came into view. Each stall had a clipboard hanging on the front, a clear plastic page holder listing the animal's name, height, weight, and status. The first horse they came to looked back at them with neutral impartiality.

A green band of vinyl tape peeked from the side of her halter. The plastic sleeve adhered to the front of her stall read:

*Ethereal Emme*
*15.4 hands*
*4 YO Quarter Horse*
*Mare*

Emme's ears gently revolved toward each person in her human audience. The horse seemed comfortable despite the fact she had a large pack watching her, and lowered her head as Jason scratched between her ears.

"In many situations, Hammond seizes several horses from one place. We can house around eighty to ninety horses on average, but we have satellite locations if we need to keep more. Every horse receives shelter here. No animal is left out in the cold," he said affectionately.

"When the horses arrive, they're named alphabetically, and once we've gone through the initial twenty-six letters, A, B, C, we go through them again, doubling the name in the sequence, then tripling and so on. For example, Emme here is the thirty-first horse of her herd to come to Hammond's, making her a double-E name."

After giving a final pat to the mare, Jason led the group down the row of stalls, detailing the operations and giving a quick introduction of each of the obedient greens, who all looked like they were patiently awaiting their food.

"So now that you have an idea of how it all works, I'm going to let you get started," Jason said. He beckoned to one of the younger kids in the group to get the first assignment. Jason made quick work of divvying everyone up, pairing human with horse. Kelly stayed at a distance, letting everyone get tagged until the number of people dwindled, leaving her the last one standing. She scanned the aisles, all the greens were taken.

"Hang on a second," Jason said, jumping to a solution. Bounding out of the main barn, he disappeared into the beams of sunlight, returning a minute later.

"We've got one for you. Follow me."

Kelly trailed behind Jason as he led her down a long corridor, the stalls going from occupied to empty as they trekked to a smaller auxiliary area adjacent the main building. Kelly's head popped up as a loud whinny shook the rafters. Poking her head around the corner she caught a flare of movement in the last stall.

She turned back to Jason, whose attention was pinned to another volunteer who'd approached, talking animatedly about some kind of brush shortage going on in the tack room.

"Okay— I'll be right there." Jason paused to direct one person at a time. "Sorry to do this to you, but can I ask you to take one flake of hay and wait by the guy on the end? I'll be right back."

"Sure." Kelly stared down at the scraggly pile of muted green at her feet as Jason hot-footed it to the other barn.

The hay bales were pre-cut by machines and bound into squares by twine. Kelly popped a bale free using a pair of scissors she'd found on the ground, and separated one layer of hay in her hands. Loose strands caught flight as she carried the food down the quiet passage. Passing one empty stall after the other, Kelly picked up on the sound of heavy breathing: the inhale sharp, the exhale skipping and labored.

*A few of the horses are in recovery,* a mental voice repeated from orientation.

Rounding the hub to the last stall Kelly held the hay to her chest, the stuff scratching at her neck as she peeked in.

The animal that peered back at her from behind the bars brought her heart to a stop.

The horse towered over her, the base of the thoroughbred's neck slightly lower than Kelly's forehead, her mind pounding out the math, converting feet and inches into the equine height translation of hands. Abnormally thin, the horse had a muted chestnut coat, his fur a blanket of spots under a matted film of dust and dirt. The textured covering stretched over lean muscles and stark bones, all deep brown except for the four white socks above his hooves. Dust motes swirled in the beams of light shining through the opposite side of the stall, breaking around him as if he were the center of their universe.

"Hi there," Kelly said softly, trying to stow her uneasiness for the horse's sake. Animals could sense tension. She struggled to wipe her slate clean before she stepped into his space.

She assumed he was a boy by the way he watched her, with level, instinctive eyes. He surveyed her apprehensively then pinned his penetrating gaze on the hay, his lean physique confirming that he must be eager for what she'd brought.

"I'm Kelly. I'm here with your dinner." The words came out the way she intended: gentle, comforting. In response the horse went motionless as a sculpture, the flare of his nostrils the only sign of life emanating from him.

Peering through the bars, the vinyl strip of green on his halter shone in the light. The bare stall front offering no plastic sheets or clipboards, which gave Kelly no name to call him. She watched him breathe with exertion, her free hand resting on the steel lever of the gate.

He didn't exude the same tame air as the other horses, but maybe she had surprised him?

She was a new face, and he was isolated in a separate stall, all by himself. By the look of his coat, no one had been in to groom him in a while.

The brown orbs of his eyes remained focused on her: serious, cautious, unblinking.

*Storytelling eyes.*

With a slide of metal, Kelly let herself into the stall, turning her body to hold the food away from him until she could reach his bowl. Relocking the door behind her, a huff of hot air blew down her neck. On contact her instincts screamed.

Jason hadn't told her to go in. He'd told her to wait outside the stall.

She'd done something impulsive.

The heat on her shoulder blew again. Hotter, closer.

She'd done something *too* impulsive.

# CHAPTER 4

Kelly froze, her hands gripping the hay, a heavy breath heating her neck.

Her eyes shifted to the gate that caged them, the deserted hallway beyond. It'd be a few minutes before Jason would return, but that would be enough. The safety waiver she'd signed so frivolously waved invisibly in front of her face as she rolled over all the various ways the animal could retaliate.

*Stupid, stupid move.*

Maybe she should just drop the hay and back away slowly.

*That sounds like a good plan.*

She could sense the animal's position from the steam gusting behind her. Taking a deep breath, she turned.

The reaction was spontaneous; no sooner had she squared her body had the horse whipped his neck, thick lips curling back, wide teeth snatching up the hay. Kelly let go and stepped back, holding her hands up in surrender. Watching the horse's lean muscles in action, his broad neck hoisted up the tangled square of food. With a vigorous shake of his head the lump disentangled, the hay snowing knot-like strings to the bare floor.

She kept her hands in front of her, the remnants of tossed food clinging to her clothes and hair as the horse retreated. Time slowed in contradiction to the speed with which he chewed; the rotation of his circular cheek keeping a separate pace than the wary eye he had trained on her.

The horse finished his first pull and craned his neck to the floor, fetching the remainder that had fallen, his guarded stare constant as he backed into the corner of the stall. Kelly exhaled as the light from the window above spilled over his body revealing protruding ribs, a thinning coat, and a low body weight. Her gaze followed his legs down to the floor, where no bedding lined the stall. No straw, no sawdust, just a stretch of black rubber mats.

Her escape plan forgotten, query flooded Kelly's mind.

There were few reasons why you couldn't put straw down for a horse....

She saw his emaciated body anew, her heart breaking.

Without thinking, she reached out a hand, propelled to touch him. The horse pulled back with a jerk, letting out a startled outtake of breath. She stepped back, tracking his reaction.

"It's okay," she said, keeping her distance. "I won't take your food away."

He seemed to calm at her words but protected his meal, jutting out a boney shoulder as if he wanted to block her access until he could stow it away.

"You're so hungry..." she murmured. Sympathy radiated in her voice as she stepped to the side, keeping in his line of sight, the two of them staring at each other. "What's your name?"

The horse let out a soft breath as a pair of urgent footfalls echoed up through the outside corridor. Jason emerged through the grate of bars, Pippa right behind him, an expression of anxiety etched on her face.

"Oh no," Jason uttered, craning his neck to get a good look. Turning to Pippa he whispered, "That's not Hopscotch, that's *Keegan*."

The horse's head popped up at the name, coming to attention with his notice of the new visitors.

"Are you okay?" Jason paused with is palm on the latch, eyes darting from Kelly to the horse and back again.

Protective, Kelly held up a hand to stop them as Jason went to open the door. "I'm fine. Uh—I gave him the hay," Kelly admitted, guilt trimming her words.

"That's all right," Pippa replied calmly, her eyes cautiously pinned to the horse. "We need you to exit the stall now, Kelly. Jason's going to step in and I want you to walk out at the same time, okay?" The woman moved as she spoke, rolling the gate open just enough for Jason to slip in.

Keegan's eyes went wide at the shuffle of movement, his ears pointing at Jason as if fearful that a militia were coming for him. Jason pivoted his body and looked the horse over.

Agitated, Keegan snorted loud and launched into a series of hacking coughs. Kelly felt her feet go limp, an act of revolt against leaving as a warm grip latched on to her forearm.

Pippa leaned into the small space, her hand steadily guiding Kelly to the door. Jason followed them, backing his way out. The trio looked in at the animal from the hall, watching Keegan heave, the hacking sounds disconcerting and phlegmy.

"I'll let Sophie know; we'll call Dr. Althea," Jason said with a nod to Pippa, disappearing out of the barn in a rush.

"I'm so sorry," Kelly said. "I fed him—"

With a final hiccup, the gagging cut off as Kelly watched, stunned, a hand on her own stomach as Keegan continued to take ragged breaths; his mouth scouring the ground for any stray pieces of hay.

The stuff made him sick but he wanted more.

Kelly turned on Pippa. "Did I hurt him?"

"Let's walk," she replied, tugging on Kelly's elbow.

Not a *no*. What had she done?

The two were out in the main paddock before the conversation started, Pippa choosing her words. "There was a mix up. Keegan's a new rescue, not evaluated yet. He just arrived two days ago. Keegan snapped his halter out in the paddock this morning, and a volunteer grabbed a spare one that had a green band on it. We're glad you're all right."

Both their heads snapped the direction of the barn as Keegan let out another air-cracking whinny. Kelly's eyes traced the window of the last stall. "Did I *hurt* him?"

"No, he's in the same shape as when he arrived. After his evaluation, we'll assign him special food, a liquid diet." Her eyes turned serious. "Until we can wean him back onto solids."

Kelly winced. The hay she'd handed over was solid and then some. Way too harsh on the horse's system. Like a human, Keegan needed to be eased back into regular eating after what he'd gone through.

"I didn't help." Kelly flipped her stare back to other woman.

"He's got a physical scheduled today, him and the other five. We can gauge it, please don't worry," Pippa replied, turning toward the main barn.

"The other *five?*" Kelly asked, following her.

"Keegan's one of six horses found abandoned on a racetrack," Pippa said softly, a hand coming to rest on her hip.

Silence rung in Kelly's ears as her breath held. So she'd been right about the malnourishment. "For how long?"

"From what we can tell, two, going on three weeks. We got an anonymous phone lead. They were found wondering the circuit, scavenging for whatever food they could find. From what we've seen they were turned loose and left for..." Pippa's expression stayed level, steady, giving Kelly the eerie impression that she must have discussed worse in her time at the rescue.

Kelly felt her heart lurch.

"Look, how about we let you go home. You've had enough of an introduction for one day," Pippa said, the woman's smile a thin line of concern as she reached out and touched Kelly's arm.

"*No*—please," Kelly objected, not wanting to leave. "I'd like to stay, if there's a horse for me," she added in a softer tone.

Pippa dropped her hand, her brow furrowed. "Okay, if you're sure."

Kelly nodded.

"Just so you know, you handled yourself well in there. You stayed calm, that's rule number one with horses. Most volunteers would be shaken going up against an unevaluated their first day."

Kelly glanced back at the auxiliary barn.

"You're sure he'll be okay?" Kelly breathed.

"He's here now. We'll take care of him." Her tone was so resolute, so certain.

Kelly turned, taking in the horsewoman's face. She saw how the woman had come to be senior staff with her calm demeanor and dark, knowing eyes.

"I'd like to stay."

Pippa's eyes crinkled at that, her mouth turning up at the edges. "Okay. But let's find you a quiet one this time."

Twenty minutes later Kelly stood in another stall, her "quiet" horse more than earning his moniker. Pippa had called the horse Moe. Standing as motionless as the model had in orientation, the horse's ears were the only things that moved, silently following Kelly's movements like fuzzy satellite antennas.

*Sweet Moe.*

Kelly ran a curry comb in broad circles over the horse's back, getting a little shoulder-shimmy in response. Moe's coat went silken with every pass, the horse's warm brown body a contrast to an ebony black mane and tail, topped off with a splash of a white down his long nose. Moe stood still and calm, emitting a peaceful sigh as Kelly brushed her way around the animal's long body.

*So different from Keegan*, Kelly mulled, unable to forget her encounter earlier. The horse in front of her now seemed to know that food and care would always be provided; Keegan didn't.

Her heart squeezed a little at the thought that he may never know that amity.

Kelly grabbed a hoof pick from the carrier tray and trailed her free hand over Moe's side, feeling a padded ribcage under layers of healthy muscle. She prayed that Keegan's body would someday show the same level of rehabilitation.

And how long had Keegan suffered mistreatment?

As a racehorse, his background had to be logged—his history documented somewhere... Kelly's mind lit up at the lead into Keegan's past.

Maybe Pippa would let her look into it.

Kelly tapped over Moe's croup and down a back leg, palming a hoof. As she got down on her haunches the horse made the job easy, lifting his foot so Kelly could pick out the dirt. From her riding days Kelly remembered that some horses were sensitive about their feet, so the obedience was nice.

"Good boy!" she said, standing up to give Moe a pat.

Then she heard it—a bass chuckle. *Someone laughing?*

With a hand on Moe's neck, Kelly treaded to the front of stall.

Sure enough a man stood leaning on the gate, his forearm resting high against the frame, an amused expression pulling at his lips. She recognized the tall, lean body.

Blue Eyes flashed from his strong face as Kelly held in a gasp.

"He's a *she*," he said, speaking first. His voice was just as she'd remembered it, deep and resonant and...

"Excuse me?" Kelly muttered, a little stunned by all the—*him*, standing there in the flesh.

Blue Eyes pushed off from the door; his posture straightened, illustrating wide shoulders and an even balance, his tight body tucked into well-worn pair of Levi's and a navy blue, cotton short-sleeve. Kelly had to peer around Moe to stare.

"She's a mare. You know, there's—" his eyes dipped to the underside of horse and then back up "—nothin' hanging."

*How did he—Wait. What?*

Bemused, Kelly did a discreet duck, checking out the horse's undercarriage. She froze, rising again slowly, whispering, "I'm so sorry, honey," to Moe's face.

Placid as ever, the horse just breathed, taking no offense to the cross-gender implication.

Blue Eyes gave another chortle, regaining Kelly's attention.

"A girl named *Moe*?" Kelly said, unable to hold in the riposte. "Let me guess, her girlfriends Larry and Curly are a couple stalls over."

His mouth remained tight, but she could tell that her quip prompted a smile.

"It's short for *Modest Mona*, she's the double-M of her group," he explained, crossing his arms and returning to his *GQ* pose against the stall's gate.

"Oh," Kelly muttered, going back to her gawking. He looked so natural, so *real*. Like a celebrity photographed on the street, the fantastic made corporal. In the clarity of daylight the blurry snapshot from her night in jail didn't compare. He had the same square jaw, the same tousled dark hair, same deep blue stare trained with no-nonsense intent. Only now she noticed the small shadows under his eyes, the furrowed brow. Those weren't there before, but then again she hadn't even caught his—

"What's your name?" she blurted, her cheeks starting to heat.

"Aidan Wright. I'm an arson detective for the county," he answered, his voice authoritative as if he were laying down ground rules or something.

*Aidan.* So the eyes had a name. And a badge.

Well, that explained the lack of a uniform and the air of superiority; how he remained unfazed by the way she watched him. Questions sparked up in her mind like a stoked fire.

*Why would an arson detective be hanging around a horse farm?*

"I was at the precinct the night you were brought in," he said, seeming to follow her train of thought.

"I remember." The memory had haunted her for over a month.

His jaw ticked at that for some reason. The reaction took Kelly back to an airless interview room, to the peppering of questions about how she'd gotten to the party, who she'd talked to, who invited her. An onslaught of *who, who, who*, as she'd told Officer Carson everything she knew.

What else did the police need from her?

"Mr. Wrigh—" *Okay,* not *calling him that.* She back-peddled. "Detective—"

"Aidan. Aidan is fine," he corrected.

Kelly absently stroked Moe's neck, trying to get comfortable with being on a first name basis with the man. Bringing up the night in jail seemed like a sure-fire way to kill the budding conversation. The *so, you saw when I was faced* ice-breaker a bad lead-in.

*Keep the questions open-ended. Let him do the talking.*

"What brings you here?" Great, now her voice sounded strangled.

*And like a cheeseball, pickup line.*

"Visiting a friend," he replied, his voice vague. "I'll be—around during your service."

"Around," Kelly repeated, stunned.

The idea of him hovering, observing her while she performed rudimentary farm chores made Kelly nervous, and not just because he'd be seeing her knee-high in more than mud.

Her intuition twitched.

It didn't make sense.

The other half of her brain, the less rational part, gave him the stamp of approval to hang out, effective immediately.

"Given the community service"—he pushed his chin out—"I figured I'd introduce myself."

*Well, hi there. My name is...uh. It's, wait, I know this...K-something.*

Kelly's brain kicked back into focus as he stood up straight, angling to leave.

"I want to come back later and ask you some questions," he said, more a directive than a request, his voice full of the base grumble she remembered.

"Questions." The word rolled out of Kelly's mouth, her bewilderment achieving the impossible—striking her mute. "Detective Wright, I told Officer Carson—"

"*Aidan*," he repeated. "And I know what you told Carson."

"Okay," Kelly replied.

*Something is really off here.* But she'd let it ride.

"Good. I'll see you around," he said as casually as if they'd agreed to meet for brunch. And in a flash he stepped away, quick footsteps sounding down the hall.

Kelly blinked a minute and poked her head out of the top of the stall gate to find the corridor deserted. The man appeared and disappeared at his leisure.

The ghost of hangovers past.

Kelly turned to Moe, her newly confirmed *girl*friend. "I bet you don't get this enigmatic crap from the geldings."

Moe stared up at her with soft, passive eyes and long eyelashes. Kelly went back to work cleaning Moe's hooves, the physical activity doing little to help corral her rampant thoughts. The guy who had been popping up in her dreams decided to pop up during her community service. And he didn't state for how long.

*What were the chances of this happening—six million to one?*

Kelly pet Moe's cheek, her brain rolling. The encounter was no accident. Kelly felt her chest open as if a belt were being released from around her heart. Aidan's presence had to be related to what happened at the field party. His assignment to her didn't seem voluntary either, given the short-answer routine and his sullen disposition.

*Or maybe cops are just like that all the time.*

Kelly gathered up the grooming brushes and patted Moe goodbye.

A temperate wind gusted through the graying sky, blowing through the empty main paddock. The cool dark of the tack room welcomed her as she dropped the brushes and tools back into their corresponding bins, stacking the empty grooming tray atop a colorful pile.

Kelly documented her time on the clipboard at the vacant volunteer table and glanced up at the old outdoor clock hanging on the wall. *Four hours down, ninety-six to go.*

The encounter with Aidan stuck on mental replay, she walked out to the parking lot, his face branded into her memory.

*He'll be around.*

Kelly settled in behind the wheel of her Honda, anticipation threating her pulse.

Maybe her summer wasn't going to be so boring after all.

Gravel crunched under Aidan's boots as he strode back to his car, the sound akin to his grinding thoughts. His "introduction" to the girl didn't go well; he could see it in her wide eyes, hear it in his raw voice. His words sounded stilted, rusty with the whole "getting to know you" bit, but screw it. He'd never been the real easy-going type.

No one would call him charming, either.

Aidan had gotten accustomed to the daily no-BS exchanges with other guys on the force, the small talk proof that he wasn't completely anti-social. Aside from the mandatory conversation, Aidan's co-workers avoided him most of the time, too. He was a loner by nature. Paul was the interpersonal one, the one who'd check in, follow up on injuries. The one who cared.

*Paul.*

His partner had been approachable from the very beginning, since Paul and Aidan had been thrown together as roommates back at the Academy.

Aidan tried to recall exactly when they'd first become pals, drawing a blank. Like gravity or physics, the two of them simply fell into balance with one another. Whenever Aidan got gruff, Paul could get him to lighten up. Cases got solved when they worked together, their camaraderie cementing them as official partners on the force.

God, he missed his friend.

A lot of people did. The quiet that echoed in the month following Paul's death was a sentimental torture. Many of their colleagues wore black, the flag out front of the station hung at half-mast. After Aidan's release from the hospital, he'd had to reacquaint himself to the office space they'd shared, the place empty, hollow. Aidan had hated how the vacant desk made him hurt, every bauble and paperclip reminding him of some experience with his partner, the man gone.

A week later the notification arrived that Aidan had been transferred to the arson division. Aidan had taken the following two weeks off, cleaning out both his and Paul's desk, wiping clean the memories, erasing all evidence that his friend ever existed.

In a numbed-out daze, Aidan had driven the box of his late partner's things to the guy's house. Paul's wife Angela had answered the door, her eyes puffy and red. Handing the lot over, Aidan watched her fingers roll the gold of her wedding band around and around, not wanting to take the thing off. He'd been unable to look her in the eye. Aidan had heard that later she'd moved back home to Ohio. To mourn, to heal.

And he began his new position in arson as if he were a different person. The new Aidan Wright less accessible than before, his detachment amplified. Not that his job ever suffered from the fault in personality. In law enforcement, being soft was the chink in a cop's armor, and the dealers he arrested viewed the vulnerability as an opportunity.

Thinking back, Aidan hadn't started out in life with such thick skin. The calluses had accumulated over time, life beating the ability to cooperate with other human beings out of him.

Sometimes he wondered what Paul would think, seeing him now, and the emotion poked at him. His partner wouldn't have liked the man Aidan had become: hard, withdrawn.

But the world was already down one good guy. More would follow if Aidan and the other hard-asses weren't there to stand guard.

He assuaged the guilt by telling himself that compassion didn't fit the job description of a narcotics detective. Not when the majority of his days were spent cracking down on criminals and flunkies. Sure, the move to arson put him around people more, got him in touch with victims and their families. But even the one-on-one cases were brief and to the point: a small show of empathy followed by a long disclosure of information, hardly deep-bonding stuff.

Funny, he handled his job the way he handled his love life: quick, non-committed. A new face for a short time. His last real relationship had been a while ago, the woman ending it with him shortly after the funeral.

A year later there'd been another quick fling—what was her name—*Megan, Melanie?*

He crowned himself an asshole for not remembering even though the woman hadn't wanted a relationship either. And the passage of time surprised him.

Had it been two years? Yeah, it had.

But the first year following the shooting had been a raw one. His physical needs had taken a back seat to his grief, and he didn't blame either of the women for not sticking around to watch the meltdown. After Paul, Aidan had let a lot of things go. He'd continued going to the gym because he had to pass his physicals, but everything else he'd purposely let slide: going out, making friends, watching sports, *running*.

He loved to run. The sensation of it, the speed, the sense of power, of forward motion.

Somewhere in the chaos he'd stopped, when everything he used to like ceased to bring him joy. In the beginning he knew that he'd spiraled into depression, still healing from his own injuries. Then it was as if a layer of steel had grown over his body, over his heart.

He rolled his shoulder, felt a tug of resistance.

He shrugged and added *get a date* to the mental pile of crap he had to do.

It'd be a nice distraction.

If he could find a woman who wanted to spend three hours with him.

But then talking to women had never been a challenge for Aidan in the past. Many of them overlooked his hard disposition because they liked his eyes and his body, which got him phone numbers.

The Monroe girl liked his eyes, too.

He could tell from the expression on her face—which was half the reason he'd come across so rough when he'd talked to her. If his baby blues landed him case information, he'd use them. What he hadn't banked on was her response. He replayed the conversation in his mind. She'd seemed unsuspecting, surprised. Watchful too, which made him question her motives.

She had smart eyes, and a smart mouth to go along with them.

Aidan knew that intellect didn't make a person a criminal, but it stoked suspicion when they were potentially involved in a drug case. His reason told him that if the girl were in cahoots with the Dove distributors, she'd have kept up a better cover, but either way, Aidan didn't trust anyone.

Close to a decade's worth of police work had taught him that criminals excelled at appearing ordinary. Average was a red flag, a sign of the guilty trying to blend in. Major felons had an "approachable" look about them, predators luring in their prey. Victims could attest to the charm of some of the worst offenders. And for cops, misplaced trust meant a funeral procession.

Innocence on the outside made Kelly Monroe one of two things: a serious adversary or a bystander with piss-poor luck. Both scenarios spelled trouble.

Aidan pushed the image of the girl from his mind. He was close to the answers; he could feel it. He just needed to keep his findings objective.

As he rounded the small administration building, Aidan stopped and cursed.

Five feet, ten inches of dark-haired, uniformed authority stood blocking his car. Eric Carson stood at the driver's side door, a regular poster model for police decorum, feet planted on the ground with his shoulders rolled back.

The casual air didn't fool Aidan one bit.

*Time to take care of business.*

Aidan sauntered forward as Carson's legs did a swift reposition, his stance widening. The cop's broad chest topped off a pair of wiry legs, his physique sitting the fence between lean and bulk. Aidan had a few inches of height on the guy, but he'd bet the two would tie in the contest of who had more muscle, in both body and will.

Carson's dark eyes measured Aidan's approach, the cop's appraisal like walking through an x-ray machine. He seemed to know all your secrets in a single glance, a talent that made other people uncomfortable.

Not Aidan.

That was the one perk of being an open book; Aidan didn't *have* to hide. His opinion on everyone and everything was obvious. But Aidan could tell that Carson operated differently.

Aidan had crossed paths with the cop for the first time the night of the bonfire, when the guy had been put in charge of interviewing the girl. A uniform for the county, Carson's reputation for research had circled the water cooler over in the arson department. The cop noticed everything, and the evidence he'd collected for his cases was always airtight and indisputable. His penchant for taking criminals down in the court room put him on the detective fast-track.

That, and the guy's relation to the current Dove lead stood as reason enough for Aidan to show a little respect.

*As soon as the blue boy steps off from my ride.*

"What are you doing here, Carson?"

"Need to talk to you," Eric replied, his voice low, neutral.

"About?"

Eric didn't respond, just continued to eyeball Aidan as if he was the one with all the answers. Aidan stared back, the silence permeating.

"This doesn't involve you," Aidan said, making a move for the door, stepping to the side to avoid knocking the cop in the shoulder. An unmoving block of flesh, Carson didn't flinch.

Annoyed, Aidan turned his head, glaring. He admired the uniform, but he sure as hell didn't answer to him. Eric's expression went grim, stepping over to allow Aidan access to the driver's side.

"Capt. Reeves knows you're here," Eric said, crossing his arms as Aidan moved past him.

Aidan went still, one foot in the car. He squeezed his eyes shut, and opened them again. "He wants me off the case."

"He wants you supervised," Eric countered, his tone calm. Aidan recognized the *stick to the facts* police demeanor instantly, he used it on a daily basis in his work. He never expected to end up on the receiving end of it, as if he were the victim.

"I haven't asked her any questions," Aidan threw back, irritation clipping his words.

"You're going to."

"She doesn't know anything."

Carson didn't reply, his face skeptical.

Aidan's eyes narrowed. "And Reeves thinks I need a babysitter? Who gets the honor?"

Eric exuded more of that smooth composure. "You?"

When more silence came, Aidan lowered himself into the car and slammed the door, his thoughts baking.

Carson—they sent *Carson*, a goddamn bloodhound to watch him, to shadow him as if he were some rookie recruit.

This was the approach the captain chose to take with him?

Coerced cooperation—what a team building exercise.

Aidan connected the dots. Reeves would allow Aidan to question the girl under the guise of community service as long as the intel was handed back to him, and the NARCs assigned to the Dove case. Carson had been thrown into the mix so the uniform could gain some field cred working with a detective. Aidan got to work out his grief by pseudo-working the case.

While they put him on a leash. *What a win-win-win situation.*

Aidan wanted his own private meeting with Reeves. In a boxing ring with gloves on.

That'd be a few hours of good therapy.

A knuckle rapped at the window. Aidan could feel his teeth grind as he let the glass come down, Eric's face filling the empty space. He weighed the merits of rolling the pane back up to block the guy out, positive that would get a reaction out of *Mr. Serene,* but he held back, knowing that would only kill his chances with the Dove lead.

"This is to help you," Eric said, his face serious.

"I'm fine on my own."

Eric stood quiet as Aidan stared out through the windshield, trying to keep it together.

"Let me enunciate—*I don't need a partner.*"

Eric straightened at the remark, his expression hardening. "I'm not here for that."

Aidan turned his head at the rebuff. Carson had to have done a background on him, had to have seen the file on Paul. To the guy's credit he didn't let any empathy show, although Aidan could sense it.

From the crook of his elbow Eric flipped out two fingers like a magic trick, a business card pinched between them. Aidan scowled at the tiny rectangle, flipping his eyes up to the cop's emotionless face.

"No reporting. The sharing of information, that's all. You tell me what you find out and I'll do the same."

"What can you tell me that I don't already know?"

The uniform's mouth twitched, picking up on the bluff. The cop had jurisdiction over police files involving the party, and the girl's testimony. If Aidan tried to research the Dove case in any way, he'd get blocked. Possibly banned.

There was a moment of hard silence and Aidan snatched up the card, crushing it in his palm. Eric nodded and stepped back. Silent as a shadow he turned to leave.

*What if this is a mistake?*

Aidan felt the pulse in his neck go rapid-fire as he leaned out the window.

"What if I don't contact you?" he called out.

The cop turned around, the weight of his gaze a visual punch to Aidan's face. A shrewd smile creased the guy's mouth. "Then I'll find *you.*"

The four words hung in the air as Aidan watched the uniform's shoulders disappear between the cars.

*Blue boy has a little crazy in him. Great.*

Flipping open his palm, scratches of blue ink marked Eric's personal cell phone number at the bottom of the crumpled card.

Off-the-record reporting for his off-the-record surveillance.

With a huff Aidan tucked the mangled strip of paper into his pocket, thinking that if his life got any more complicated, he'd need a fire extinguisher to put it out.

# CHAPTER 5

Kelly woke up at six a.m. without the help of her alarm clock. Her body ready to go, she hopped out of bed, washing her face and dressing with an efficiency she usually saved for workdays. Not even a week ago she would have clobbered the hell out of the snooze bar and slept in on a Saturday morning. Given the small amount of sleep she'd gotten, she should've still been face-down and unconscious. Instead her overactive brain had her wide awake most of the night, asking questions she couldn't answer. Most of them revolving around what interest an arson detective would have in a wayward girl from upstate New York.

Sometime around two a.m. she figured that she had ninety-six remaining hours of community service to either get her answers or go insane.

Spitting out the toothpaste, she moved on to her makeup, taking care with its application. For the first time in a while she had a reason to look pretty.

After orientation at Hammond's, Kelly had run to the store and purchased a pair of inexpensive rain boots, a temporary alternative to real riding footwear, but one that worked better than her old sneakers. Shoving one foot into the knee-high rubber, the material encased her leg at the calf, the soles sturdy enough for work out in the paddocks. Adjusting into the heel, she tamped down, gauging its comfort before fishing around under the sitting bench for her other sock.

The early morning light shone through the window over the sink, illuminating her gray apartment, the room bright but bland. The unpainted walls and sparse artwork stood as a stark reminder that she hadn't lived there long.

Relishing the quiet, Kelly recalled with clarity how noisy the place got at night, another reason to make rising early part of her regular routine. When she'd first relocated to Maryland she'd searched for reasonably priced housing, all the rentals surrounding the school asking ridiculous amounts for rent. The three-level complex she'd gone with was built on the shoulder next to a major thoroughfare, the whir of cars speeding by at all hours just one of the many sounds that she had to adjust to, the apartment's paper thin walls amplifying the noise. She heard her neighbors' every thunk and slam, their laughter raucous as they loitered outside late at night.

A few of the episodes had gotten bad, with an unexpected crash of a thrown bottle or the blast of someone setting off firecrackers, but Kelly did her best to tune it all out. Noise complaints to the police were an everyday occurrence, and once made, the offenders simply disappeared back into the shadows.

*Only temporary,* she reminded herself. Sock still in hand, she vowed to look for something better after her six-month lease expired.

The sun crept into the room, lighting up the oval mirror of her vanity tray, showcasing a small collection of makeup, two perfume bottles, and a container of one-a-day vitamins. The rainbows projected by the facets landed on a blue envelope, multi-colored fingers tapping on the closed flap.

Her mom wrote to her every two weeks like clockwork, sending news along with small support checks—traditional correspondence despite the modern standard of text messages and phone calls. Her most recent letter had asked when she could come to visit.

Kelly cringed at the thought. She'd divulged the apartment's address so her mom would have a source of contact, not so she could tour the place. After six months of living independently, Kelly didn't want her mom seeing that she was scraping along, not attending classes. The fact felt like defeat.

*The long road.*

It seemed liked everything came hard-earned with Kelly for some reason. A late bloomer at twenty-six, she'd worked her way through college.

*A really late bloomer.*

It was a wonder her petals hadn't fallen off by now.

She thought of her peers. Over the years she'd watched as other people her age accomplished time-appropriate goals:

established careers, got married, had kids and adopted dogs, bought houses.

The realization struck that she'd never even had a pet.

And Kelly liked animals; dogs were cool, cats self-sufficient. However the decision to have one always came down to time and dedication. She had a day job, college classes, and homework to fill her hours, which took away every minute she had to give.

The sacrifice adding another thing onto the forfeit pile.

*Aw, knock it off.*

She had no right to complain. Raised by a single mom with the help of her grandparents, Kelly knew the merits of working hard, and that continuing her education would be tough. Since graduation the previous summer, the plan was to plod forward with a master's program, the advanced degree giving her a shot at a better starting salary in the biology field—a better income for all the living she needed to catch up on.

She just had to *earn* it first.

It'd take all of her energy, would put the dream of a house, a dog—a boyfriend, on hold.

Blue Eyes came to mind.

*Temporary hold.*

Booting up her other foot, she stood up.

She'd made it through school once, she could do it again. And The University of Maryland's biology program was named one of the best in the country, the reason she'd packed up and moved. A carrot dangling from a stick, her master's degree application was due to be approved by the biology board any day. The spring semester had wrapped up, and the professors would be reviewing the stack of applications for fall.

Kelly just had to wait for her magna cum-laude GPA to land her a spot in the program.

With luck, she'd have an acceptance letter as early as next week.

The happy thought had her stepping lightly over to her closet. From a spread of loosely spaced garments she grabbed her favorite, beat-to-hell, cotton short-sleeve off the hanger. Pushing her arms through, she did up the bottom buttons, the faded plaid pattern closing over the flesh-colored tank top she wore. Tucking the worn tails into her jeans, the loose strings of thread tickled, the unraveling seam creating a pocket as her finger filled it like a tiny person tucking into a sleeping bag.

And new clothes joined the list of things that diligence would bring.

She breathed in deep and walked over to a small plastic pot sitting on the ledge of the kitchen window. Her seedling tomato plant was making progress, but would be much stronger if it had more direct sunlight.

She repositioned it for optimal exposure and peeked outside, noting the sprawling clouds through the mottled glass. She pulled her phone from her worn pocket, and saw that the weather was showing a thirty percent chance of a thunderstorm later that afternoon.

*Better bucket the leak.*

She popped open the kitchen cabinet and grabbed a lone saucepan, the thing plucked from her mom's stainless steel set years ago because it'd come with a lifetime warranty. As she lacked the domestic gene, Kelly had yet to use the pot for cooking, the microwave being her kitchen appliance of necessity.

The Saucenator in hand, Kelly eyed a corroded spot in the ceiling, the radiating circle a sickly mustard color. When she'd first moved in Kelly had counted herself lucky to have gotten a top floor unit, back before the leaky roof and rising summer heat had set in.

The apartment complex had a full-time maintenance guy, but trust in the man had waned quickly after Kelly moved in. She'd overheard shouting matches with the management company about personal effects being mislaid following service calls. A couple of weeks prior, the woman downstairs had called up in a screaming rage, insisting that someone had been in her underwear drawer and that one of her gold chain necklaces had gone missing.

Unwilling to take any chances, Kelly did her own home improvement after that.

Granted, the only object worth Kelly's concern was the solid gold signet ring that her mother had bought her for graduation. She locked it up in the closet because it held the most monetary and sentimental value of anything she owned. And while she doubted that her plain-Jane cotton underwear would appeal to anyone, she would still be devastated if either were manhandled or stolen.

She aligned the pan on an unopened moving box, attained a good position based on trajectory, and nodded.

*No mopping today.*

She made her way to the door and performed a final look-over, pocketing her license and money. She locked the deadbolt behind her just as a faint stirring came from the unit across the hall.

Kelly looked up and down the dated mauve walls. The lackluster borders seemed to confine her, to hold her in. She raced down the stairs, the crisp morning air filling her nose as she burst through her building's front doors, hitting the street in a torrent.

For once, she had a place to go, the thrill of something new.

The destination gave her a sense of purpose, and something else she couldn't define.

It was the excitement of getting up early for summer camp. Except a farm, a horse, and a detective awaited her.

She'd promised to be on time.

*Why not get there early?*

# CHAPTER 6

Aidan hated hospitals. To him the tranquil art on the walls did little to alleviate the pain deposited in each of the rooms, a false sense of peace in light of all the recovery.

He tried to not view the building as a prison for the sick, but take away the hotel-esque atmosphere and bottom-shelf coffee, the four walls jailed him. The mental images of blood-stained sheets paired with the smell of rubbing alcohol made the walk from the hospital's waiting area to the patient rooms an exercise in desensitization.

The high note of the visit was that Josh Moreland did look better, his mottled skin smooth like melted wax, but healing. The kid moved around and spoke, able to relay a few extra details about the night of the bonfire, and went on the record that his friend Mike had been the one who'd bought the drugs. The information helped, even if it left only two potential witnesses to who'd dealt the powder: Mike and the Monroe girl.

Aidan huffed in frustration at the fact. It put more pressure on his talk with the girl, the *other* visit he needed to make today. The knowledge that he could've gotten her interview over with the other day gnawed at him, but at the time he'd followed an instinct to wait. Something told him to approach the girl slowly, to ask the right questions, to not spook her. Which was odd, because he never waited to do anything.

As he stood by the hospital bed, Aidan watched Josh stare down at his own marred hands, a vacant expression filling the kid's eyes.

After their talk, Aidan walked back down the spotless hallway, trying to shake the image of the boy. He knew firsthand that chance dealt you crappy cards sometimes—he'd been given one hell of a bad hand himself. But Josh's situation seemed harsh for some reason, unforgiving. Not that dabbling with drugs was ever smart or condoned. Aidan had witnessed the aftereffects so many times before with his job that he considered himself numb to it all. The signs of addiction and the radius of pain it caused. The chemical provided a brief check-out in exchange for a hell of a lot of grief. The ones who did it found an escape from life. But drugs weren't a winner's game, more like an egg-timer's wait to misery.

There was little rhyme or reason to when and how hard the repercussions hit, but watching a twenty-one-year-old boy man up to his consequences had stirred something in Aidan.

Before he left, Aidan checked in on Mike. The second victim had a ventilator breathing for him, the boy still incoherent after a month of treatment.

Another glimpse of how heavy handed fate can be.

As he spoke to the boy's mother, Aidan learned that the kid had had the longest exposure to the flame—more than a minute—resulting in major skin damage, which required several surgeries. He was lucky to be alive. Aidan remained silent a few minutes by the boy's bedside before he left, sliding the patient room door carefully behind him.

*The roulette wheel spins, and one night of stupidity costs a lifetime of penance.*

And the number of victims would grow if Aidan didn't stop the Dove ring, *now*.

As Aidan drove down the west back roads his mind returned to when the rash of cocaine sales had first started up three years ago, the deals going down at college parties. Evidence of the group's involvement was obtained when he and Paul had first started on the case: sample-sized plastic bags marked with a small gray Dove stamp found next to the bodies of boogered up students. The Dove brand made a quick reputation for itself with the drug's purity, lab reports revealing that the dust lacked beiging chemicals, which resulted in more deaths as buyers did larger quantities of it, expecting it to be less refined.

Aidan and Paul worked well together, each of them doing what they did best. Aidan performed the research while Paul made the arrests. Within months they'd busted three of the ring's biggest dealers. Then a few weeks later Paul had spotted a brunette woman recruiting new pushers. Rachel Lancaster.

It'd taken Aidan a while to locate the woman's criminal records, her past buried in numerous case files. True to bad guy form, Lancaster's behavioral tendencies filled the bill: reckless disregard toward others, quick temper, manipulation.

Aidan learned that Lancaster was adopted at two years of age, and that her indiscretions had begun early. A bully in elementary school, her anger problem quickly led to fights and acting out. The paper trail of her juvenile record culminated five years later with numerous underage drinking charges coupled with attempts at running away. The offenses intensified once she hit eighteen, the crimes filed under different names in order to mask her permanent record. With weapon and drug arrests spanning several states, she eventually settled in Maryland, establishing a connection to one Marcus De Silva, a figure Aidan had long suspected to be the guy running the show.

Unlike Lancaster, De Silva maintained an airtight profile, his records including convictions in Florida for drug and arms profiteering under other aliases. De Silva had only been identified in Maryland once, the witness killed shortly after, the murder driving home the message that the Dove group didn't play. In turn, the judge helped the NARCs send a message right back. De Silva's flunkies were sentenced to life sentences in jail.

While their ring leader got away.

But De Silva was smooth, hard to catch. Deadly.

In the months following the arrests, the drug lord's skill at evasion had left Aidan and Paul in the dust. They'd come close to taking him down several times, missing him in the raids by minutes. And while Aidan had never seen the criminal in the flesh, there were surveillance photos. Tall, tan, with an almost easy-going look about him, De Silva had black irises that exposed him as a devil. Two black holes, devoid of compunction or repentance—Aidan could feel the cold in the man staring out from the photograph. Like Rachel, the man didn't care who he hurt, or to what extent.

Days after their last near-bust, De Silva went further underground. It was Rachel who surfaced now and again, acting as the ring's moll and middleman.

But Aidan had seen her in person, one time...

Aidan knew the woman's facial structure: the shape of her nose, her dark hair; the evil mug shot branded into his brain. He'd go to his grave knowing her brown, almost-red, remorseless eyes. The sound of the gunshot replayed in Aidan's head, a stab of pain that echoed as his shoulder twitched.

The shooting was a hit to both sides: law enforcement and the distributers. Paul's death put serious heat on Lancaster, so she followed in De Silva's footsteps and vanished. Drug activity slowed to crawl, the distribution of the Dove product virtually disappearing.

*Until now.*

Aidan was unaware of how long he'd been sitting parked in the farm's visitor lot. Turning off the engine, he felt strange, as if his pilot light had gone out and needed to be relit.

*By some other hand than fate*, he hoped, getting out of the car.

He walked down the back side of the main building as something flickered in the center of his chest. Maybe he should have taken more time before approaching the girl, but he struck down the thought. He'd never needed a break between interviews before, and he damn well needed to get back into his standard pattern of operation.

*And it's an interview, not a date, so why the nerves?*

Besides, the jump back into the case felt invigorating, to a point. The return to work stoked him, he just wished he didn't have to work with an observer.

With a huff, Aidan thought of the other piece of business he'd taken care of over the weekend. He'd broken down and called Carson, which to his surprise went better than expected. The blue boy answered his phone by the second ring and didn't come off as smug, proving that they both might survive their little working arrangement.

Carson kept his usual measure of calm the moment Aidan spoke, the cop launching into a quick run-down of facts that he'd dug up on the girl, followed by an inquiry on Josh Moreland. After the slow-healing status update on the burn victims, Carson wrapped up the call with an astute, "Okay, I'll have more next time."

Aidan looked at his phone after they'd disconnected, impressed. He liked the direct exchange. No sugar-coating, no bullshit. The

less their alliance/collaboration/*whatever*-you-
called-it weighed him down, the better.

Somewhere in the hospital Aidan had let go
of his reservations regarding the cop, an
agreement to the unspoken terms of their new
pact.

With his own stipulations, of course.

Carson wasn't his partner, and by
"cooperating" Aidan had one ground rule—he
wouldn't answer anything he didn't want to.
Carson could ask, but Aidan chose to answer.

Not that either of them had much choice.

Aidan strode under the pitched arch of
Hammond's main barn, the mid-morning sun
speckling the floor through the notched holes
and crevices. Planked with wood and tinged in a
classic faded red, the inside carried the aura of a
country painting. Practical and inviting, the
walls were reinforced with rafters that sheltered
a broad row of stalls. At a glance Aidan could
spot the few places where small renovations had
been made. He could see that the building itself
would benefit from a full remodel, the project
likely delayed given the farm's budget.

"G'morning." Sophie's voice brought Aidan's
head around. She entered the barn behind him,
her eyes glinting chocolate brown as she stepped
through the light.

"'Mornin'," Aidan offered with a smile.

"You here to check in?" she asked.

"Yeah." She opened her mouth to say
something just as he threw a glimpse at the
ceiling.

"How long have you been working out of this
building?" he asked.

Sophie paused, appearing to mentally add up the time. "Twenty years. The infrastructure is as solid as they come, and the roof has held up. If the girders were steel instead of wood we'd be in better shape. These humid Maryland summers warp everything." Her eyes traced the lines of the beams, nails pinning the planks at the corners. "We'd planned to utilize the ground space for a training ring after Mr. McAllaster sold us the parcel of land next door. Many of the volunteers have already offered to help build, we just need to raise the funds to cover materials. We may get to it year after next, if donations allow."

His eyes skipped over the familiar length of the walkway, drifting over a massive stack of bales that fortified the far wall. The plaque that hung on the wall read:

*This Barn is Maintained for the Comfort of the HORSE.*

The realization that Sophie had run the place for over thirty years struck him.

"Spending is always a balancing act. It's hard to make the necessary cuts, this year especially. The cost of feed goes up all the time, and this month we have fifteen more mouths." She appraised the hay, as if tallying up how long it would last. "Add in the medications, supplies, replacement items. And we're still dealing with some legal issues right now," she added under her breath.

Aidan turned to her, not liking how worried she looked.

"Issues? With the racehorses? I thought they were abandoned, that calls for instant seizure—"

"The track is claiming that they had no knowledge of the desertion," Sophie explained as Aidan bit his tongue, irritation flashing.

Aidan loathed how low capitalism could make people sink. It was typical that a corporation would keep the horses tied up in legal while a non-profit was caring for the animals.

"It's horseshit, I know."

That got him to crack a smile. Sophie knew when to call it.

"Can you get Bill to fight it?"

Bill Swanson was the farm's pro bono lawyer. Providing his services as a donation to the farm, he'd saved Hammond's thousands in attorney's fees over the years. He was a damn good advocate, and Aidan had witnessed the man's handiwork with previous abuse cases. But even with the legal backing, the farm would be paying out of pocket for horses that were lawfully owned by someone else. Worse, if the track won in court they could reclaim the animals, leaving them susceptible to more mistreatment.

"Yes, but until we can prove negligence, the state can't give us full ownership. It's been a struggle." She let out breath, her shoulders falling.

"If there's anything I can do to help." Aidan's tone went soft.

"We'll get by, we always do. But thanks."

The two meandered to other side of the barn, stopping at the mouth to peer out into the stretch of main paddock, sunlight radiating in a wide beam over the open spread of woodchips. Sophie passed through the spotlight without so much as a squint, unfazed by the blast of illumination. "Kelly's right there."

Aidan stayed in the shadow of the wall, concealed as he caught sight of the girl. Bumping his shoulder into the lip of the door's frame, he let his eyes run over her. Hair up in a high ponytail, clad in an old shirt and an older pair of jeans, Kelly slowly led a sickly looking horse into the paddock of the adjacent barn. A staff member followed her around the small patch of dirt. A lanky, young kid—*Jason*, if Aidan remembered.

"She's been doing a good job," Sophie commented, noting where Aidan's attention had gone. "Spent all day Saturday observing and most of Sunday working with greens, a few yellows."

Aidan watched as the girl kept a loose hand on the lead rope, conversing with Jason over the horse's weathered back, motioning to the animal's hind quarters. The male aide smiled at something she'd said.

Aidan frowned as the recognition hit him. Jason Wallis, the son of a local business owner. Barely twenty, the kid had started with the farm a few years ago, some fresh muscle to help Hank with the heavier farm chores. A known charmer at the fundraiser events, the boy's social prowess had never bugged Aidan before. But for some reason watching the guy practice his lines on the girl pissed Aidan off.

"Something wrong?" Sophie chimed in.

"No," Aidan responded in a dead tone, wishing he could iron out his face. He'd never been good at bluffing. He watched as Kelly ran a gentle hand over the horse's back, Jason finding the action a perfect cue to prop his hand up, too.

*Real suave.*

An ugly sound came from Aidan's throat.

Sophie dipped her head, hiding her amused grin.

"So, she's been working out okay?" he asked, changing the subject.

"Yes," Sophie said with a nonchalant cross of her arms. "She catches on quick, is polite. The staff has nothing but good things to say, Pippa and Jason especially."

Just as the sentence left her mouth, Aidan watched the boy steal another glance from around the animal, the girl unknowing; her sole focus on the horse.

Yeah, Jason liked her, all right.

*Player.*

Aidan wasn't sure what irritated him worse, the fact the kid had game or that his own skills were toast. With a grimace, Aidan turned his eyes to the thoroughbred. The horse was thin as hell, its protruding ribs and a stomach so sunken that it blurred the form made by the animal's matted coat.

"Which horse is that?"

"King's Keegan, he's one of the five."

"Five? I thought there were six?"

Sophie's voice dropped. "We lost one." There was a beat of silence before she spoke again, clearing a frog from her throat. "Kelly specifically asked to help with Keegan's rehabilitation—she's fond of him, and he's calm with her."

In the distance Keegan lifted his head, sniffing Kelly's hand.

"She's been bringing him his food, a mush that's easy on his stomach. It'll be a while before we can give him anything solid. It's baby steps for right now. I didn't see any harm in her working with a purple, as long as she's supervised," Sophie said, observing the pair with sage authority.

Aidan watched as Jason ran another roaming glance over Kelly, looking enthralled with his assignment.

"Can't she work with Pippa?"

Before Sophie could reply a sudden buzz of talk erupted, Kelly pointing to something on the ground and reverently petting Keegan, reciting more of the adamant "Good boy" praise she'd given Moe. Aidan cocked his head, trying to make out what monumental achievement had taken place.

"Bowel movement," Sophie replied, answering the unspoken question. "Means his intestines are healing."

"Oh," Aidan said, noting the steaming pile that had not been there a moment earlier.

"I'm going up to the house for coffee, you want some?" Sophie offered.

"No, thanks."

"I'll be in the office if you need anything."

Sophie's footsteps faded as Aidan went back to observing. The girl continued to shower affection on Keegan, the horse soaking it up; his ears forward, eyelids low as he lowered his neck to allow her more access.

Covered in dust, boots thick with mud, the girl didn't fuss about being dirty, her attention occupied by the horse. Aidan recognized the expression she wore, having seen it before just that morning with Josh Moreland. She wanted closure for the animal, for him to recover.

*She cared.*

The observation didn't surprise him. The background check that Carson had run on the girl had come back squeaky clean. A decade-plus honor student and cum laude graduate from college, the girl didn't have as much as a parking ticket. One address aside from her current had popped up: a townhouse up in central New York State owned by a Lynn Monroe, a RN at the local hospital. No listing of a Mr. Monroe, no variance in surname.

*Raised by a single mother.*

The missing father figure put a single checkmark in the girl's con column, as a lot of juvenile crime began with instability at home, but the one statistical fact hardly outweighed the pros. Her academics said a lot: smart, hardworking, goal-oriented.

It was unlikely that she'd throw away a decade of school to fall in with the Dove dealers, although Aidan knew there were few lengths people wouldn't go for fast money. When poverty hit he'd seen average folks take the slide into dealing and prostitution. Any work they had to do to shelter their families, to put kids through school, no matter how illegal.

He didn't like to think the girl capable of it, but given the length of time it took her to complete her undergraduate, she must of paid her way.

And in life, you couldn't rule out need.

His thoughts traveled back to the first night he'd met her in jail, mascara smeared down her cheeks, her eyes suspicious. She'd seemed disoriented but still aware, which put him on guard.

Had she witnessed something that night? Was she a part of it?

Aidan watched the girl now murmur to the horse, running a gentle hand over the animal's gaunt flank, her face kind.

His eyes traced the lines of her profile, and Aidan had to admit that she was sort of pretty. About five-foot-six, and lean underneath the baggy, inexpensive clothes. Her dark hair flashed copper in the sun, a long coif of bangs falling free of the ponytail, flopping in her face like the forelock of a mane. When he'd introduced himself in the barn was when he'd gotten his first real impression of her: apricot skin paired with round hazel eyes, all set in an oval-shaped face. She'd worn little makeup that day where he could see her features. Simple, noticeable.

Aidan pushed off from the wall to go to her when Jason picked the same moment to encroach, walking up to the girl, beating him to the punch. Kelly finished up her petting and handed off the lead-rope. The boy reached out his hand and leaned in close, speaking to her as if giving some kind of instruction.

*She can hear you, pal. There's this thing called* personal space.

Before Aidan could voice the objection, Kelly gave the boy a nod and waited as Jason escorted the horse away, circling once before she headed toward the main barn.

Toward him.

*Oh, crap.*

Aidan paused, stepping back into the dark of the space.

A minute later Kelly passed through the ray of sun, her hair going aflame in a highlight of crimson before dimming back to deep brown.

*Auburn hair.* Her natural color, he figured by the absence of dark roots or the chemical tinge of hair dye.

She walked past him, not noticing that he hid in the pocket of shade.

Aidan opened his mouth but nothing came out, her closeness fascinating him. She stood a few feet away, her back facing him while she perused the stacks of hay. Preoccupied, Kelly leaned down to examine one bound square, pulling out a few strings to roll between her fingers before bringing them up to her face. The exertion made her legs go taut against the back of her jeans, revealing the trim silhouette of her slender thighs.

Aware that the longer he stood there the more of a creeper he became, Aidan craned his head, trying to poke into her peripheral vision.

No luck.

Oh, for crap's sake, it never took this much effort for him to approach a girl.

He rotated his jaw in an attempt to find his voice. He needed to announce his presence, but didn't want to startle her. Oblivious, she kept to her business, bringing another handful of the thread-like food to her nose, smelling it, murmuring some kind of disaffirmation to herself. Flipping her sights to the top of the hay heap, she dropped the unsatisfactory sample and started to climb, her lithe body making the hike appear effortless.

Aidan gawked.

*What is she doing? She's passing up ten-plus bales at the bottom for something at the top?*

Kelly scaled the heaped pile, appearing to find what she wanted at the summit. Tugging free another tester from one of the squares, she verified it, fisting the cords binding the block with both hands. Hauling the load by herself, Aidan watched as she wobbled under the thing's weight, trying to keep her foothold on the stringy bricks as she descended.

"You want some help?" he spoke up as she reached the halfway mark.

She saw him then, her eyes darting up and flaring. Gasping and dropping her cargo, the messy hunk tumbled off to the side as she began to lose her footing.

*Real smooth. Way to scare the hell out of her.*

Kelly strived to regain her balance, her foot shooting forward to brace her body when the unsteady surface gave way, throwing her into a freefall.

*Oh...no!*

Aidan lunged forward as Kelly hit the ground, landing flat on her back with an audible *Ooof!*

"*Shit*—don't move!" he directed, rushing to her. His emergency medical training took over as he kneeled beside her, keeping one hand close to her neck and one near her waist.

Clearly winded, her eyes were peeled wide, staring up at him in shock. Her hair lay in a splayed out aura around her face as he scanned her body, not detecting any broken bones. Aidan moved in close, sliding his palm under her neck and gently palpating her skin, while visually checking her ears.

*No fluid making a halo on the ground, no immediate swelling.*

"Are you okay?"

She stared at him, her muscles still. He pushed down his panic and moved in closer, feeling the soft column of her throat with the pads of his fingers. "Kelly, does that hurt?"

Something in the use of her name got her to come around. She shook her head slowly, proving she hadn't broken her neck. Aidan looked down, realizing how close their noses were, almost touching. He forced himself to lean back.

*Personal space.*

"Do you feel pain anywhere?"

"No," she said, blinking at him.

"Did you bruise anything?"

"Yes, my pride." She moved to sit up.

"Here, let me help you." He pushed his weight onto his heels, extending his hand. Their palms met and with a sturdy draw he had her on her feet, both of them swiping at the fresh dirt that dusted her clothes.

"I tried to catch your attention," he said, retracting his hand with vigor as one of his wayward swipes came close to her butt. Her *nice* butt.

*Hey, no touching.* He retracted his hands with an awkward jerk.

"I didn't see you," she said, continuing to brush herself off.

"I know," he retorted, looking for the hay she'd dropped. Her eyes bored into him as he stepped over to it, plucked the block off the ground with ease and delivered it at her feet.

"If you saw me, why didn't you—"

"Why didn't you just grab a bale from down here?" Aidan cut her off.

"We needed hay," she replied, not skipping a beat.

*And all this?* Confused, Aidan pointed to the abundance stacked around them.

"*Hay*, not straw," she said gently, as if he were missing something.

"The scratchy stuff on the floor." Aidan felt comical as he pointed.

She giggled, the sound disarming as she crouched down and picked a green splinter from her bundle. She dipped again, plucking another stick-looking fragment from the floor to hold side-by-side, displaying the comparison. "Hay has a full head on its stalk, like grain. It's more of a green color, it smells sweet."

Aidan smiled. It'd been ages since he'd been schooled about something.

He bothered to listen because his teacher was cute.

"Straw is coarse, the hay's discarded shell, the chaff." She held up the yellowish looking stick. "It's used for bedding, while the hay is what the horses eat—" She stopped as if correcting herself. "What healthy horses will eat." For some reason she got quiet. Sad.

The expression didn't look right on her.

"Everything okay in here?" Jason appeared in the doorway. "Oh, hey...Aidan." The kid's eyes lingered over them, the two standing less than a foot from one another.

Aidan stepped closer to Kelly.

"I fell getting the hay. It was my fault," Kelly piped up, the reply hurried. "Dect—Uh, *Aidan*, helped me up."

And where was lover boy?

"The bales are too much for her to carry alone," Aidan said, his voice stern but he didn't care. No one sent a woman to lug something that heavy.

"Here, let me get that for you." Jason pegged Aidan with a hard look as the boy stepped forward, blocking Aidan from the dropped bale.

Aidan wanted to stay and talk to the girl, but his chance got slapped away now.

He glanced at Jason, the kid kept up a cool front while he eyed Aidan as if he were an intruder.

*Not so cool underneath all the smooth social exterior.*

Aidan could see Jason's attitude seething underneath and wished he knew how to put on

a mask of charm like that. A man of little
pretense, if Aidan was angry, you knew it.

What you see....

"I have it—" Kelly bent down to lift the bale.
Still wobbly from the fall, she circled the floor,
drawing in a deep breath. Aidan's moved to
help, his eyes darting to a line of yellow-green
sticking out from her hair. He beat her to the
hay, lifting the square easily, carting the bundle
past Jason.

*Hay isn't the only thing that looks green,*
Aidan mused as he dropped the heap into the
wheelbarrow waiting at the mouth of the barn.

"Thanks," Jason said dryly as Aidan strode
back, stopping in front of Kelly.

"Thank you," Kelly said, her smile fading as
Aidan stepped up close, reaching for her. Her
soft hair brushed his hand, silk against the
calloused pads of his fingers. Entranced, her
eyes followed his movement, watching as he
gently disentangled a thread from the top of her
head.

Aidan held the greenish looking string up for
inspection. "Hay or straw?"

Kelly's smile lit up the space, the sight
making Aidan's chest open.

She leaned forward, eyes narrowed in
examination. "Hay."

Aidan grinned as a blush touched her cheek,
a swish of movement behind them making her
turn away. Jason waited by the wheelbarrow,
his face dour as if he'd been slapped in the puss
with a wet mop.

*A little friendly competition never hurt
anyone.*

Especially when Aidan won.

"We'd better go. We're making food rounds to the other barns," Kelly said, caving to Jason's impatient stare. Aidan stepped in between them, his body a physical block to the censure.

"Will I see you later?" Aidan asked, relishing how Kelly couldn't peer around him, making it just him and her.

"Sure." She blinked, giving Aidan a dopey half-grin before she stepped tentatively around him, falling in step behind Jason as the boy pushed the wheelbarrow with renewed fervor. Aidan tracked them as they made their way across the paddock, the girl looking back at him from midway across, her eyes bright.

Aidan watched her as he rolled the hay between his fingers. Glancing down at the twist of green, he smiled.

So he had a little charm left in him after all. Good to know.

"There you go." Kelly took the bucket Pippa gave her with sure hands. She glanced into the pail, watching the soupy, gray feed slosh around like watered down oatmeal. Kelly knew that the mush contained vitamins and nutrients that would help Keegan's insides heal faster, but it smelled as appetizing as it looked.

*No wonder Keegan jumped at the hay.*

"Main barn," Pippa instructed. The senior staff member stepped over a line of pails lining the concrete floor, her destination a rack of metal shelves that held a medicine cabinet full of horse supplements.

"Will do." Kelly turned and did an abrupt halt. "Wait, where's Jason?"

Since her fiasco with the wrong halter her first day, Kelly was assigned company when she visited Keegan, to act as a backup in the event the horse became ornery.

"He's in with Soph." Pippa kicked out the reply, her eyes honing in on a glass bottle with an eye dropper top. Unscrewing the cap she hovered over two of the meal buckets, counting the number of drips falling into each of the plastic tubs.

"That goes to Keegan," she reiterated, moving on to the next supplement.

"Right." Kelly stared down at the mash, waiting.

"What's wrong?"

"Someone usually goes with me."

Pippa paused, perception taking root in her eyes. "Do you want help?"

"Uh, no. I mean, can feed him by myself. If you say it's okay."

The woman smiled, her olive skin warm in the early morning sun. "I think you can handle Keegan."

"All right." Kelly felt as if she'd been knighted making her way to the main barn. There was an elation to doing a job well, and being recognized for it.

Like a graduation, she relished the sense of growth.

Peeking through the bars of the horse's stall, Keegan stood in the center, his ears perking as he heard her approach.

"I came with grub." Kelly unlatched the door and ducked in, the close quarters no longer intimidating. Keegan crowded her back like he had at their first meeting, all *Ooo, food!* But she knew the rules of the game this time. Tucking the bucket like a football, she pushed at his flank, prompting his thin body backward.

"Step back, Keegan."

The snort he gave her was droll, his nose nudging her shoulder as if saying, *That's for ME. Mine. MY food...* Kelly deftly blocked Keegan's attempt to knock the bucket out of her hand, which was his Plan B. His next move would be lunging his head into the bucket.

Kelly switched hands in preparation.

"Keeg, you know the drill. Back it up, buddy boy." She pressed harder against his chest, her palm meeting bone and thin muscle. Keegan took a meager step in reverse, more reclining than moving, so Kelly kept up the resistance until she saw his hooves come off the ground. The three steps he'd conceded opened up space in the room. Keegan twitched but remained still, his face a look of *How 'bout now? Good? Happy? MY FOOD.*

"Good boy." Kelly dumped the bucket into his feed tray in one deft movement and stepped out of the way.

Keegan made a head-dive into the dish, rummaging around and re-emerging with a mustache of gray painted around his mouth. Rolling his tongue around, his face went content as if saying, *You know, if you mix in a little alfalfa, this stuff is pretty good.* Like a little kid delving into a grand dinner, the munch-munch-munch was sweet music to Kelly's ears.

*Eating, not choking.*

A replacement to the gagging when she'd given Keegan hay her first day at Hammond's, the memory was hard to erase. She watched as Keegan lipped up the pâté mash, relieved that although the mush was no more than runny oatmeal, he could swallow it without struggle and wanted more. Kelly trailed her eyes over the jutting bone of his shoulder, the line of dots revealing the vertebrate of his back. In her head she could see the nutrients running through his internal organs, like a diagram in a book, the skeletal example present in front of her. She flipped her gaze to his face. Keegan ate with concentration, a look of survival hard on his face.

But the horse wasn't a graph or an illustration. Not an organism to be studied.

*He's a living thing.*

Kelly chided herself for having never spent time around animals before. At school she'd studied them: anatomy, genes, cells, but she'd never bothered to analyze the outside. The *real.*

Keegan's withered flesh glared at her.

*What did he look like before?*

She envisioned layers of muscle, of healthy cartilage and bone. Strong hooves carrying him over the dirt as if he were flying.

The malnourished body before her now was so battered, deteriorated.

*As if he'd survived a war.*

Kelly reached out a hand, not thinking. You didn't touch a horse while they ate, especially one that had been starved. But Keegan didn't flinch, didn't snap at her as Kelly laid a palm on his neck. His tendons flexed under her fingertips as Keegan chewed, letting out a heavy exhale. He closed his eyes, his body calm, at rest. He let her touch him.

*A sign of trust.*

Kelly had never received a sweeter gift.

She stroked his shoulder, a vow igniting within her. She would be there when Keegan regained his strength, when he healed. She wouldn't leave until she saw him able to run again. She pulled her hand away, allowing him to eat in peace. Just as she let go Keegan's head turned, his eyes guileless. She realized what the expression meant.

Everyone Keegan ever trusted had left him. His owners, his handlers....

"It's okay, boy. Finish your food. I'll be here when you're done."

Kelly stepped into his line of sight and leaned against the wall. The horse stared a minute, as if waiting for her to take the offer back. She held still, ready to hang out, and for the first time in her life she was content to not be in motion.

In the quiet she could sense a similarity between them, a camaraderie. The two shared the same weathered skin and sky-high hopes.

Two explorers who'd veered off the beaten path.

She leaned back, watching him watch her. "I'll stay as long as you want me to."

And with that Keegan let out a reverberated sigh and went back to his breakfast.

# CHAPTER 7

The next morning Kelly kicked her feet out under the hub of her desk, dodging her purse. Giving her workspace an once-over she mentally ran down the department's checklist. The *Biology for Beginner's* workshop notes were typed up, and in Professor Moore's mailbox. The invitation flyer for the department luncheon was ready to be passed out to the students next week, and the grades for the spring sub-semester in the queue to be finalized and distributed.

She turned to look at the clock on the wall.

*Ten more minutes.*

To quell her nerves she gave creative visualization a work out, repeating, *a good outcome,* in her head. She envisioned Prof. Keene shaking her hand in congratulations.

*A good outcome...*

Kelly's palms came to rest on her thighs, accentuating their inactivity.

The biology department's office stood quiet in the way that holidays and the gaps between classes always made school. The floor-to-ceiling windows on the opposite wall cast rays of early-afternoon sun across her desk, dappling everything with flickers of soundless light.

Restless, she stood up, her booted footsteps carrying her to the large center window, the blinds pulled up to let in the sunny day. She peered out, the field at the center of the University of Maryland's main campus sprawled out before her in emerald green grass. The scene was like oil-painted Americana, its rolling lawn bordered by red-brick sidewalks and stone-mortared short walls. The roundabout in the distance displayed an immaculate letter M constructed of deep red and pure white flowers, surrounded by perfectly pruned shrubbery.

The bodies of students dotted the ground: some propped up on elbows, lying with laptops and cups of iced coffee, throwing footballs and hovering over open textbooks.

*College life.*

She scanned the field of fresh-faced twenty-year-olds, and a familiar drop behind her sternum verified that she was what had expired. A decade behind everyone else, her youth had become a big part of the investment she'd put into her education. The cost involved more than money. It took time.

*Too much time.*

Back in New York she'd waitressed full-time, living a dual life between night classes and homework. The lifestyle leaving her with all the responsibilities of the adult world but none of its pleasures. She'd never resented the lack of freedom, but she had to admit, a little fun now and again would be...nice.

Her eyes traced the white columns that shouldered the buildings, the walls of sturdy crimson brick indented with clear windows and crisp paint. Her gaze settled on a girl nestled off in the green. Tied around her waist was a windbreaker with UMD stitched in bright red, black, white, and gold silk, the colors shimmering in the afternoon sun. Kelly recalled seeing the very same jacket in the bookstore the other day.

It looked comfortable. Beautiful.

*Expensive*, which one glance at the price tag had affirmed.

Pulling out the mental scale, the one that made an appearance every time there was a need-versus-want situation, she knew the garment didn't stand a chance, the thing stamped with the label *extravagance* along with luxuries like steak dinners and pricey hand lotion.

Yeah, a week's worth of food took precedence over any new article of clothing, even if it did show school spirit. Plus she hadn't registered for her grad classes yet, which threw marked-up book and tuition costs into the mix.

*No pretty new jackets.*

Wrapping her arms around herself, Kelly stroked the worn fabric of her plaid shirt with her thumb. She wore the short-sleeve on a regular basis; it was her favorite. She hoped it lasted a few years longer. By then she could maybe afford to splurge on a good replacement. But even then it wouldn't be as nice as anything from the bookstore, she thought with a sigh.

*Pining over clothes.*

God, the violin playing behind her had to stop.

Bringing the mental pity parade to a halt, Kelly realized that she was standing on the grounds of her first-pick college—*working* there.

*How many people are standing where I am now?*

She had to give herself props. Even though her position was temporary the placement of the job was perfect, in the university's biology department, right where she wanted to be. One of those "good on your résumé" bargains, where in exchange for the time, she'd gain experience, and maybe make an impression on some of the professors while she was there.

A flash of longing tugged at her as Kelly recalled the biology lab back at SUNY Albany, the day-long trips she'd taken to gather samples and study habitats. The memories opened her chest. She had won over all of her New York professors with her drive to learn. She'd found the work interesting, exciting. The thrill of exploring new things nudged at something warm and deep within her, fanning the spark into a tiny flame. Like heat raising a hot air balloon, Kelly felt lighter just thinking about it. She loved school; it made her feel alive.

And to give herself credit, she *had* been around some of Maryland's biology professors.

*In passing.*

Greetings and thank yous exchanged over documents delivered. Requests made and acknowledged. During the impromptu encounters, Kelly had considered saying more, trying to ask about her application status or to even just talk a little shop, but remained careful not to push. Other grad students had taken the same tack, and didn't get anywhere by annoying those in charge.

Glancing over to her computer, she was beckoned by the screensaver with the school's logo. The sight helped rally her thoughts as she walked back to her station, noting the time.

She needed to get going.

Locking up her credenza with a little more force than necessary, she pivoted back to her computer and signed off. The speakers played a shutting-down decrescendo as she threw a guarded look behind her.

She was alone.

In a single slow movement she pulled a paper from the pocket of her jeans, the letter worn at its folded edges. Flattening it against the desktop, Kelly stared down at the letterhead of the state of Maryland. The laser jet print was commonplace, but the phrases *suspected possession of illegal drugs, no prior record,* and *hundred hours community service* seemed to glare up at her.

For being a reprimand, Hammond's had become her safe haven. A snapshot of Keegan flashed in her mind. His long nose dipping down to the bucket and popping up, muzzle covered in mauve-tinted mush, the expression of *MMMmmm* broad on his face.

Kelly grinned at the memory.

*That horse.*

Then cobalt blue eyes appeared. Aidan Wright's tall, lean body emerging next. Kelly's brain turned over the hazy reenactment, her body tingling at the memory.

*That man.*

Aidan had been absent at her hearing, and Kelly suspected that the one night in jail was it, that she'd never see him again. Then the guy started showing up at Hammond's. He needed to interview her and appeared to want to conduct it on level terms, to make her comfortable.

Although *comfortable* hadn't been the outcome.

The two times he'd sought her out had been a disaster: first with Moe, and again in the barn, the graceless nosedive she'd done in front of him spearing her confidence. The tumble had caught her by surprise, and distorted her perception. Her heart had trembled like a bird from the shock of fall, then pounded for a different reason. She couldn't shake how, fast as a blink, he'd hovered over her, all authority and concern. She could still feel his arms braced on either side of her, the heat of his skin bringing out the woodsy smell of his cologne.

But none of that compared to his eyes. Up close his cerulean blue irises were dark, like the Caribbean Sea at night. He'd looked at her with consideration, heating her blood, making her feel....

God, she couldn't recall the last time she'd noticed a man like that, with passion.

Kelly pushed down her enthusiasm at the memory.

He'd been making sure that she hadn't knocked herself unconscious, nothing more. The man needed a coherent witness, not a new friend.

Although she liked the idea of being his friend.

*Come on, common sense. Feel free to step in any minute now,* she thought, the over-optimistic, cheerleading section of her head taking over. Her hand found its way up to her hair, running over the length of her ponytail. Catching the action, she pulled back as if the strands had burned her.

What questions did he have for her anyway?

She doubted that the officer who'd interviewed her the night of the party had left anything out, but if Aidan wanted additional information... And it'd give her a reason to talk to him.

She let her imagination off its leash. Maybe they could go out for coffee and talk.

Not a date. *Coffee.*

With a sexy arson detective.

He'd get his answers, and maybe she'd get to know more about him.

Then, like the first time she'd laid eyes on him, he'd disappear.

Great. *Now* her common sense decided to show up.

*Killjoy.*

Her chest ached at the shutdown. She didn't know why all of it bothered her so much. She'd gotten into trouble for the first time in her pathetic existence, the result of which involved a cute detective. She needed to clip the pie-in-the-sky anticipation. No romanticizing.

None of Aidan's interest in her was personal. Or probable.

*You'd think that being accused of drug-dealing would be enough to kill off any feelings of attraction...*

The image of him suspended above her lingered, the thought of him sparking every time she dropped her mental guard—

"You leaving?"

Kelly crushed the letter in her grasp, whirling the direction of the sound.

"*Rebecca.*" The word came out a gasp as Kelly crammed the letter-ball into the purse at her feet and rushed to stand up. "You scared me. I didn't hear you come in."

As if the top and bottom halves of her face operated with different muscles, a smile stretched Rebecca's lips while everything north of her nose remained cool as an igloo. The woman's dark curls fell below her shoulders, her deep colored eyes darting to the open purse on the floor and then back up to Kelly's face.

"We seem to keep missing one another."

Kelly had only been working at the office a few weeks when she'd first met Rebecca. The woman had stopped by to introduce herself, a graduate intern from the earth science department next door. Kelly had noticed her before, both of them about the same age and pursuing related fields of study. The social resemblance ended there, however. The quintessential socialite, Rebecca attended all the college events and private-parties.

The girl who had invited Kelly to *the party.*

Kelly took a step backward, bumping into her chair, sending the thing into a full swivel. "Yeah, I've been busy, uh, finishing up the semester..." she said, stopping the wayward seat with her thigh.

"Of course." Rebecca waited a beat, side-stepping the brush off. "Well, I wanted to see how you were." She enunciated the tail end of the sentence with a flourish. A bridge into some new invite, Kelly sensed.

And the answer to that would be a big, fat *no*.

*Talk about your knee-jerk reactions.*

Kelly winced. There was no justifiable reason for her to dislike Rebecca. Well, other than the fact that the woman had played hostess to Kelly's night from hell.

*Other than that...*

"I wanted to see if you were free this weekend—"

Kelly felt her brow furrow as Rebecca continued. Ignoring the response, the woman's flow of speech ran over Kelly's trepidation, the effect smoothing, disarming.

Practiced.

"I don't think—"

"It's a small get-together at my house. A few of my closest friends," she retorted.

*Small get-together.* Kelly figured that constituted half the campus.

Rebecca's eyes narrowed on Kelly as she tacked on, "Leslie Nelson is coming. She's working on her PhD in bio—one of Keene's golden candidates. I bet she could tell you all about..."

Kelly's ears began to filter out the words even though they interested her, watching Rebecca trudge on with the party sales pitch. Kelly looked up into Rebecca's face as she went on, the woman's irises catching Kelly's attention. A unique shade of brown, the mahogany hue was a gradient that looked almost red, garnet embers against her pale skin and dark hair. To any biology student this would be fascinating, a trait to analyze, but after their many encounters, Kelly found that no warmth radiated from those crimson eyes, only a creeping chill.

"So, you think you can make it?" Rebecca finished, transferring her weight from one foot to the other.

"Rebecca—" Kelly reached for a polite decline but couldn't conjure one. Honesty was all she had left. She retreated back into her desk. "I can't. I—I want to avoid the scene for a while, but thank you for thinking of me."

As the words came out the aura of the room shifted, morphing from congenial into coercive. Kelly avoided the icy eye contact. Reaching down, she lifted her purse to her shoulder, turning the direction of the exit.

"Okay, I understand. Where you off to now?" Rebecca asked the perk in her tone contrived.

"A meeting." Kelly tossed the response back, making a break for the door.

"Where?"

"Nowhere important. I'll see you." Kelly waved an awkward goodbye, trying to come off as casual and failing miserably.

"Kelly," Rebecca started, stopping Kelly halfway. The woman's tone dropped its pretension. "Look, I know you must hate me for what happened that night. I had no idea that it was that kind of party and I hope you're okay."

Kelly felt her chest tighten again, wishing it were all in the past. What happened that night was no one's fault, but she couldn't shake the vague discomfort she felt around the woman. Maybe it was the disingenuous smile, or some conditioned response. Whatever the reason, Kelly just wanted to be left alone.

"Look, I appreciate you bringing my car back." The desk cop at the police station had been kind enough to drive Kelly home after her interview with Officer Carson. And Rebecca had returned her purse and car keys a few days later, at school.

"Sure," Rebecca said, following up with another well-versed show of teeth, the action sucking all the heat out of the room.

Kelly noticed it then. The woman's body stood loose, her muscles relaxed—except for her hands. Her fingers were balled into fists at her sides, a reinforcement of her red stare.

"We could get together to talk about it. It can be just you and me. I'm free this—"

"*No*," Kelly cut her off, silencing them both. "Sorry. I have to go."

The temperate air of the hallway hit Kelly like a heat lamp, smoothing the goose bumps that had appeared on her arms. She shuddered as if the movement would slough off her uneasiness. The pressure to hang out seemed to increase with every encounter with the woman, even more so since the night of the party. Rebecca had returned Kelly's missing purse and car keys, so all things considered, there were no ties, no reason to maintain the façade of friendship.

Ease filled her as Kelly sped down the hall, the distance clearing her head. Rounding the corner, Kelly slowed as she reached a door with outdated graduation cards taped all over its surface. She composed herself before knocking.

"Come in," a voice came back.

Dr. Keene looked up as Kelly entered, offering a cordial smile. "Kelly, thank you for coming. Sit down."

*Good outcome,* Kelly thought.

She closed the door and took a seat. The professor shuffled papers, leaving a closed file folder marked MONROE laid out on the desk.

"I first want to say that we are flattered by your interest in our program," Dr. Keene began, the cadence of her voice professional. "Your grades from SUNY at Albany are impressive."

Kelly felt her cheeks flush at the praise. "Thank you."

The professor's face went neutral.

*Not a normal response.* Kelly took a steadying breath. The Rebecca run-in must have shaken her.

"Well, the entire board gave your application careful review." The professor paused, a stone-faced reserve taking over. "I do have to inform you that, due to a failure to meet certain criteria, we are unable to approve your application at this time."

Kelly blinked as her mind ground to a halt.

*What?*

*That can't be right.* She'd reviewed every qualification, analyzed every subparagraph of the program. Her scores and experience were more than enough to—

"Dr. Keene, I don't understand—My GPA is far above average, I have recommendations from several of my New York teachers. I was careful to meet all the prerequisite requirements." She caught herself sputtering, etiquette taking a backseat to her astonishment.

"Yes, your grades exceed guideline expectations. We took serious consideration of them before making our decision."

"I don't understand," Kelly repeated.

Flipping open the folder, the professor lifted up a paper from the top, turning it to where she could see. Kelly stiffened as the letterhead registered, a match to the wad of paper stuffed in her purse. The verbiage stated the same verdict but in select areas the terms "misdemeanor" and "internal document" were listed next to Hammond's address. Her eyes honed in on the wide scrawl of a signature at the bottom: a broad A stringing into the clear surname, *Wright.*

Kelly felt all the blood drain from her body, leaving her a clammy shell of skin.

"It states here that you were aware of the sentence," Dr. Keene said softly.

Kelly gave a wooden nod, her voice dead. "I've—I've been serving the hours."

"The university holds a strict policy on personal conduct. The expectation here at Maryland is that our students behave in a responsible manner in and out of the classroom. I searched the bylaws for an exception, but unfortunately there is no recourse."

Kelly nodded her head again with slow acknowledgement, her ears staring to ring. "Yes. I...understand. May I have a copy of this?" She tapped on the letter. "And of the rejection, too. If that's okay?"

Dr. Keene plucked up the papers, pivoting in her chair to a small Xerox machine stationed behind her. The whir of the machine filled the silence as Kelly stared at the now blank desk.

In five minutes the aftermath of one night had set fire to eight years of her life. Someone could have stabbed her and she wouldn't have felt it.

Her future. Gone.

The professor turned, stapling the slips together, handing over the still warm copies.

Kelly took care in tri-folding the papers, her hands quivering. "I'm assuming—" The words came out a whisper. She cleared her throat and tried again. "Will this also forfeit my aide position in the biology department?"

Dr. Keene's face went grave. "I'm so sorry, Kelly."

The realization that she needed to breathe came as Kelly stood, lightheadedness making her weave on her feet. Dr. Keene got up, ready to offer a hand. Which was not the handshake Kelly had envisioned.

"I'll clean out my desk today," Kelly said, ignoring the gesture as she found her balance. "I appreciate your time."

"If anything changes—"

"That's okay," Kelly heard herself say, the words lost in a vacuum as she stumbled out the door.

The hallway air had turned cool, unwelcome, adding to the frozen cavern behind her ribs as Kelly stared down at the written rejection clutched in her grasp. How harmless the papers looked from the outside, like the sheets she filed—*used* to file.

Staring through the scroll's hollow center, she caught a glimpse of the signature.

*His signature.*

The halo of good-natured integrity burned away from the image of a pair of blue eyes. The corrosion made her want to cry. She'd thought that the hours were voluntary. A testament of good will that wouldn't go on her record. But he'd forced her to perform the service.

WHY? To corner her?

She put one numb foot in front of the other as she made her way back to her empty office. The sunset had left the space in a wide band of shadow, as if the sun had come to reclaim its light. The packing up of her few personal items took all of five minutes. Her purse stuffed, she left the office key on her desk and exited without looking back, preferring not to linger in the disgrace.

She barreled through the doors to the parking lot and glanced up. The opulent exterior of the campus no longer seemed impressive, but foreign and overcast. In a flash the setting of all her dreams had become a place where she no longer belonged.

She'd been banned. Exiled.

She reached her car, threw her bag on the passenger seat with her keys in hand. The vehicle's need to warm up forced her to sit still, the immobility making the fire in her chest surge, the mental fog lifting a little as a course of action started to smolder and fume.

Less than thirty minutes earlier Kelly had wanted to talk to Aidan, to tell him everything she knew. He had questions and she couldn't avoid him, couldn't refuse seeing him...

So she'd talk to him.

Yeah, the next time Aidan Wright showed up at Hammond's, she'd give the man his answers.

Right after he explained why he was sent to incinerate her life.

# CHAPTER 8

Aidan popped his head into Hammond's break room.

Pippa didn't bother to look up from her bag-o-lunch, she simply pointed east and said, "She's taking Keegan to his stall. Main barn."

"Thanks." Aidan gave a nod of acknowledgment and popped back out, not sure if he should be self-conscious. No one bothered to ask who he was there to see anymore, they all knew.

The morning air fed his thoughts as he walked, a literal breather from the last two days he'd spent cooped up with office paperwork. Digging through the stacks of interviews, reports, and investigation notes—the post-fire fact checking was his least favorite part of detective work. The burial in the standard eight-and-a-half-by-eleven had never appealed, but made up fifty percent of the job requirements along with "other duties as assigned," which included getting shot at, which oddly, he preferred. When an additional fact about the case would surface, then all the paper pushing served its purpose, as it had yesterday. Hidden in one of the interviews was a note from a student at the scene, an annotation Aidan had overlooked at first. A UMD sophomore at the party had stated that, standing a few yards from the fire, he'd heard chanting.

Kicking out thoughts of monks in brown burlap robes singing in monotone, Aidan wrapped his head around that tidbit of information. He'd gone to college; it'd been forever since he'd attended any toga parties, but he doubted the practice had changed much.

*No variations that involved group-sung hymns, anyway.*

Mulling over it, he moved on to the photographs of the party site. The scene's aftermath looked like any typical, outdoor drink-a-thon. A backyard-scale Woodstock with stomped-down grass strewn with cups and beer bottles. The only illegal parts were the arrests made for underage drinking and the slew of Dove-stamped drug baggies. No sacrificial altars, no out of place symbolism. No rituals of the non-collegiate kind.

Aidan had even checked in with Carson to be sure, the brainstorming sessions between the two becoming more frequent. Despite the imposed pairing, Aidan found it hard not to include the guy. Aware of the emerging pattern that had formed in the few weeks they'd worked together, he had to give the uniform credit. For one, Eric had patience. Throw in the blue boy's eye for detail and Aidan got a damn good second opinion. And while taking time to check-in sucked, the budding reliance on Eric seemed like a small price to pay for the support Aidan got in return.

Aidan snorted a laugh.

As a reward for the help, he'd even started calling Carson by his first name.

After examining the witness interviews Eric had reached the same conclusion: the dealers appeared to have targeted the field party, maybe even hosted it, in order to push through a mass drug sale. The first rehash of Dove activity in three years, an indication that there was more product to be moved. Aidan had a feeling they'd try to distribute again, but he needed more evidence.

The girl was their strongest lead.

*The girl.*

His mind darted to the image of Kelly after her fall. Sprawled out under him, hazel eyes staring up, appraising, her smooth skin framed by hair splayed out in an auburn halo. The event remained stuck on cerebral replay for the last forty-eight hours as Aidan tried to focus. Despite the piles of police reports there to occupy him, the picture of her continued to flicker to the forefront.

As he walked into the barn, the environs fueled the déjà vu, the layout and stalls setting the stage. The mental snapshot burned as he approached the hill of hay bales. He stopped to stare at the pile, stirring at the memory.

The girl was pretty, sure. Youth gave a glow to those in their prime, but something else tugged in his chest, demanding to be defined.

The women he'd dated had always come across as self-confident, blatant. The girl struck him as different. With her there were no showy displays of flirting, no social pretense or game-playing. His mind sparked at the realization. She looked at him with frank appraisal and appreciation. With *honesty*.

He called her a girl but that stare of hers said otherwise.

Crouching down, he picked up a bent up string off the ground, examined it. A green, sweet-smelling thread.

*Hay.*

Smiling, he wondered if this was the same strand he'd pulled from her hair.

A metallic clanging sound brought Aidan to his feet and over to the opening of the barn's double doors. As if completing the reenactment, Kelly led Keegan out of the gelding field. She shut the gate behind them, the sunlight streaking her hair with claret red.

He liked the color, a compliment to the green in her eyes.

She took measured steps, watching the ground as she moved. The faded jeans she wore overwhelmed her small frame, a muffin-top cloud of material stuffed into inexpensive, vinyl boots. The same beat-up pair she'd had on the last time he'd seen her. The shirt deviated from before but appeared to be another thrift store find. He frowned.

*Does she own any clothes that fit?*

As she trudged up the cedar-chip walkway, Aidan took care to stand in front of the hall in presentation, determined not to scare her this time.

With one step over the threshold, Kelly glanced up and froze. The expression that hit her face flared through the corridor, heating the air. Kelly's bright eyes, once open with curiosity, went level with suspicion. Her nostrils gave a slight flare before her lips flattened into a grim line. The look was like the after-burner of a jet taking off, more than enough to singe eyebrows.

Aidan squashed the urge to turn around, curious if he'd find a scoundrel standing right behind him, one who'd warrant that stab of a greeting.

On the pivot back he gave his shirt a quick check. Nothing but empty air and well-worn, pre-shrunk cotton; No factious dictators, felons or animal abusers in the barn, although he suddenly felt like he was all three combined.

"Hey," he said, raising his hand, fighting the impulse to lift the other one up, too, for some reason.

"Hi." She came back, the word dismissive. She walked Keegan into the wide expanse, releasing the slack of the lead-rope as she snapped tethering lines from the bordering walls to each side of the horse's halter.

*Okay.* She was pissed. About what, he had no clue.

He took a mandatory step back as Kelly pulled the second lead-line out in front of him, banishing him to the outside of the rope. Eyeing the cord, he craned his neck to catch her attention. Ignoring him, she moved at a clip, pulling a grooming tray from a neighboring station and going to work on the thin horse with a curry comb.

"Is now a good time to talk?"

"Sure," she said, her voice hard, a contrast to the gentle touch she gave the animal, dust misting the air.

"If you want, we can—"

He stopped midsentence as she pegged him with hard eyes, a visual punch in the face. Aidan leaned back. The girl who he'd helped off the ground was gone; in her place stood a woman with the same shrewd eyes, but with defenses mounted, as if she were threatened.

"Let's get this over with." She turned back to Keegan, hiding her anger.

*Whoa.* Maybe the girl had something in common with all women: the pendulum-swing of estrogen that could level a man. Guess that came standard.

What had changed in two days?

"Whatever you want," Aidan said staying on his side of the rope. He felt safer that way, the once well-formulated questions he'd had lined up in his head dissipating like smoke from a fire.

A bonfire. "I need to ask you about the night of the party."

She nodded, the comb in one hand as she stroked Keegan's mane with the other. The horse's breath added a shuddered backbeat to the exchange, a staccato rhythm like the drum beat to a song of war.

"I was invited to the party at the last minute," she said, bringing Aidan's focus back to the subject.

"By who?"

"Rebecca LaCorte. She works at the school." Her voice sounded numb, but at least she was talking.

Aidan leaned forward, his chest brushing the rope. "What does Rebecca look like?"

Kelly turned her head and met his gaze, her hazel stare holding no pretense. "Five-six, brown curly hair, brown eyes. Pale complexion— I gave all of this information to Officer Carson." Her response came out clipped, short.

*She has a temper.*

"How well did you know her before the party?" Aidan drove right over her objection, not caring if she was mad. He didn't want rehearsed, ironed-out commentary; he wanted what she saw.

She disregarded the question, dropping the curry comb into the bin and unlatching the ropes. She directed Keegan, the animal's lean body reinstating the wall between them as she guided him into the stall, turning the horse so that he faced forward.

*Why the secrecy?*

Aidan put his hands on hips, waiting, as if staring her down would make her talk. He tried not to think of it as an interrogation. He watched Kelly move, her small body and steady hands working in the quiet. Shifting his feet, Aidan's hand went to the back of his neck, rubbing. He reminded himself that silence didn't mean that she was hiding anything. It didn't mean that she was involved.

*But what does she have to be hesitant about?*

Impatience surged as she fiddled with fixtures inside the stall.

"I hardly know her. She goes to my—*the* school," she said at last, the words stilted as she continued to busy herself. Aidan knew that the conversation would be awkward, but her dragged out replies made him antsy, stoking his restlessness. He circled the space to take the edge off, stopping a few feet away.

He stomped back, trying to be diplomatic and failing. "How—"

The smell cut him off, hitting Aidan's nose before the mushy consistency under his foot had registered. His movements went slow-mo as his eyes rolled down in tandem with the lift of his boot. The visual eval proved that—yeah. He'd stepped in it.

The horse was a four-legged manure machine.

A stifled giggle brought Aidan's head up. Kelly patted Keegan's flank, the animal's face full of *Look, Mom! LOOK* enthusiasm.

"Good boy," Kelly said loudly, lathering up the positive reinforcement.

Aidan glowered at his boot. Yeah, real good.

*Pain in the ass horse.*

"*Thanks,*" he said, shooting them both a glare before he hobbled over to the corner where a boot brush shaped like porcupine awaited him. Giving the cast-iron rodent a few vehement swipes, he thought about the smell. It'd linger in his closet for weeks, at least.

*Frickin' great.*

Kelly seemed to have recollected herself by the time he returned, hiding her amusement when Aidan pointedly side-stepped the pile on the double-back. The air turned sober as he walked up to the stall.

With a final rib of amusement, the girl stepped out of Keegan's area, securing the gate. She turned and looked up at him, her emotional armor back in place.

*Ready for round two.*

Aidan would have respected the show of strength if the verbal arrows weren't aimed at him. And if he knew what he'd done to deserve the assault.

"Next question?" she asked, her arms crossing her chest. Another barricade.

In a blaze of resentment Aidan matched her hostility.

*She wants to be tough,* FINE.

"Have you hung out with Rebecca since? Have you had any other run-ins with her?"

"No." Kelly pivoted, switching places with him, a reluctant dance, the last step inching her toward the door. His civility overshadowed, Aidan's head reeled through the links, the detective in him taking over.

*What if the Dove group has networks established through the college?*

He looked into Kelly's eyes, the flecks of green making his mind falter.

"Did you see any drugs dealt that night?"

*Are you one of them?*

Conviction hardened her gaze. *"No."*

"Witnesses at the scene said they heard noises—chanting. Do you remember that?" Aidan barked, making Kelly freeze. "What did they say?"

Her shield fell as she blinked, her eyes going glassy. "It was a refrain, they repeated it—

"What? What did they repeat?"

"Fire walker. They said *fire walker*." She put a hand on her head like it hurt.

Aidan's brow furrowed. "Fire walker?"

"Yes."

Confusion shorted out his thoughts.

*Is she making this crap up?*

"What the hell does that mean? I need to know what happened that night—I need you to be straight with me," he said, the words harsh. The moment they were out, he wanted to take them back but it was too late. Her expression darkened and his heart sank. He could see her frustration, anger, and pain.

She was telling the truth.

"You want me to be straight with you? How about you be straight with me! You're the detective—you're the one who's got this all figured out!"

His jaw fell as she threw out her arms, opening herself up.

"You said—"

"No, *you* tell *me*! I should know what a fire walker is, right? Why? Because I drank *one* glass of wine at a college party? No. It's because I *look* like a drug dealer to you?"

The emotions flashed across her face. Injury, offense.

He'd hurt her.

"I never said—"

With a snap of her hand she yanked something out of the back pocket of her jeans, a tri-folded piece of paper. As she slapped the stack to his chest Aidan popped one hand up, pinning the thing to his sternum while she turned and marched for the door.

"*Kelly.*"

The use of her name made her stop, the light of the door creating a silhouette around her slight form, the rapid blinking of her eyes a slice to his heart. She pivoted toward him, her face hard; her shield pulled back into place.

Caught in her beam, Aidan couldn't find his voice. Her presence flipped it off, staking an irrefutable claim on his attention.

There was only one woman he knew capable of that feat. Sophie.

"Don't you feel like one of them sometimes?" she asked softly, her voice sad. "Like you're playing with the flame and don't expect to get burned?"

Aidan stood mute as she walked out.

After what felt like years, he unfolded the paper she'd thrust at him. Reading the words with care, he flipped over to the second page and exhaled a curse.

*Expelled.*

The letters on the paper fogged over as Kelly's words rang in his ears, the tone merging with images of moths and horses and bonfires and victims.

*Fire walker.*

Aidan felt his molars grind.

Josh Mooreland had gotten burned. Now Kelly.

Refolding the papers, Aidan turned. Keegan poked his head out of the stall, ears trained on the man, the horse's dark, round eyes that of an arbitrator's. The animal let out a heavy snort, the huff of noise sounding like the word, *Jerk*.

Aidan couldn't argue.

With a glance back down at his feet, the stench of horse manure invaded Aidan's nose. The shit on his shoes summed up the situation perfectly.

And boy did it stink.

# CHAPTER 9

The next day Kelly stood mesmerized as Keegan bounded into the paddock, his hooves lifting and pounding back into the earth as if it were his personal mission to kick up dirt. Securing the gate, she edged over to the wood fence to get a better seat for the show.

The former racehorse didn't disappoint, his bone-lined stomach constricting to let out a loud whinny. He followed up the trumpeting with a seamless transition into an animated trot, his tail whipping in circles like a propeller.

*He must be happy to be out of the stall.*

Kelly scanned the expanse of the arena. Three times larger than a traditional paddock, the farm had utilized the space as an area for horses that needed physical therapy.

Not that Keegan appeared to need that at the moment.

All the jumping and prancing made it seem as if the jutting bones and sagging skin were some kind of a bad Halloween costume. Keegan stopped in the center of the ring, air leaving him in ragged puffs as he let out a wheezing cough that contradicted the healthy façade.

*Not as well as he wants to be. Not yet.*

Ready to enter the ring and settle him down, Kelly heard another sound ring out over Keegan's din, a soft neigh. The railing to the mares paddock bordered one side of the arena, the two planks of fencing sidled up next against each other. Beyond the divider a smaller horse waited, watching Keegan with rapt attention. The sweet disposition coupled with the height and markings identified the mare instantly. Moe.

*Ah, a little over-the-fence canoodling.*

Keegan took slow strutting steps toward the girl, like a guy embarking on a hot date. His tail flicked as he craned his neck over the doubled line of fence, the two muzzles making contact, sniffing and brushing against one another. Kelly layered her arms on the rail, propping her chin on top her hands.

Most the animals at Hammond's were fixed, with Keegan being an exception until a time when he would be strong enough to undergo the procedure. As long as the guy had people there to monitor, and a fence in between, he was allowed to visit with Moe. With the hardship a lot of the horses faced, the making of a new friend was encouraged as well as a joy to watch.

Keegan nuzzled Moe's neck, appearing content.

*Maybe Keegan's new owners will change his name to Casanova when he's adopted.*

Kelly winced at the thought, reluctant to think about the day that they'd have to part ways. The truth remained that whoever got Keegan would have the right to do whatever they wished with him: rename him, train him, race him, put him out to pasture. She was okay with all the scenarios as long as they treated him right.

*As long as they give him love.*

Kelly's eyes gauged the horse's withered body. Pippa had told her about the licit issues surrounding Keegan's ownership, hinting that with the legal fight outstanding, plus the time it'd take for rehabilitation, it'd be a while before the farm could find Keegan a home. Although court battles weren't ideal, Kelly took solace in the delay. She had time left with him still.

Her feelings were selfish, but there was no arguing with them. In her few weeks at the farm, the horse had become her rock. What she clung to in the midst of a lot of unwelcome change.

*Like getting kicked out of school and losing your job in the same day.*

Her chest expelled a breath, the force of it making her head bob as she did the mental math. With her day job gone she'd been free to plug away at her community service hours, the calculator total for the week reaching about fifty hours if she added right.

*Half done.*

The remaining fifty was a mere week and a half's worth of work if she went full-time. And once logged she'd have no reason to stay. She could volunteer after that, the plan a fairy tale given that dedicating her time without pay didn't cover her bills, and that she should be using the down time to hunt for employment. The money she'd saved up for tuition provided a cushion with her rent for one to two months, minimum, making it decision time.

She could rebuild the tuition savings, but the dilemma with school still left her cornered. If UMD rejected her application for the misdemeanor, other colleges would do the same, leaving her with nowhere to go.

All her carefully laid plans disintegrated like paper thrown into a fire.

Kelly felt her neck tense, a lump of lead manifesting in her chest at the meager options she had left. Something died inside of her at the thought waitressing again. Her go-to security blanket of a standby; the twelve-hour, stand-all-day, live-off-scraps reserve that she'd been forced to return to year after year.

*The inevitable.*

The step back made her want to scream.

Not even a step, but a shove that landed her on her ass. The imagery of falling took her back the barn, to a handsome face surveying her. She tried to shake off the thought.

*Why doesn't that man go away!*

As much as she wanted to believe that Aidan's involvement was an accident, that he didn't intend to turn her life upside down on purpose, he still signed the papers that fried her chances. He'd left her to deal with the repercussions.

And *why*?

Kelly shook her head. After a decade of work, her harvest seemed forever delayed. No matter how hard she tried to get ahead—her degree, her experience, meant nothing if supporting herself meant a lifetime of retail labor.

To escape her mind, Kelly looked up at the sky. The water-colored stretch of deep blue was far from threatening, and yet it seemed to tower over her. The cotton-like puffs toddled along in harmless disregard to the human woes down below. No steel-colored clouds or angry sky there to beat her down, and yet she wanted to shun the canvas because the blue reminded her of the man's damn eyes. Aidan's face seemed to form in the atmosphere, a manifestation that wanted to lock horns with her for purposes she didn't understand.

She hated how the road lay forked in front of her, one path a retreat, while the other offered her no certainty. It used to be exciting, a journey. Now she felt...lost.

Under her hands and feet lay common dirt, the buildings and troughs all structures she recognized, but in a pang of desperation she searched, her eyes needy for the familiar.

If by finding she would be found...

She checked on Keegan. Unmoved, the horse continued to dote on Moe, his tail the only part of him in motion, a constant flip as his head touched hers, the pair spooning over the barrier of the fence. Melded, like one entity.

Kelly watched them, wishing that love truly worked that way. That two spirits found one another, connected, and stayed together evermore. Her common sense cut off the fantasy. Her life and education had taught her that truth long ago. All animals, horses and people alike, were out to serve their base needs. The males were polygamous playboys by nature.

Keegan, endearing as he seemed in that moment, had an instinctive motive. So did Aidan.

When they got what they wanted, whatever the goal: sex, companionship, *information*— they'd move on. Kelly felt a deep frown crease her lips.

"Mind if I join ya?" The voice warmed the air.

Kelly came to attention as Sophia stepped up, resting her hands next to Kelly's on the slatted fence. The woman's skin glowed with a golden tan, the tint an accent to her deep brown hair and eyes. Beautiful in a fearless way.

Kelly scooted over, making room.

"It's amazing to watch, isn't it?" Sophie took in Keegan, the horse's head bridged over the barrier with Moe's.

Kelly nodded, the sight a rare moment.

"You learn so much observing them. The herd is so defined. Each horse falls into a role," she continued. "The boys have to compete for the girls a lot. The thrashing tail, the display of prowess, it's to show off their vitality and strength. Keegan, here—" she inclined her head "—*wants* that girl's attention."

"I'm sure he'll get it." Kelly's voice went hollow.

"Maybe," Sophie said, her tone assured. She cleared her throat, shifting gears. "I wanted to thank you for the great job you've done with Keegan."

Kelly's head snapped around before she could stop it. The last time someone started in with praise, the follow up had been getting canned.

The fear must have shown because Sophie's eyes softened.

"You have a great manner with him and it's my hope that you'll stay with us."

Kelly exhaled unaware she had held her breath.

"I know that the last few days, have been...challenging." Sophie chose her words with caution.

"The barn has ears."

"And legs and tails." Sophie's kind chuckle lightened the weight in Kelly's chest. "I don't mean to pry. I know that Aidan can come across as tough, but please know that he has a good reason for it."

Kelly lifted her head, the brown of Sophie's gaze was a well of wisdom and—comprehension. The woman was holding back, as if keeping a secret not hers to tell.

"I'm sorry the ruling caused you trouble," Sophie said, her compassionate stare unwavering.

"I wish I can say that it's okay, but..." Kelly glanced at her feet, toeing the ground. "When my hours are over, I—" A moment passed and no words came. For once in her life she had no response, no direction.

She'd drifted so far off track.

"I understand." Sophie's attention went back to the horses, then returned to Kelly. "In the meantime, I wanted to see if I could get your help with something."

Kelly faced the woman as Sophie laced her fingers together, propping herself up by an elbow. Calm, lenient. Kelly wished she could harness that kind of serenity.

"From what I hear, you're good with research."

Kelly paused, her curiosity stoked. "What kind of research?"

Sophie pushed off from the fence, unleashing her bright smile. "That's what I'd hoped you'd say. Let's go."

Aidan mumbled a foul word under his breath as the floor beneath his feet let out a loud squeak, his preemptive attempt at stealth thwarted by aged wood.

It was a good thing he'd gone into law enforcement, because he sucked at sly.

Inching down the hall, he peered around the corner. Kelly sat at the head of the round oak table, her face lost in thought, papers scattered around her.

She must have taken the noise as normal, the old building's token of age. Thankful for the moment of concealment, Aidan took in the sight of her. Her hair down, the length was longer than he'd first guessed, a curtain that joined the wave of her bangs, a line of smooth brown she'd parted to one side. He imagined her as she pulled the elastic off, combing an aimless hand through it, shaking the locks free. Her face was natural, free of makeup that he could tell, and smooth, perfect. Not a girl, but a woman.

A woman Aidan had wronged.

With a grimace his mind reeled to that morning's attempt at making amends. He'd called the college, tried to reason with them, while the school board did nothing but shut him down. University rules rivaled some of the bi-laws Aidan had heard lawyers spout in court, the stuffed shirts. Even the proposition that he retract the ruling didn't work, the offer brushed off with the stock response, "The transgression has already gone on record." And so the ruling stood against Kelly.

Who actually used the term *transgression* in normal conversation?

*A well-educated bunch of idiots, that's who.*

Kelly settled into her seat, unaware she had company, which earned Aidan the titles of both cad and creeper. He never thought that she'd be negatively affected by the service. True to form, he'd acted first and thought later.

Well, he didn't *think* about it.

That was his talent in life: jump first, *then* figure out how to land.

And while he didn't care if he went splat, he never intended to take others with him. And now he'd robbed Kelly of a reason to stay. She was under no obligation to answer his questions; she could up and leave at any time. And tell him to go to hell before she went, too. Like he could blame her.

Hell, she could appeal the community service and go now.

Kelly leaned forward, the ends of her hair brushing the table's surface. Aidan thought of how that would feel against bare skin—

*Stop it.*

Thoughts like that kept popping up at odd moments, cauterizing all the reason in his brain.

*Leave.* The follow-up command stung in his gray matter, a harsh solution but the right thing to do. He'd done enough damage, he needed to leave her alone.

He hovered in silence, perplexed by his need to be around her, an inkling screaming inside of him, telling him to keep close, to *protect.* Tracing over her once again, his eyes found their way down to the table. Pages with graphs and other documents littered the round top. The papers full of grids, sheets marked with both print and pen handwriting from the look of them, some old-looking, the edges yellowed. As his gaze trailed closer to the center of the weathered oak, Aidan squinted.

To the side of the jumble of paper sat a line of white plastic. A rounded utensil—a spork?

Leaning forward his boot caught the corner cubby, nudging it across the floor, a loud scrape sounding out. Kelly's body perked, her eyes still trained on the files, her hand moving to jot down notes as she spoke. "I'm almost done..."

Aidan went still.

She thought he was someone else, probably Sophie, or Jason.

Letting out a breath, he stepped into the room.

"It's me." *The asshole.* "Can I come in?"

Kelly looked up slowly, pausing a second before giving a nod of agreement. Beneath the cascade of hair she wore rimmed glasses, and she plucked the frames off her face as he came forward.

"I thought you were Sophie," she said quietly.

*Better Sophie than lover boy.*

"No. I can get her for you when I go, if you want. I wanted to—talk. Briefly."

*No questions*, he mentally tacked on, noting her stiff body language.

She watched him, the stare different than before, unwavering, expectant. The flare of anger from the last time they'd met dimmed to that of a candle's flame.

"You came to apologize." There was no malice in her voice, just statement of fact.

But something about her saying it out loud still made him feel like an ass. Regret and forgiveness weren't his areas of strength on a good day, and it wasn't like he had a ton of friends to practice the crap on. The sentiment of emotion felt sloppy and excessive in his business, but for that moment, with Kelly, he found it—bearable.

"Yes."

"Okay."

Aidan waited for the "now get out and never speak to me again," but it didn't come.

With an awkward cough he decided to drop it all on the table.

"I didn't mean for—" He faltered, wondering where his cool went.

Since when did he ramble?

She studied him, probably stunned by his verbal ineptitude.

"What?" he barked, reverting back to his traditional hard-and-fast speech. "Shit—Look,

I'm no good at this. I'm *sorry*. About your school
and the service. All of it."

Anguish stained her face, throwing another
jab into his larynx. "I talked to Sophie before
coming in here. She threatened bodily harm if I
said anything to upset you. So, I can go now if
you—"

"I don't know anything about you," she said
sitting up. Her body squared, she regarded him
with contemplative interest. "You show up out
of nowhere with a badge—actually, I still
haven't seen one of those yet."

Aidan stopped. Blinked.

If flashing his brass got him off the shit list,
sure.

"You never asked," he said as he dug into the
interior pocket of his jacket.

She shot him a look that said, *don't BS me.*

Suppressing his grin, Aidan obediently did
the flip and flash, holding open the leather-
backed shield as she extended her neck to get a
closer look. He tucked it back into place after
her head bob of affirmation.

"Appears legit," she said, leaning back. He
watched her shoulders roll back, spine in perfect
alignment. No passive little girl, a woman
taking control.

He liked that more than he should. "Anything
else?"

"You asked your questions. Now I have a
few." The superior look she shot him didn't come
across as haughty, but as if it were her given
right to know the answers. He motioned to the
chair, and she gave him the go ahead. Aidan sat,
anchoring his heavy legs with knees open, arms

propped against his thighs. The guy-at-ease position.

"Hit me."

Her shrewd hazel eyes landed on him like a spotlight. She interviewed the way he did, with no pretense or bluffing. Direct and to the point, the girl's honesty was like fresh air, fanning him.

"What's your favorite color?"

The corner of Aidan's mouth twitched.

"I'm starting simple," she retorted, impervious to the taunting expression that played across his face.

Before he could stop it, Aidan's eyes flipped up to her hair and back, the glint of copper winking. "Red."

She halted, her brow furrowing before she continued.

"How do you know Sophie?"

"Her and my mother are close friends."

"Have you always been a detective?"

"I started as a cop. Climbed the ranks to become a NARC," he said, his answers blunt. She followed his replies deftly, unfazed by his gruff tone. Her approach was a compliment to the exchange, made it authentic, comfortable. A tingle in his chest made him eager for the next question.

"Do you like it?"

That stopped him. He thought of Paul, the stain of red blood seeping through the memories.

"If we can skip that one. Please," he tacked on, not meeting her eyes.

"What do you do for fun?"

Hmm. That took him a minute. *Fun?*

Convicting drug-dealing murderers and cursing.

*No. Yeah.*

Well, anti-social should be in there somewhere. He pushed himself to think. He had hobbies. Three years ago.

Where the hell did his life go?

"I used to run. I might get back into it." The wistful note in his voice echoed.

Slowing, she glanced down, giving her pen excessive attention as she threw out the next inquiry. "You have a girlfriend?"

The grin hit Aidan full-force. "Not currently."

"Why not?" She looked up at him, the hazel of her eyes a double punch when studded against the red of her hair.

*Beautiful.*

His train of thought snapped, costing him a minute to answer.

"My interpersonal skills need improvement." He threw her a lopsided grin.

She let out a soft laugh, pulling together the papers. He focused on the documents in her hands. "What are you working on?"

Kelly relaxed her hold on the piles, pulling out a sheet to show him.

"Sophie gave me Keegan's file." Her voice was full of gratitude. "Everything they got from the seizure. Half of it makes sense." She scanned a paper that looked like a birth record.

"What's that?" Aidan bent forward, the crest of a big-name breeder embossed on the top.

"It states that Keegan was born on a small farm outside of Lexington, Kentucky. He was sold and moved to Maryland when he was a yearling. There are strange notes here and there." She pointed to what looked like a family tree scratched in pencil on the back of a bill of sale. The names "Tiz" and "H&G" printed several lines below the word "A. Flag."

"On the front it says something about Glen Riddle Farm."

Aidan had heard of the place through news stories and the history books. Located out near the Maryland coast, the farm had been the birthplace to racehorse legends Man O' War and American Flag. The stallions went on to sire generations of offspring over the years, their descendants boasting the pedigree. Glen Riddle was said to have had a race track built on the property for training. The last Aidan had heard the place had faded from its former glory, the buildings deteriorated and abandoned.

"Does it say who his sire is?"

"No, just his dam, a filly named Celosia. He was born a few years after Glen Riddle was bought out and turned into a golf course." Kelly's forehead wrinkled as she laid out the sheets, as if trying to link the sporadic pieces of Keegan's life. "He has a tattoo inside his top lip. It links us to some of his racing records. Keegan finaled in the Preakness, and he has files at Charlestown, but who knows where he went after that." Her gaze landed on a lined form, a recent health evaluation from Hammond's. She added to the notes, a timeline of when the horse started rehabilitation, his eating habits, and other observations.

Born to a filly and thrown into a life of racing at one year of age. Keegan must have been a surprise pregnancy, and sold for the money. Fatherless and left to make his own way.

He and the girl had a lot in common.

"Has he seen a vet yet?" Aidan cocked his head to read what Kelly was writing.

"Once." Her sigh was audible as she jotted down comments about Keegan's digestive issues.

Aidan pointed at the blank space below the aim of her pen. "Shits like a demon—*write* that."

That got a chuckle out of her, a contagious giggle.

The most beautiful sound Aidan had ever heard.

Her eyes flipped up to his, still narrowed with amusement. "We still need to do a sonogram to see how his lower intestines are faring."

"My boots say his intestines are fine."

Her lips twisted as she wrote *regular bowel movements* in small, uniform script.

"Good?" she asked, displaying the entry.

Yes, and it'd be even better as soon as he got reimbursement for his shoes.

"Looks great. Now when am I getting new boots?"

"Never, you had it coming." Her dismissal was casual as she stood up, gathering the mass of papers, tapping them together against the tabletop before placing the stack back into the folder.

Emulating her, Aidan got up, searching for a way to help. He reached out for the spork that lay on the table, ready to throw it out as trash.

"*Wait.*" Kelly's eyes went wide, lunging to grab the thing.

*Okay, she's fond of plastic eating utensils.* "It's not left over from lunch?"

"No, I'm saving it," she said, her tone muted as if embarrassed.

They both went motionless, staring at each other as Aidan held up the white plastic. On a breath, she moved to take it from him, their fingers brushing.

He didn't let go.

"One question."

She flinched at the inquiry, pulling on the spork in his steady grip.

The reaction pained him. No doubt she thought he was out to grill her again, to barter small talk about himself in exchange for more interrogation about the party. He joggled the utensil that joined them. "What's with this?"

The tension in her face drained away, replaced by a faint blush. He stared, the color gorgeous.

"I have saplings—in small pots." He released his hold, watching her tuck the spork in her palm. "It's good for cultivating the dirt, like a little Garden Weasel." She dipped her chin, her flush deepening.

"Oh." Unable to step away he stared down at her, noting how her head was level to his chest.

*How easy it would be to scoop her up and...*

"Thanks." She collected the last of the documents, wiping the area clean. Something about the scene jabbed at him. Everything would be that spotless when she left Hammond's.

*As if she were never there.*

Stealing a final glance, Kelly took small steps toward the exit as Aidan fought the absurd urge to beg her to stay.

He had to let her go.

*Now and...later.*

She stopped at the door, turned. "Aidan?"

"Yes?"

"I don't hang with her. Rebecca. I met her at the college. The night of the party was the only time we'd gone out," she said, her voice hushed.

"Kelly, you don't have to—"

"I know," she cut him off, their eyes locking.

God, she had every right to stay mad, to shut him down.

"Why the second chance?" he questioned.

She paused, as if giving the words consideration. "If Sophie trusts you, so do I."

Aidan smiled. "See you around?"

"See you tomorrow." She blushed again, giving him an awkward wave before scuttling out the door.

"Good night..."

He waited until Kelly was out of earshot to add the "beautiful."

# CHAPTER 10

"I'll wash out the buckets," Andrea said.

Kelly watched the girl collect the multi-colored pails by their wire handles, the empty hubs playing percussion as she toddled over to a metal spigot protruding from the shed.

*What a good kid.*

The teenager launched into a careful method of rinsing and brushing, ensuring each container got rinsed clean. The collar of her shirt lay in a pile between the girl's shoulders, covering up a long French braid of dark hair, the front of the tee branded with the bright, painted name of her high school. A month into fifteen, Andrea had been the girl Kelly sat behind their first day at orientation. Drea had seemed jittery and uncomfortable, and after talking with the girl's mom, Kelly learned that Drea had a phobia of horses that stemmed from a random incident when she was ten. After hearing what had happened, Kelly noticed that Drea never came within a certain distance of the animals and appeared to focus on her breathing.

A young girl working out her anxiety. Kelly had to give her props.

*How many kids would be that brave?*

The odd thing was that when Kelly asked how Drea ended up at the farm her mother got quiet. It appeared that Drea hadn't volunteered.

Curious, Kelly discreetly asked around, trying to find a simple answer—one that wouldn't invade the girl's privacy. As expected, Jason, the head cog of the rumor mill had the details, although Kelly felt a twinge of guilt asking for the full story. Fresh out of a divorce, Drea's mother had moved to Maryland for a new job. In a new place and starting the dirge known as high school, Drea had stepped out of her comfort zone to make new friends, which apparently blew up in her face. A month into school Drea had been busted by mall police for having a stolen necklace in her pocket, and ended up serving the community time.

*Talk about a rough start. The kid ended up in juvie.*

According to Jason, when asked about the theft charge, all Drea would say was that she hadn't gone to the mall alone and that she'd never stolen anything before. If Kelly had to guess, someone had pushed her to take the necklace, or told her to pocket it when the police arrived.

Kelly had only known Drea a few weeks, but the kid didn't seem like a thief. The girl's kindness showed, doing menial work while keeping her distance from the horses, as if she'd chosen assignment to the farm to help iron out some of her fears. The teen arrived three days a week with her mother, ready to perform her chores without complaint, with no mention of outside friends or activities.

The parallel to the girl reminded Kelly of her own situation. Like Drea, Kelly had met a lot of fellow students at school, but the only people she could call friends were the folks she'd met at the farm: Sophie, Pippa, Jason, Drea, and the volunteers.

And it seemed like everyone had a story for being at Hammond's, a few of the histories tainted.

In the distance Drea squatted down and balanced herself on the balls of her feet, crawling around while she scrubbed, rinsed, and stacked. Loose strands of her hair dangled down her cheeks as she got lost in her duties.

*Afraid of horses, but caring for eighty of them.*

And Kelly thought she had it hard.

The defense Sophie had given Aidan's actions sprung up in Kelly's memory.

*He had his reasons.*

If Kelly viewed her predicament from a different perspective, like if she were in Drea's shoes, she wouldn't blame Aidan for having his suspicions. Having her motives scrutinized was no party, and Kelly knew how it felt to be put on trial.

How would he have known that she wasn't involved in the bonfire?

Giving him the benefit of the doubt still hurt, though. Images of Aidan's face played in a carousel in her head.

During her night in jail Aidan's features were an impenetrable stonewall; when he'd accused her in the barn, his expression had been upset and torn. The other day when he'd sat down to answer her questions, he... A smile pulled at her lips. The man she'd met that first night had caught her eye, but the Aidan who she'd interviewed in the break room was a force of nature, capable of emotionally disarming any woman he wanted.

Missile codes had nothing on that man's undivided attention.

And he'd told her what she wanted to know without bargain or trade. A gut feeling told her that their little Q&A session had been a gift. An apology, although Kelly sensed there was more. And Aidan had changed since she had first met him. He was still as dynamic, restless, but something in him had shifted. She didn't know what had sparked the transformation, but she liked the man he'd become.

Returning to her own chores, Kelly pushed her sleeves up, leaning in to run a wire hand brush over the empty ceramic belly of the large water trough in front of her.

Throwing more force into the scrubbing, Kelly swiped at the slippery lining, the thought of Drea being set up as a scapegoat making her fume.

*Fifteen.* An age of development and change.

But there was no cosmic rule that said that youth included joy. And no doubt, Drea's eagerness for companionship had made her venerable, and oh how Kelly could relate to that. She'd been just as impressionable at twenty-seven.

The need for acceptance must know no age limit. It seemed unfair, though.

"I'm going to grab that one," Drea called out, pointing to a lone, red pail that hung off the side of the fence bordering the mare shoot, a long channel where the girl horses were steered down from their field.

"Okay," Kelly called back, watching the girl slip through the gate, bent on the container's retrieval. With the clang of the lock, Drea walked up, unhooking the empty bucket.

Kelly propped her elbow up on the lip of the trough as a flash in her peripheral vision made her head pop up. Sophie came down from the main house, doing her midday operations check.

With no company of the gorgeous arson variety, Kelly's heart calmed. Performing an appraisal of her tasks, Kelly noted their progress with the buckets, her attention moving to her dingy clothes. Sophie never expected the volunteers to look glamorous; in fact, a good day's work showed by how dirty you got.

A brown cloud of dust erupted as Kelly gave the side of her jeans a swipe, an unspoken tribute to her work ethic. The attempt at dispelling the layers of dirt that caked her body was futile after she'd groomed Baker's Dozen that morning. Everyone who knew the gelding called him *Pigpen* because the horse liked mud, and as if equipped with a radar for the grimiest puddles, he was eager to give himself an allover muck mask. Once the stuff had dried the brushing session that followed became a full body workout, and no manner of cleaning, short of a dip in suds, was able to get the grime off.

Doing a quick smooth down to strands of hair that no doubt just sprang back up in frazzled defiance, Kelly gave up, presenting herself for filth assessment.

Sophie had just reached the mouth of the main paddock when the eerie *thunk* of a bucket hitting the ground made them both turn. Sophie's face jerked toward the mare shoot, the welcoming grin she was about to give Kelly fading instantly into concern.

A caramel-colored hurricane barreled down the canal. The volunteer at the other end of the channel looked on helplessly, failing to check if the area was clear before letting the animal loose. Kelly recognized the mare by her markings and size.

*Callisto.*

A Belgian draft horse, Caballine Callisto towered at seventeen hands, the base of the mare's neck exceeding Kelly's height, her mass earning her a name based on Greek myth. Good-natured and inquisitive, the mare's bad habits stemmed from the fact she knew her own size. The red tape on her halter was a caution to others that her strength, when unchecked, came across as raw power.

Unfazed by the breach in protocol, the mare's muscled legs covered the tract of ground at a vaulting pace, mane and tail flagging in the wind she created, heading straight for Drea.

Crossing the space in a fury of steps, Kelly rushed to get to Drea first. Sophie honed in on the girl too, motioning to the volunteer at the top of the chute. The closest person to the channel, Kelly threw out an arm to signal the other staff members to stay back. The cavalry would only spook the horse, and like Kelly's first encounter with Keegan, there was a lot of Callisto to work up.

Sidling up to the gate, Kelly could make out Drea's back flat against the gate's slats. Dead still, the girl's hands were the only limbs that moved, her fingers trembling.

*Too late.*

Kelly held her breath as Callisto came to an abrupt stop in front of the petrified girl. With a jut of her powerful neck, the mare poked her long nose into the teen's face, appraising Drea with a series of wide-nosed sniffs.

Drea recoiled as if the encroaching muzzle were a venom-drooling alien sizing her up for lunch. The horse moved her focus to the bucket lying sideways on the ground, and gave Drea's arm a hard nudge, the girl seeming to stow her shriek for help. Bowing her head, Callisto lipped at the edge of the plastic.

"Drea?"

The girl jumped at Kelly's use of her name, the mare preoccupied with the empty pail.

"*Easy*—don't make any sudden movements, okay? I'm right here."

With a wooden nod Drea fell still again, seeming ready to burst into tears.

A panicked girl trapped with a headstrong horse. *Fantastic.*

*What to do...What to do...*

"Drea?" Kelly kept her voice soft, imitating Pippa's trained cadence.

*Calm. Soothing.* It helped.

"Yeah?" The word was said with a gulp of air as Kelly watched the girl's face drain of color.

"Remember what we learned in training?" Kelly inched closer through the slats and leaned down low, anchoring herself. Ready to jump in if things escalated.

"Y-Yeah."

"The horse's ears—" Callisto nudged Drea again, harder this time. The girl gasped like she wanted to crumble right there.

*Okay, not working. Plan B.*

She had to help Drea get comfortable with the horse—

"Her name is Callisto," Kelly said. The Belgian raised her head at the sound of her handle, reclaiming the space muzzle-to-nose with Drea, the girl cringing. "*Easy.* Easy now. We're cool."

Drea sucked in another lungful of oxygen as the horse assessed her, the animal's body language neutral; the mare's nose so close that Kelly could make out the caramel color of the velvet fur.

"She's not going to hurt you. She's curious."

"She's...*huge.*"

"Remember in training, where are her ears?" Kelly kept talking. The logic was working, keeping the girl focused.

Drea paused, appearing to soak it in. Unfurling, she dragged her eyes the long trail up to Callisto's head, settling on the horse's broad crown.

"Her ears are on me," Drea said.

"Yes."

"And on the bucket." The answer came back stronger, Drea's eyes running over the horse's body with awe. "She's big."

"The largest mare we have," Kelly replied, holding tight to the honesty.

*Way to desensitize, right?*

The event was one hell of a test, but like a flame growing in strength, Drea tilted her head, taking in all of Callisto's dimensions, tensing when the horse moved. With another hard push, the mare thrust her nose into Drea's palm.

"She thinks you have food," Kelly said, almost forgetting that the gate separated them.

"I *don't*," Drea shot back.

"Show her." Before the girl could reply, Kelly crouched down, picking up the bucket through the gap in the gate. Turning her head, Drea frowned.

"What are you doing?"

"Here." Tilting the pail, Kelly pushed the handle against Drea's clinched fist. "Show her it's empty."

Eyes glued to Callisto, Drea loosened her grip long enough to take the offering, the horse's response instant. Drea held it up for the horse to rummage, wrapping her arms around to hold the tub steady, the action jostling them both. Not finding what she wanted, the animal popped her head out, stepping back, her head dipping in disappointment.

"See, empty," Drea managed, measuring the horse with newfound courage. "*Not* dinnertime."

The horse smacked her lips, emitting a heavy exhale like a shrug.

"Later," Drea said, tucking her chin as if embarrassed to be holding conversation with a horse.

"No, that's good—talk to her. I think she likes your voice."

In a bold move Drea lowered the bucket to the ground and turned her palms up. Taking the invitation, Callisto pressed her nose to the exposed skin and inhaled. To Kelly's surprise Drea let out a delicate laugh.

"That tickles," the girl said, one palm cupped around the horse's broad muzzle. "You're... soft." Bringing her free hand up, Drea hovered next to the round circle of Callisto's cheek. Kelly watched the girl's fear melt into wonder as Drea's eyes trailed over the horse's musculature.

"She something, isn't she?"

"Amazing," Drea murmured, her free hand up where Callisto could see it. Drea's fingertips quivered, outstretched and ready to make contact.

Beyond the horse's flank, Kelly caught sight of a volunteer opening the gate, approaching them with a lead-rope in hand. Ready to evacuate. Kelly watched Drea stand in frozen animation, Callisto lowering her head as if in anticipation of being touched.

*They need another minute.*

Kelly held up her hand and the volunteer paused at the signal, waiting.

*Don't break them up, not yet.*

Hesitant, Drea reached up, the pads of her fingers landing on Callisto's flat cheek. Elation spread across the girl's face, the delight radiating at the gentle touch. Standing next to them Kelly felt a warm sensation spread throughout her chest at the sight of Drea's— *courage.*

"Good girl," Drea murmured as the horse held still, the teen maintaining gentle strokes over the expanse of the animal's jowl. "You're a big softie under all that beef, aren't you?"

"She'll let you cuddle her all day," Kelly said. The volunteer moved in again, calling an end to their little party. "Time to let you out, Andrea."

Drea's brows knitted together as if just noticing the other persons standing there. In one concise movement the volunteer clipped a lead-rope to Callisto's halter. Kelly could almost hear the *beep-beep-beep* like the backup of a sixteen wheeler as the volunteer prompted Callisto to take withdrawing steps.

In the new space Kelly opened the gate a crack, allowing Drea to exit. Dazed, the girl complied, closing Callisto in with the handler. It took Drea a minute to follow Kelly out, the girl stealing backward glances, the horse doing the same from the opposite direction as the volunteer led her away.

"Did you see *that*?" Drea gushed, her questions not made to be answered, but to have someone share in her pride. "How she just came up and—" Motioning with her hands, Kelly grinned at her animation, blown away by how well the girl handled it.

Kelly walked in a zig-zagged pattern, letting her shoulder bump Drea's in jest. "I'm calling you Epona from now on."

The girl let out a glorious laugh, turning again to get a final glance at Callisto, and pivoting forward to complete the twirl with exuberance. She looked up, beaming, like she'd plugged into a hundred volts of self-esteem.

Happiness looked good on her, a birthright. Sophie had the same shine.

The two fell in step next to one another—
*Crap,* she'd forgotten about Sophie!

Kelly had waved the woman off as if she were a subordinate. The possible repercussions sent a shot of fear through her as Kelly's head sprang up. She found her boss standing yards away, leaning in a casual pose against the fence, a broad smile stretching her face.

Sophie gave a nod of consent that seemed to say, "I'll check in on you later."

*Okay.* That must mean that Kelly had dodged any reprimand. For now.

Turning back, Kelly set the concern aside and playfully linked her arm with Drea's, the girl leaning into her as the pair three-legged it toward the main building.

"I think you've earned a break," Kelly said, standing back so Drea could climb the steps first. "The bottled water is on me."

The road was open and clear for the drive home, awaiting Kelly like a crowning reward for an afternoon of good work. She'd spent an hour with Drea talking as the girl glowed, looking like she felt invincible.

A small smile creased Kelly's lips.

What glory came from facing a fear, as if staring it down took away its power.

Her car cut off the thought, the engine groaning as she pressed the accelerator.

Over the last week the sounds and sluggishness had gotten worse, but losing her source of income had bumped an auto checkup to dead last on the priority list. With a glance at the dashboard, the temperature gauge read hot while a high pitched grating sound started up from under the hood.

*Crap.*

Car repair was a death rattle, especially when your vehicle was old as dirt.

The meager surplus of her checking account might be enough to cover a basic diagnostic, but Kelly added a silent prayer as she checked the time on the dash. Summer nights froze the clock with its wealth of daylight hours, but if memory served she had less than thirty minutes to get to the repair place down the street from her apartment.

Pressing the gas, and her luck, the Honda whimpered its way past five exits, rolling to a stop in the deserted parking lot of a strip mall. Anchored at the end of a retail row which included a bakery, sports bar, and an optometrist's office, Al's Auto Repair stood as a bright beacon against the putrid yellow of parking lights. The car bays illuminated from the inside, the Plexiglas squared doors were trundled open, looking like an amphitheater with the suffusion of blue-white glow.

Kelly locked up her car as a precaution and treaded up to the open area, poking her head in. The place appeared deserted, the tools and chests all secured for the night. With the room's high ceiling and wide, echoing walls, she felt like a mouse exploring new territory.

"Hello?" she called, her voice bouncing off the metal racks and coils.

Kelly noticed an array of dingy cloths laying on a neighboring counter. Maybe they were finishing a few jobs before going home.

Or maybe her car could make it until tomm—

Before she could move to leave, a head peered out from a splay of tools in the corner.

Okay, someone had the closing shift. And *hello,* she had the pleasure of being his pain in the ass, last minute customer.

Guilt tugged in her chest but her car needed the emergency doctor's visit. That she couldn't help.

The face remerged attached to broad-shouldered body, the man wiping his grease smeared hands as he stepped up to greet her. Rangy arms and legs were encased in a zip-up uniform, the durable material a deep navy blue that set off the man's crop of dark brown hair and eyes. Kelly guessed him to be close to her in age.

The guy didn't compare to Aidan, but the term *cute* did come to mind.

"Can I help you?" the guy asked.

"Sorry to show up right before closing but—" Kelly stopped mid-sentence as the guy's eyes flipped up, pegging the dark breadth of the parking lot behind her right as a big, expensive-looking SUV rolled past.

Maybe that was his last appointment of the day. *Worth the wait,* Kelly thought taking in the car's sleek lines and gilded edges, its flash was like a Roman candle in the haze of July air. Eyes glued to the vehicle, the guy's attention didn't wane; following the beams of the giant's headlights until they cut through the dark and disappeared. Judging by the man's disappointment the last thing he wanted was to spend his evening working on her relic.

She'd better talk fast.

"I don't have an appointment, but I've been here before for oil changes. My car is acting strange."

"What's it doing?" he asked, his demeanor that of a specialist.

Kelly described the sounds, and handing the guy her keys, he drove her wheezing vehicle up into his work area, each cough of the muffler sounding fatal.

Given leave to hang out in the waiting area, Kelly watched the mechanic put her old Honda up on the lift, professional speculation on his face. She pushed through the door, on a mission to find some distraction. A steel beast of a coffee maker welcomed her, stationed next to a papier-mâché nest of picked apart newspapers. She found a solitary fashion magazine buried under a stack of *Sports Illustrated* and *Car and Driver,* and forty minutes of worry reprieve came in the form of catching up on trivial social news. Not the current month, but standard fodder as far as media fluff went, the projection that spring pastels were in, the fashion recycled to appear new every year. Kelly laid the pink polka dots aside, not ready to return to her not-so-glossy reality when her mechanic entered the room a while later.

She gauged his expression, it appeared that he'd came back with questions.

*Not a death knell. That's good news.*

"Hi," she greeted.

"Hey. I ran a short test and I got a P0440 code—the problem's related to the gas tank."

Hmm. She'd heard of certain models having weird defects over time, but never something like that. It explained the crappy gas mileage, though.

"And there's this—" He raised a gloved hand, the smell of gasoline permeating as he rubbed the substance between his fingertips, the stuff more grainy than greasy. "I drew out a sample."

"That's my gas?" It looked like facial scrub, sugar soaked in petrol. "Is that normal? What would cause that?"

Her mechanic shrugged, perplexed. "I don't know. I've never seen a sample like this before."

"Can it be fixed?"

"I'm not sure. We'd have to disassemble the tank to find out."

Fantastic. Kelly wanted to let her head fall back, drop off her body where this nightmare would end. The labor costs alone would leave her homeless.

"Have you considered trading it in?" The mechanic's dark eyes were kind.

Mulling it over, Kelly had bought the Honda used, suspected that it had four years in it, tops. It had been good to her, reliable until the end. Maybe it was time to trade up.

"The body and muffler are in good shape, but I wouldn't drive it much longer until we get a better look at the problem, or it could go systemic and cause damage to other areas. If you want to shop around, a few blocks down is a

place called E-Z Auto Retailers. They specialize
in trade-ins. They may be able to salvage what's
left and give you some money toward something
new. If you go, ask for Luis. Tell him Ben sent
you."

She stared unseeingly at the wall a moment,
her mind dazed with options.

"Thanks." The words came out on a breath as
Kelly retrieved her wallet from her grubby back
pocket. Flipping it open she fished past change,
pennies mostly, to get to the plastic, the card
worth marginally more than whatever credit
she had linked to it. "What do I owe?"

Ben's calloused hand motioned for her to put
it away. "On the house."

*No.* While the dirty clothes and five cent
savings spelled out broke as a joke, she didn't
want pity. He'd done the work and he seemed
like a nice guy.

"Please, I kept you late." She handed him the
card but he stepped back, refusing the payment.

"Keep   us   in   mind   for   your   future
maintenance and we're square."

Kelly retracted her hand, watching him. In
his mid-twenties, brown hair shiny from the
day's work, the working side of life had added
premature creases around his warm eyes.

They had industriousness in common, and
he'd given a fellow working-man a break. He
handed over her car keys. "Your Honda's out
front. Talk to Luis, he'll find you something
dependable."

"Thank you so much."

Ben followed her out, monitoring until Kelly
got into her car. Sitting a moment, she watched

him return to the shop. Another SUV passed
behind her, a white Lexus the size of a whale.
Ben's head popped up again, his expression
crestfallen as the vehicle's tail lights glowed
crimson and faded into the night. He turned
back to the cavern of the shop, picking up rags
and shutting down machines.

Kelly hoped that whomever Ben was waiting
for showed up soon.

Good guys were hard to come by in this
world.

She pulled out of the parking lot and rolled
up to the exit. Taking a deep breath she turned
right, opposite the direction of her apartment.

A new car would be another radical change,
like she needed more crazy, but she had to get
back and forth to Hammond's until she finished
her service. Plus, no school and no job, made no
mode of transportation a *no go*.

She'd owned a jalopy before the Honda. Not
an automotive paragon, but it ran.

She went easy on the accelerator as the neon
sign of the E-Z auto retailers came into view.
Kelly uttered a silent prayer for something
decent, although she'd take whatever she could
get.

Driving back to New York in a beater was
still better than taking the bus.

# CHAPTER 11

Aidan rolled the spork from his lunch between his fingers, wondering if he should save it for Kelly. Having a backup never hurt, in case the one she had got broken or got thrown away by accident. The resulting smile crept up on him.

He stilled the movement when he felt eyes watching, and glanced up to peg Eric with a return stare. The blue boy said nothing as usual, just performed another one of his trademark squint and scans from across the break room table, then went back to his lunch as if Aidan's preoccupation with plastic utensils didn't faze him.

He did that a lot, Aidan noticed. Conversation wasn't required because the guy's hazel-brown eyes were better than any radar bought or sold. Over the last month Aidan had tried to launch into the *let's talk* spiel several times, but like a fox, Eric never went for it. Carson could know all a person's secrets by simply standing two feet away, but damned if he'd allow an outsider to know his.

*Not dumb. Not an open book. Plenty of brawn.*

All of it made the guy a good candidate for the cop job but it also made him one hell of an enigma.

Eric took in another steaming forkful of the heavenly smelling beef and rice dish laid out in front of him, the stuff bulging with whole new potatoes and baby carrots. Aidan looked down at his own lot, the processed Tex-Mex sliding around its plate of wax paper. The cheese whiz dripped off the refried beans in a visual confirmation that the crap contained no nutrients whatsoever.

Eric ignored him, taking measured bites of his meal, the feast a la Rachael Ray spread out in a plastic container brought from home, prompting Aidan to check the guy's left hand for the millionth time.

No wedding band, no indention or tan line. No mention of a woman.

But then again Aidan couldn't get Eric to spill his age much less anything else, the guy dead silent on a good day. That and maybe-partners weren't allowed to be nosy.

Not that that stopped Aidan from asking.

"Something on your mind?" Eric asked, loading up another forkful.

Aidan pointed at the beef bourguig-yum with his spork. "You bring that from home?"

Eric tensed, the guy taking an extra-ordinate amount of time to chew and swallow before he gave a curt nod.

"Your mom make it?"

"No."

"Girlfriend?"

"Don't have one."

The look of astonishment must have shown because Eric reined in an eye-roll. Aidan didn't know the guy real well, but he hadn't gotten the impression that he was—

"I'm not gay."

*Okay, that answers that question.*

"Who's the spork for?" Eric shot back as if to say, *since we're putting all the personal crap out on the table.*

*Who*, not what.

The quiet resounded. Cornered with the question, Aidan felt his jaw do the open and close, no sound coming out. Eric saw right through him, knowing full-well that his preoccupation with the girl went beyond his obligation to the case. How unprofessional was it that he was thinking of Kelly that way, looking forward to seeing her. He needed to get his head in the game.

"I've been patrolling her neighborhood," Eric said, breaking the silence.

Aidan's head shot up. "What? Why?"

"We monitor the area anyway; she lives in a shitty part of town."

Aidan's indignation faded, not so angry with the fact that Eric was watching out for her but that he wasn't the one doing it. He'd already bent the rules to oversee Kelly's community service, and an arson detective had no jurisdiction in running security patrols.

Carson had the beat rights, not him.

The rounds gave Eric the case data, and at least the guy was cool enough to share.

"Dope deals go down in her complex." Eric's words were direct, factual. "A lot of her neighbors have drug records. No big flake that I've seen, but marijuana gets wheeled and dealed."

"That doesn't mean—she's paying her way through college. She barely eats and her clothes are second hand. That's not the lifestyle of a dealer," Aidan said, his jaw ticking. Funny that Aidan was defending her against Eric's suspicions when he'd harbored the same doubts about the girl. But he no longer believed Kelly capable of being in cahoots with the Dove dealers, not after getting to know her.

"I don't think she's involved, but she's living in the middle of it." Eric's eyes met Aidan's in a visual struggle, the guy's orbs sincere.

Eric pulled his gaze away, doing a quick search of the break room, ensuring that no one was listening. He leaned back in, voice low. "Reeves lets me patrol to keep tabs. I do rounds to make sure she's okay—a lot of domestic shit goes down over there at night."

Eric leaned back, all nonchalant. Aidan squashed the urge to clap hands with the man. Eric had been supportive, helpful from the very start.

A sudden doubt stabbed at Aidan. He had to know. "Why are you helping me?"

A frown dug ravines around Eric's mouth, his expression sad, haunted. He formed the syllables with care as he spoke. "I don't like to see good people get hurt."

The emotion that came off the guy was like standing through a crashing wave in the ocean, pushing Aidan back, and confirming all of his assumptions: Eric Carson was no wimp, and the man had known pain the way Aidan had, the rip your heart out kind.

His maybe-partner had a story, a dark one. And it'd take Aidan a while to pry out the details.

"Any unusual activity at her apartment?" Aidan asked, going back to Kelly.

Eric crossed his arms. The placid surface back in place, he shook his head. "I see her car parked out front, no visitors that I can tell. She's smart, locks up after sunset. The rest of the tenants scramble when I show up. A lot of airheads floating around. No open dealing that I've seen, not yet."

Aidan tossed the remainder of his lunch and tucked the spork into his palm, holding it tight. Eric's eyes flickered down, tracking the action as Aidan pocketed the thing.

"You stopping by the farm today?"

"This afternoon."

With a scrape of his chair Carson stood up, crossing the room in a few steps. In one economic move he opened and closed the break room fridge, returning with a plastic container identical to one he'd been eating from. Eric slid the thing over the table. Aidan peered through the clear top, seeing layers of pasta in a red sauce. Lasagna. Enough for two.

"In case you guys get hungry later."

Aidan got to his feet, picking up the gift. The room stayed quiet except for the sound of a heavy hand landing in admiration on Eric's shoulder.

Aidan walked out the door, his mind running like a locomotive. Carson had proved himself to be more than a good cop; the man had become the one thing Aidan had been without for so long. A friend.

Aidan didn't know everything about the guy's past, but he knew enough to make an important decision.

From then on, when it came to Eric Carson, Aidan would remove the prefix *maybe* from the term *partner*.

# CHAPTER 12

Kelly stomped on the clutch. The wayward car's mechanism responded with another horrible popping sound as she disjointedly rammed the shifter into second gear.

Or she thought it was second; it was northeast on the stick-thing. She didn't dare take her eyes off the stretch of back road to check. She was less than a mile from Hammond's, so the nightmare was almost over.

The unnerving jumps of movement and grinding sounds seemed to ease for a second, the demon going quiet, her cue to keep up whatever she was doing. Like a crying baby she was trying to pacify, and the monster that was her new car liked being in neutral, but neutral wasn't going to get them into the farm's parking lot.

"Look," she said to the steering wheel, "just get us back and I won't drive you ever again. *Deal?*"

As if in agreement, the car managed a plaintive silence as Kelly pumped the clutch, carefully moving the shifter into the center area while turning onto the farm's gravel driveway. Kelly used the last of the thing's momentum to coast halfway down the bumpy stretch before they slowed to a crawl, the gravity of the incline making them drift backward. Kelly pumped the brake and a loud grating followed a reverberating thump through the floorboards.

A chorus of, *you're doing it wrong—WRONG!*

"*Crap!*" Kelly spat out, reverting back to her trial and error petal shuffle, her hands and feet doing a dance of shifting and stomping.

She popped her head up. A figure stood at the end of the driveway—a man centered at the middle of the path, watching with his hands on his hips, the stance all authority. Even from a distance she could make out the Mediterranean blue of his eyes.

*Shit.*

Yet again the detective was going to bear witness to her epic failure. Like his opinion of her wasn't already in the toilet.

Why couldn't she screw-up in private?

Kelly let out a puff of breath, her focus back on bringing her hunk of metal in for a landing. Throwing the shifter into first gear, she touched the gas pedal.

"*Shit—No!*" Kelly hollered as the Jeep bounded over the leftover distance of driveway, Aidan's stationary form going from small to full size as the raging vehicle lunged toward him.

Panicked, Kelly slammed her foot on the brake, and the keening wail of brake pads heralded their abrupt stop. In a cloud of brake dust and steam the Jeep's body bobbed like an old playground ride on its shocks. Kelly held stock-still in her seat, dazed and winded, uncertain if the ride from hell was over.

Blinking out the windshield, she cranked on the emergency brake.

Aidan's composed face greeted her, amused.

The man had no sense of self-preservation. *Whatsoever.*

In a burst of reanimation, Kelly flung the door open and scampered around the vehicle's nose, running concerned eyes over Aidan's body. She glowered at the Jeep's bumper, the beam of metal a mere three inches from the man's knees.

*Any closer and—*

"Are you insane?! Why didn't you move?" Kelly heard her voice escalate into something high and squeaky. An isolated thought told her that she may want to stop screaming at her would-be probation officer, but logic trumped the misconduct, like how she'd just dodged vehicular copslaughter by three inches.

"What were you going to do if I didn't stop in time—*jump* out of the way?"

He wasn't that fast—was he?

It dawned that Kelly had never seen Aidan in action. On previous occasions she'd noticed that his gait was smoother than normal, very controlled, but it wasn't like the man could dodge a charging car.

"You traded in your Honda?" he responded in a light voice, staring approvingly at the Jeep.

"I could have killed you," she said to his shoulder as he stepped past her, eyes fixated on the car.

"You weren't that close," he muttered, a smirk pulling at his lips.

Kelly silently added *showoff* to the growing list of descriptors she had compiled for him. Next to *cocky, daredevil,* and *jerk.*

Her pulse throbbed in her temple as she tried not to imagine Aidan a foot shorter.

Aidan ignored the censure as he moved to the open driver's side, poking his head in to check out the interior. The backseat and roof was enclosed with the soft-top panels that Kelly had been shown how to set up back at the auto dealers. The exterior paint was a faded, garnet red color with minor specks of rust. "Garage kept" as Luis had called it.

She'd been careful to look everything over before signing any papers, but outside of the aesthetics, it was obvious that Kelly knew little about cars. Her sales guy, the one the mechanic had suggested, took her for a test drive. He'd walked away a little wobbly, too, but gave her an upfront deal with a three-day, no-question return clause. The five speed saved her three grand on the price, the option seeming smart.

*At the time.*

Footsteps approached as Kelly turned to see Hank emerging from the repair shed, pulling off work gloves.

"So this is all the commotion," Hank said viewing the Jeep with a grin, rounding his way to the front where she'd nearly buffed the license plate with Aidan's kneecaps. "I haven't seen one of these since—"

"—1984." Aidan poked his head out of the cabin to finish the sentence.

"Oh, yeah. A CJ-8?" Hank asked.

"9, I think. The 8's were longer. Had a flatbed like a truck," Aidan answered, his voice muffled as he continued to peruse the contents of the brute's glove box.

"Pop the hood while you're in there, Aidan," Hank instructed.

Kelly disappeared into the background, the conversation centering on the brute's rebuilt engine, gas mileage, the overhead something-or-the-other. The men combed the Jeep over, checking for everything from body damage to weak belts and hoses.

Never mind the fact that with a viable witness less than ten yards away Kelly had nearly turned Aidan into road-pizza. Of course that wouldn't be enough to interrupt the male bonding over her new mode of transportation. Aidan examined every gauge on the dashboard, pressing buttons and throwing an occasional question out to Hank through the steel of the propped up hood.

Watching the guys work for her set off a sensation in Kelly's chest.

She'd never known her father and didn't fare well in relationships with men, her schoolwork taking the place of a long-term boyfriend. Whenever the loneliness set in she just pushed it away, writing it off as too much solitude. She'd learned early that life was work, and that simply getting ahead had to be her reward.

She'd never allowed herself to linger on the idea of a man looking out for her, like a father for his daughter, or a husband would his...

Hank inspected under the hood while Aidan sat in the driver's seat, pushing back into the bucket's padded back, testing its resistance; his face was serious, absorbed. He was making sure it was safe to drive, for *her.*

She tried to remember a time a man had ever done something like that for her before, drawing a blank. None of her previous boyfriends were ever that committed, and she rarely asked for the help. It seemed like the men she attracted knew that, too. As if they expected independence of her.

A suspicion planted itself in her mind, confusing her. She'd always been her own man, but what if someone came along and wanted to take over the role?

With one long leg hanging out of the cab and his hand on the shifter, Aidan turned her way. "You bought a car with a manual transmission?"

"It was all I could get for my trade," Kelly said wrapping her arms around her stomach. Looking back, she had to admit that it was an impulse buy.

*More like a desperate buy.*

She didn't expect to have to explain her decision to anyone. And she'd liked how the car looked tough, durable. Dependable sounded good. But in the light of day she felt far from empowered, she felt foolish.

"I have three days to give it back...if it doesn't work out," she answered, her voice regretful. Her eyes trailed over one of the brute's oversized tires.

"Have you driven a manual before?" Aidan asked, as if trying to suppress his opinion.

Like he hadn't been witness to her kangaroo hop down the driveway. His blue eyes trained on her, he waited for an answer.

"A few times. A friend taught me in high school, I thought I could pick it back up again," she said. She looked up to find that his eyes had softened, blue irises glowing, and for a moment Kelly let herself get lost. Aidan reached out and touched her elbow. Under the warm weight of his hand on her skin she couldn't breathe. The dark pupils of his eyes went wide, dilated, and Kelly felt her head tilt in disbelief.

*He couldn't be. He couldn't possibly...?*

"Hey, Hank?" Aidan called out, flipping his cobalt stare away from her.

"Yeah," Hank's voice retorted around the rugged metal sheet of the brute's hood.

Aidan gave Kelly's arm a gentle squeeze before releasing her and walking over to where Hank stood holding an oil dipstick.

"Hey, would Sophie mind if I borrow Kelly for a few hours?"

"She's picking up feed at the supply market, won't be back for at least another hour. I'll let her know when she gets back," Hank said, throwing Kelly a gentle smile. "You're going to help her practice?"

"Yeah," Aidan replied, rubbing the back of his neck. "My place has a long driveway. I think it'd make a good track, if that's all right."

"Fine with me," Hank replied with another smile as he reinstated the car's pieces, mashing the hood shut with the meaty palms of his hands.

"What are you doing?" Kelly asked as Aidan returned to her.

"Hop in."

Aidan ushered her into the passenger seat. Tracking his return trip through the glass of the windshield, Kelly watched as he took the driver's side, fastening his seatbelt and ordering her to do the same. She obeyed, watching as with a flip of his wrist the engine came to life without protest, letting out a constant idle as Aidan's hands and feet effortlessly shifted the demon into reverse.

*Traitor,* Kelly thought at the dashboard.

The brute had to be adhering to some underground guy code:

*Thou shalt behave for fellow men but not for overachieving, demanding women.*

So male.

Kelly shrugged, crossing her arms again and turning her mind to the country scenery that was soon passing outside her window. She felt like an idiot. If previous events this year hadn't already confirmed that she had a full dance card with Murphy's Law, she should know by now that any attempt at succeeding, at anything, was futile.

Why was she so unlucky?

The center of her chest coiled again, her subconscious playing Marco-Polo, taunting her with hints that she was getting "warmer." It had to be some cosmic lesson in modesty. Like she'd been too smug and deserved to be demoted.

Broke and struggling, she couldn't imagine that a lower rung even existed. She recalled her best moment, when she'd walked across the stage to receive her diploma. With every accolade, she never once felt better than anyone else, quite the opposite. No matter how much she achieved she felt behind the pack, below par, years behind everyone else her age.

She was no stranger to striking out. She thought of the dusty clarinet sitting in her closet back home, the time she'd nearly knocked herself unconscious falling off the balance beam in gymnastics.

She added in, *the time she bought a car that she couldn't drive....*

Kelly squeezed her eyes shut, letting the sense of failure permeate.

"We can go back if you want. Do this some other day." Aidan's level voice came again, calling her away from her gloomy thoughts. Navigating the car effortlessly, he glanced her way, his expression concerned.

"It's...nothing."

*Nothing a steady job and some common sense can't fix.*

She inspected the road in front of them, struck by the multi-acres of surrounding land; the five-minute drive had dropped them in another world. Farm-like plots lay beautifully spread apart, little houses anchoring corners of sprawling green fields, some with barns and horses; others with large gardens and areas of vegetables springing up in carefully cultivated rows. The residential street they traveled was lined with tall, aged trees and free-standing mailboxes, rolling lawns of grass and rancher-style houses.

Kelly fell silent, taking in the splendor. Growing up in suburbia, she'd only known her mother's little townhouse. She'd seen bigger houses in passing, but never envied the grandiose homes, the modern fraction-of-an-acre McMansions built so close together that they came across as more excessive than opulent. She recalled the few older farmhouses out in the rural parts of New York, the brick-faced homes appearing so sturdy, like no storm could ever blow them away.

She'd dreamed of owning one someday. A mirror of the houses on display before her now, with everything green and lush and well cared for.

"Where are we?" she asked as the Jeep slowed, turning them off onto a narrow gravel road.

"This is my place."

The rough path meandered over a hill, a long strip of land bordering them on one side. A small home rolled into view as they bounced along. A paved circular driveway emerged as Aidan wheeled them to a gentle stop in front of a stylish ranch style house. Anchored on both sides with red brick, the windows were bordered with wooden shutters painted a tasteful claret color. Connected by an arcade, the covered porch provided shade to the front door where a swing awaited use, wide enough for two. Kelly held her breath; it had to be the most perfect house she'd ever seen.

"You live here?" Kelly muttered.

"Yeah."

*Of course he does.*

He was a gorgeous man; why was it a surprise that he lived in a gorgeous house. Suddenly Kelly felt silly, naïve. A wanderer and so-called life-long student who spent half her time lost and the rest of it making impulsive decisions, then imposing on people to help her when circumstances didn't pan out. The complete opposite, Aidan had spent years in his profession. He was accomplished in the way that Kelly longed to be, with a career, and more than a ramshackle, way station of a roof over his head. He didn't need to be bringing some vagabond like her to his home. With her luck she'd jinx him.

"What's wrong?" He frowned, eyes darting between her and the house.

"Nothing. It's just..." Kelly wavered. Admittedly she felt like a burden, but it'd be rude of her to deny his help, not when he'd made such an effort. "Your house is lovely," she said, reluctantly making her mind up to stay.

"Thanks." He shot her another questioning look and then turned off the engine, leaving the keys dangling in the ignition. "Let's switch places," he said, disappearing from the seat and reappearing at her side a moment later.

Her feet hit the ground as a lungful of sweet, summer air helped clear her head. The midafternoon sun had painted the huge backyard in bronze hues, and the stretch of three acres was dotted with maple trees that waved limbs full of green leaves at her.

With the amount of land he owned, Aidan could easily have animals, which left Kelly to wonder whether he was a horse person. He hung around Hammond's for work and he knew Sophie, but other than that she didn't know much else about him. How he felt about pets, people....

Kelly reclaimed the driver's seat and felt the car cringe. She thought about the promise she'd made to the brute, the one she'd reneged on.

"You sure this is a good idea," she cautioned as Aidan settled in next to her.

"You want to keep the car?" he asked candidly, buckling his seatbelt.

*No. Yes. Crap.* What had she gotten herself into?

"Yes," she croaked, staring at the various meters, the large dials and numbers looking intimidating and foreign.

The panel glared back at her, everything bigger than what she could handle. But that had been what attracted her in the first place—the thing was steadfast on the sales lot. In the end she'd wanted to feel safe. Instead she felt like a little girl sitting behind the wheel of the huge machine.

Aidan sat up, his shoulders rolling back, locking into a vertical line of well-built posture. "Let's go then."

She blinked, distracted. Aidan's broad body took up so much space in the close quarters of the Jeep's cabin. The air warmed by the stillness, his eyes fell on her, the proximity making Kelly dizzy.

Not since her crazy night in jail had she seen him so close. She took advantage of the opportunity. Illuminated by the sun, the pigment of his irises were other-worldly, bluer than any oxide mineral. She told herself that curiosity made her angle forward, staring him down as she looked from one eye to the other. Meeting her gaze Aidan held still, allowing her appraisal. On closer inspection, his blue was like the flame of gas when ignited, hypnotic.

"What?" he asked, his voice gruff.

"I'm sorry," Kelly said, drawing back. She gave a weak laugh, feeling inappropriate, trying to shake off her awkwardness. She looked out the windshield. Feeling his stare, the heat of his attention made her blush more. "Your eyes, they're a unique color. I bet you hear that a lot."

"You know all about that, don't you?" he asked, trying to catch her attention. "In school."

"Yes. The origins of—" She couldn't look at him without getting lost. And she *could* look again, it was if he were inviting her to.

They sat sharing air, space. So...close.

Breaking the trance, Aidan's hand stirred, motioning to the keys hanging down the side of the steering wheel.

"Ready?" he asked.

"Uh, yeah." Kelly leaned away, sorry to have cornered him.

Pivoting in his seat, Aidan stayed close, his breath sending pulses of heat through Kelly's skin. "The left pedal is the clutch. Before you change gears or brake you need to press down on that first." He leaned in, his shoulder brushing hers.

"Leave the brake alone for now, we're going to learn to *go* first, then we'll learn to stop."

Kelly tried to note everything he was telling her, but the words drifted as he invaded her personal space. As he pointed to the gauges, his upper body jutted out to display a clear profile of his long jaw and strong neck. A reflective lock of hair waved down the length of his nape. She suppressed the impulse to reach out, semi-wedging her hand under her leg as a precaution, striving to pay attention as Aidan explained the tachometer.

Only inches from her nose, his tan skin emitted the scent of sweat, cologne, and from the tang of it, soap. The combination made Kelly breathe in deep, thankful that while touching was off-limits, inhaling was inevitable in such close quarters.

"Okay, let's get the engine going." Aidan reclined, taking his scent with him as he put distance between them again. "Step down on the clutch and start it up."

Sidetracked, Kelly fumbled with the key, her left foot pushing the clutch down to the floor. The engine turned over, the innocent rumble through the floorboards making Kelly suspicious. She hovered her foot over the brake pedal, awaiting more of the brute's bad behavior.

"Wait..." Aidan said in a low voice, the velvet word shockingly close—right in her ear—making her freeze. The ton of steel encasing them forgotten, Kelly could only acknowledge how Aidan's breath tickled her skin, leaving a trail of goose bumps in its wake.

"When the ignition catches, ease your foot off the clutch then let it idle. Don't touch the gas until we're ready to move, let the car start on its own," he instructed.

Kelly nodded, absorbing every word, a tingling sensation running down every single one of her nerve endings. The Jeep began to roll backward a little, but she forced herself not to react. Instead of more tutorial, the warm weight of Aidan's hand encased hers over the shifter, and Kelly shivered. His coarse fingers were a contrast to his soft palm as the touch lingered, the heat of the connection stunning Kelly motionless. She watched, entranced as his palm guided hers, shifting the car into first gear and then letting go, the air cold without his warmth.

"Now release the clutch," he said.

Her foot followed his command, the brute responding with an obedient hum of an idle; its big body coasting backward but not springing.

"Give it a little gas. Move us forward and then let it roll back. Play with how much gas it takes to move, and listen to the engine. If you hear it struggling, ease up."

Kelly followed the direction, performing a playful dip of pull and drift. The rev of the engine was like the sound of a singer warming-up with levels of humming, a deliberate and rhythmic whirr.

"Good. Ready for go?" Aidan's voice returned, the smooth cadence joining the purr, a song beautiful to Kelly's ears.

*Yeah.*

She clamped down on the small corner of fear she felt, a churning mix of tension and excitement rippling like a lick of flame under her skin. Aidan sat up, raising a hand to grip the *Oh Shit* handle bolted above the passenger-side window.

"Foot on the clutch, don't touch the brake."

Kelly took a deep breath and positioned her feet.

"Now get us out to the driveway."

With a strong, steady pitch forward she propelled them out of the circle in a solid surge of motion. It wasn't fluid, but it resulted in far less objection than her first round. Kelly let off the gas as they rolled up the gravel road, Aidan concentrating on her.

"Let's take it up to third gear on the straightaway."

Kelly raised her eyebrows at the stretch of road ahead of her and then braced herself.

*No turning back now.*

Her hands clasped the wheel as she hit the gas, the smell of dispelled exhaust wafting up around them. The brute growled and blazed onward, hauling them over the gravel, kicking up white powder. Its raw power accelerated them down the path, the speedometer registering ten, fifteen, then twenty miles per hour.

"We're topping out first," Aidan said, monitoring. "Watch your RPMs, listen to the engine, and get ready to shift."

Despite the intensity of the ride, the focus stayed on meters and vibrations, and Kelly welcomed the speed, any excuse to feel Aidan's hand on hers again; the heat of his skin like being wrapped in dryer-warm towels.

"Let go of the gas and hit the clutch," he directed, his body tethered by his arm as he tried to keep his wide body from bouncing out of the passenger seat.

In the center of the storm Kelly watched their joint hands move the shifter downward, the engine responding with a growl, projecting them faster. The wind blew through the windows as Kelly embraced the coordination and the support of the man sitting next to her, all of it making her glance down at the dashboard in awe. Elation flooded her veins, warming her chest.

They were flying.

"The road ends here. Let's turn around." Aidan pointed ahead, the path narrowing into a small loop and doubling over the same stretch of road. "Shift us into neutral."

Rotating the wheel and moving with the remaining momentum, Kelly smiled as they rounded the bend, hitting the gas when they reached the main road.

"Can you get us back?" Aidan challenged, his muscles flexing as he held the emergency brake with his free hand.

A mischievous thrill went through her.

*Okay, pal.* With a sly grin she pushed the clutch, repeating Aidan's every instruction with ease. Her heart raced as she sinuously navigated first, then second gear.

Aidan remained silent until halfway down the road, when out of blue he said, "Punch it and let's get the hang of third."

They traveled faster and faster, the pace of the car, the beat of the ground under them, all pounding in sync with her heart. The growl of the engine reached its apex as she shifted them into third with precision. The trees passed by them in a blur, Kelly's legs predicting the bounce of the shocks, and suddenly she felt a part of everything, of the brute, of Aidan. Laughter burst from her throat before she could stop it, a whole-hearted sound ringing out from deep inside her.

They raced until the side of the house reeled into view. Aidan opened his mouth to direct her again, but Kelly anticipated how to bring them to a stop. She hit the clutch and shifted into neutral, letting off the gas and pressing the brake, the brute gliding up to the front of the house like a roller-coaster ride finishing its course. She turned to find Aidan grinning at her.

"Oh my God," she said, letting out another chuckle. "That was...."

"Good job," he said, her fit of laughter making his face break into a broad smile. Kelly paused to take it in—his happy eyes narrowed, glinting with vibrant blue; his face glowing with pride. "You picked it up fast."

"I can't believe..." She'd lost all words. Her entire vocabulary had blown out the window. She was buzzing from the drive, from the way he was beaming at her. The pounding of her heart and the laughter left her...light. She felt weightless. All levity dissolved as she looked up at him with heated resolve. In the center of the storm that was her life, Aidan had given her a gift.

Did he realize how much that meant?

She stared at him, trying to retrieve an answer, unable to pull away. She had to keep a mental snapshot, of him, of the moment. As if by keeping the picture, she'd get to keep the feeling and the man.

His smile faded, his gaze becoming somber as he seemed to pick up on the change in her. In a second his eyes flashed, flipping to the glove box.

"Aidan?" She tried to reclaim his attention.

"Yeah?" he replied, eyes still downcast. She guessed that she was making him uncomfortable again.

"Thank you," she said. The appreciation was soft and sincere, but weak compared to all that she was feeling.

"Anytime," he said, his tone yielding.

Kelly traced his profile, knowing it wasn't enough. Words were just air and inflection and—not *enough*. In a flare of instinct, her torso leaned her forward, her mind shutting down. A sweet kind of panic ignited as she tried to hold on to reason, but it, too, was burning away.

What was he to her, a friend? A warden?

He was a man. A man she wanted to be close to.

And talk was not the demonstration she wanted.

He stiffened at her approach, the returning smell of him billowing through her as the rough stubble of his skin came into view. Her lips had almost reached the destination of his cheek— She didn't even catch the twist of his head—it was instantaneous, like a flicker of flame. Her lips met his in a mismatch of trajectory, her bottom lip caught between his, the two of them pursed and pressed together. A tremor of pleasure ran through her, radiating from her chest and outward to her limbs. He let her lead, a spontaneous and tender pressure.

Kelly pulled back to see his face, exhaling softly. Aidan's eyes ignited in a burn of blue, heavy with desire. She'd underestimated him, his speed.

His move was in expectation—not to avoid a peck on the cheek but to catch her lips.

*Reception, not offense.*

And it happened again. The rim of blue went thin, his pupil dilating, the dark circle opening to take in the sight of her. Kelly felt her heart kick.

She leaned in again while he waited for her; and their lips came together uniformly this time, her shaky fingertips coming to rest on his jaw. Her movement direct while he was guiding. Tilting his head, he allowed her access to all of him.

He met her halfway, leading when she faltered, resting a light hand on her arm, which sent sparks through her body. Just when Kelly thought that she'd stopped breathing, Aidan broke the contact, holding her up carefully as she melted back into her seat.

She watched his chest rise and fall as he inhaled deeply, the atmosphere thick between them. Minutes passed and he remained quiet, averting his eyes but retaining his hold on her. Kelly stared down at his thumb as he trailed a gentle circle across her skin before retracting his hand.

"We need to take you back," he said, propping open the door, a cool summer breeze clearing out the intensity hanging between them.

Kelly remained in a trance as they switched places and rode in silence on the return to Hammond's. He said nothing, as if their kiss had been a causal event, nothing of importance. Kelly started to worry more with every stop light, the silence a punishment.

Had she crossed the line? He wasn't her parole officer, but what if there was some rule about getting involved with witnesses.

Would he stop visiting her at the farm? Fear speared at her.

She expected Aidan to say something, but he sat composed the entire way, the trip short as Kelly ruminated on what she'd say when they arrived.

She had no regrets—did he? The thought ripped at her as he pulled them into Hammond's parking lot, yanking up on the emergency brake.

"Thanks," she said, opening the door, eager to get away. To cry, to scream.

She nearly forgot to collect her keys.

"Here." A familiar heat coursed through her as he grabbed her hand. She stopped with one leg out the door as he uncurled her fingers to drop the skin-warmed metal into her palm.

"Need help getting home?" he asked.

"No," Kelly mumbled, distracted by the touch and the question. Home was the last place she needed to go with him.

He squeezed once, and let her go.

The warm afternoon air didn't register as Kelly walked over to the main house in a daze, her ears perking after someone had called her name.

"Hey there." Hank appeared from the front porch, meeting her at the steps. "How'd it go?"

"Great.   Aidan's—a   patient   teacher. I'm...better." She tried to sound relaxed and wondered if she was pulling it off.

Hank was a father; he probably had radar for hanky-panky.

The old man paused, settling back on his heels, watching her. Suddenly, Kelly didn't feel like a woman in her late-twenties—she felt like she was sixteen and busted for making out with a boy. She struggled to keep eye-contact.

"Good," Hank said finally, his eyes moving past Kelly to something beyond her.

She turned. Aidan was standing next to an old truck, his eyes pinned on her. Hank gave him an affirmative wave that Aidan returned before he vanished into the vehicle's cab.

Kelly raised her eyebrows. Okay, now she felt like she was being signed over.

"Sophie's in the main barn. She wanted to see you when you got back," Hank said, stepping off the porch and launching into a brisk walk. Hank talked as Kelly fell in step behind him, his words fading into the background. The distant sound of a truck starting up dominated Kelly's attention as her thoughts raged.

*What is Aidan? A passing thrill, here now and gone tomorrow?*

A feeling surrounded her heart, a blazing premonition.

She'd always taken care of herself. It'd take a dynamic guy to get her to relinquish the role. Someone honest, strong.

Someone she could trust.

Kelly watched the red taillights fade as Aidan's pickup vanished over the hill, her instinct blaring.

*A man like Aidan Wright.*

# CHAPTER 13

"They'll catch me." Anger surged as Rachel Lancaster spit the words, pissed off that Marc wouldn't let it go. "I *told* you, another cop is casing her apartment."

Marc went back to his pacing, the back-and-forth grating Rachel's nerves. The man had his prowess in bed going for him, but no nookie, no matter how good, was worth facing jail.

*Not this time.*

Rachel crossed her arms, thinking of the badge she'd dodged the night before. Wiry, dark hair with moreno features, the new La Joda sat in his squad car as if he were holding a stake out.

And Officer Whoever was asking for it.

Rachel didn't bother learning the cops' names. Knowing a badge's handle gave them power, authority, and she be damned if she'd give that to them. The faces were all that mattered, knowing how to spot them, the brass rulebook so damn predictable. They showed up when called—if you were lucky—stayed five minutes, did their paperwork, and left.

Typical. Boring. Easy to monitor.

Variations to the pattern were rare, but with this new Po, it created problems. The badge showed up without being called, according to her radio scanner, and he parked out in front of the girl's apartment as if on guard, observing from the shadows.

He was attentive. Too attentive.

Rachel didn't have time for the bullshit. They were still catching heat from their last dead badge. And the girl wasn't supposed to still be in the picture.

Marc stopped mid-circle, staring at the floor as if trying to catch something the fissured concrete had whispered to him. Rachel rolled her eyes, taking in her environs for the millionth time. The pit of a basement embodied the hidden, the banished. The cinder block walls resembled a prison, which did nothing but stoke her defiance.

Marc ran a wide hand through his hair, disrupting the styled black waves. "You're going back tonight," he said, the command absolute.

"The hell I am—"

He moved like a specter, gone from across the room in an instant, in her face the next. He stepped in close, his heavy palm cupping the back of her neck. The lick of pain from his grip was familiar, reminiscent, holding her still. Stark light from the cage of metal above them illuminated Marc's face, making the lines of age and stress more prominent, deepening the creases; the weeks spent holed up underground fading his once bronze skin. The demand in his hard, brown eyes was a turn-on even when they looked on her with disgust, as they did now.

"We have no time." He squeezed, pinching, driving home his point. "We need that shipment cut and sold, *now*."

"No shit," Rachel retorted, tilting her head, taking back some leverage. Like she didn't know that their backs were to the wall with their supplier. The Source, as they called him. "I'm *trying*."

Marc released her, turning away, going back to his infernal foot shuffling. Rachel traced the lines of his hunched back, recalling a time when Marcus De Silva had been indomitable, regal. Powerful. He'd run seamless deals through every major port from Miami to up the east coast. A cocaine import king, Marc controlled the product and therefore the outcome, of everything.

Or he used to.

Rachel had seen his crown slip over the last few years, the man a shadow of his former glory with his rumpled clothes and slouched posture. Fear had crept slowly into Marc's worn face, with the hints he'd drop after the distribution of each new shipment, him repeatedly calling it their "last job."

The man who took his pleasure and made his money without guilt was gone, a brittle shell of a man replacing him, the metamorphosis permanent.

The drug life had gotten too hot for Marc, the pressure making him crack.

In the beginning he was the man behind the curtain, the figurehead. Rachel's job was to do the legwork, to handle the details.

With one caveat—she went to jail for no one.

She was sticking to her principles.

Marc straightened, his chin kicking out over his shoulder. "What do we know?"

"The girl's not at the school anymore. Hasn't applied anywhere else. Every day she drives out to the sticks, to some kind of horse farm."

*Horses.* Stupid animals. Pastures full of dog food.

Rachel's leg tingled over the spot where, underneath the shell of denim, a crescent-shaped scar marred her skin. She sucked her teeth, remembering the time her adopted parents had gotten her to take horseback riding lessons, the dumb beast taking a chunk out of her. Punching the bastard had won her a ride home, expulsion from the riding center, and a lingering hatred for anything on four legs. Crazy enough, the incident didn't prevent the 'rents from finding more stuff for Rachel to do, as a parade of more extracurricular bullshit followed: dance, painting—*pottery.*

Every activity an attempt at forcing her into the societal mold, a preppy, white-picketed nightmare. The couple who'd adopted her were a pair of barren, idealistic fools, trying to "save" her from an abandoned life. Rachel's real mother had gotten pregnant with her at sixteen, used by a guy a decade older than her.

*A genetic joke, all around.*

Born to an immature girl and raised by two idiots, Rachel counted herself lucky that she'd survived her eighteen years in confinement. She'd been so eager to get away.

She idly wondered if good ol' Bill and Carol knew what'd become of her. What would they say if they knew that she'd fallen in with a drug kingpin? That she'd dealt, bartered...killed?

Rachel smirked. "The car sits in the farm's parking lot during the day. There are staff people milling around."

"Then *boost* it when no one—" he barked.

"*The NARC is there.*"

Marc's head shot up. "You said—"

"He's sticking close to the girl, and he's armed," Rachel growled, done with the small talk. "And where exactly did you think I could go with a *stolen* car in the middle of the day?"

He ran his hand through his hair again, gripping it, pulling.

*That's right, keep going. Go bald, asshole.*

"You're the one who said we needed to be smoother this time. Play nice. Invite Miss Bunsen Burner to the party," she taunted, knowing it would piss him off worse.

The poking worked. Marc's face went dark, sinister.

"She was to be used as a cover, that's *it*. Plant and remove within *one* week. She's a liability now— Damn it, you know how I feel about witnesses!"

Like Rachel could forget.

The transports used to be easy. Large parcels smuggled in, broken down, and distributed within a few weeks through known dealers. The college break times making up the gravy. An efficient cycle, they did the deals and divided the cash, then geared up to do it all again.

Easy money.

Until three years ago, when the wrench hit—their activity leaving a trail. A pair of

NARCs started netting facts through dealer busts, one getting too close to their operation.

The night that Rachel had put the first red notch in her belt.

The sight of the body filled her mind, the blood. Pulling the trigger, she'd expected to feel an instant guilt, a pang of remorse. Some verification of the moral threshold she'd breached.

She'd felt nothing. And what a disappointment.

You'd think her condemnation to hell would come with some fanfare. Although it did come two-for-one. The kick of the gun, the flash of blue eyes as the one cop pushed in front of the other.

One bullet, two bodies. So economical.

She'd nudged the one who'd taken the brunt with her foot; the other watched as the cop's face paled, life blood draining away and turning him cold. Rachel had waited, but nothing came. No lightning bolt of damnation, no prick of shame.

It wasn't her fault anyway, it was theirs. They should have stayed out of her way.

Her eyes combed over Marc, taking note of his dark hair, his deep skin warmed by the steady pump of blood underneath, a polar opposite to the colorless body that'd lain at her feet.

The thought dawned. She'd murdered for this man.

Rachel wondered if the infraction tarnished her soul or his.

*Probably both.*

Marc's eyes leveled on hers, his patience gone. "Go back to the apartment. Cased or not, get the *damn car*."

Without another word Rachel carefully pulled her Ruger P89 from its holster. With precision, she opened the chamber and peered inside. The loaded clip was ready to go, and she clicked the strip of bullets back into place, returning the piece into the leather sleeve at the small of her back. She felt around for the knife enclosed in her front pocket.

She acknowledged Marc with nod and headed for the door.

"Rachel," he called.

*Jesus. What?*

She half-turned, annoyed.

"The Source knows who you are." Marc paused, his jaw ticking. "He's out to collect."

The cold metal pressed into Rachel's spine registered through her clothes, sending chills over her skin.

If the Source bumped Marc off, she'd be next.

She was no longer safe behind the curtain. They were in the big leagues now.

She gave another nod and left. As she settled into her car, her mind was full to bursting.

Two details pushed through the static, flaring to forefront: How many bullets lay at rest against her skin, ready to be used. And how many red notches she'd log with them before it was all over.

The low summer sun painted the sky a
vibrant orange as Kelly started back toward the
main barn. Squinting up through the flood of
evening sunlight, her eyes adjusted from having
spent the day outside. She stopped to quickly
roll up the water hose she'd used to refill the
mare paddock's water trough. Rushing to finish
her chores, she was eager to hear what the vet
had to say about Keegan.

Keegan had been lethargic at his morning
feeding, his nose runny, and he hadn't eaten
much. Kelly had called Pippa in to look at him,
the senior staff member advising that they call
in the doctor. Keegan's routine follow-up
appointment wasn't due for another week; a
simple health review that all the horses went
through, but the meeting got bumped up given
Keegan's symptoms. Before the health eval,
Keegan had spent the last week taking up
residence in the stall next to Moe, the two
allowed to nuzzle through the rails like
lovebirds.

Kelly smiled at the memory. Keegan behaved
in the mare's presence, letting Moe eat first, like
an attentive suitor. Kelly had never seen
anything like it before. Her college classes had
taught her about the brain chemicals triggered
by affection—serotonin and oxytocin—the
biology working the same way regardless of
species. Animals experiencing love like humans
do.A cloud of dust burst and faded as she
clapped her hands. Stepping through the mist,
Kelly secured the gates leading back to the main

paddock. With the sun at her back, in the shadow she saw that her skin had darkened, the changing color a reaction to UV rays. Naturally pale from all the hours she spent indoors doing schoolwork, the idea that she was capable of carrying a glow like Sophie made her proud.

With a glance down at her shirt, she wondered if buying something décolleté-bearing would get some of that gold on places where sexy arson detectives would take notice. She grinned, the outward radiance moving inward, as if the sunshine had absorbed through her chest.

*That man.*

The distraction of her chores hadn't been enough to keep her mind off kissing Aidan, the urge to see him again fighting for her attention. She had no idea what to say when she saw him, whether to ask about the kiss, and what it meant. The subject of commitment tended to come across as clingy, so she'd hold off. She'd wait until he brought it up, which left time for her to stew.

When not lining up ways to approach him, she spent the day mulling over girly things like what to wear. The ancient jeans and worn-out tees that made up her wardrobe hardly made her runway worthy. She planned to take more time with her hair, invest in new clothes, stuff she wouldn't get mud on. The makeover and makeup update was a complete one-eighty from her dress down mindset, but a nice change nonetheless. It'd been forever since she'd wanted to doll up for a man, since she'd felt attractive.

Yeah, she'd unbutton a bit—

Kelly stopped in her tracks. Yards away from the main paddock, she watched as a cluster of people scuttled about, cording off a large circumference around the barn, and pouring what looked like disinfectant into squat, plastic bins on the ground. A male staff member emerged from the double-doors, leading Moe into a small adjacent area.

Kelly made a beeline for the guy as Pippa appeared, intercepting her.

"I was just coming to get you. Don't freak out."

"No good conversation ever begins that way, Pip." Kelly peered past her into the cavernous main barn, Keegan's stall blocked by a swarm of bodies. "What's going on?"

"Keegan's contracted distemper."

Kelly rotated her head back, eyes pegging the woman. "Distemper, what—what is that?"

"*Streptococcus equi*, it's bacteria induced," Pippa said, her voice low.

Kelly ran the name through her head, cross-referencing it against anything she'd read or heard. A bacteria? Treatment with antibiotics would be contingent on—

"Horse strep? That happens?"

Pippa's face went solemn. "It causes swelling of the horse's throat, and it's highly contagious. Keegan's under quarantine until we can get him treatment and test the other horses. Humans can't catch it, but anyone who's been in contact with him needs to avoid giving it to the other animals."

Kelly felt her world slow to crawl, her eyes watching as volunteers dipped their boots into the plastic tray one by one.

*Decontamination.*

"I was with him this morning," Kelly said, her voice numb.

Did she need to burn her clothes? Bathe in Lysol, what?

With the precautions they were taking, the situation looked serious.

What if Keegan had brought the disease with him from the racetrack? Were the other four affected? Could Hammond's afford the cost of the tests, the medicine?

"Pippa, is he...?"

The woman's steady hand landed on Kelly's arm, anchoring her. "I don't want you to worry. We've seen this before and he's going to be okay."

Kelly mentally measured the expense, the extra hours of monitoring, the vet visits alone.

"It'll be expensive." The words were a statement of fact, not a question, catching Pippa off guard.

She let out a heavy breath. "Yes."

"But—"

"We need to take it a step at a time. So far Keegan's the only confirmed case. With all hope, Moe isn't next, and we're monitoring the others closely. It would be easier if Keegan had a sponsor, a person supporting his treatment, but we'll manage. We always do."

With an arm-squeeze of reassurance, Pippa excused herself to go help the other staff members evacuate the barn and post signs.

Kelly observed, trying to see Keegan through the fray. She stepped forward only to stop—she had no skill to contribute, even if there were a spot for her to squeeze in.

Helpless, she pulled away, drifting toward the break room. The area was empty, its inhabitants all in the main barn, where she should be, doing something. Anything. Silence screamed from the four walls as she envisioned Keegan penned up, isolated—sick and alone.

She went over to the sink, scrubbing her hands and her arms until they burned pink. She dried off with a paper towel and looked around.

Doing nothing suffocated her, like a flame of a candle denied air. Her eyes roamed the space, landing on a tall bookcase sitting in the corner, filled with reference volumes and horse care manuals. She rushed over.

*Research.*

As she scanned the row of spines, Kelly's hands moved of their volition, pulling out select tomes. She dropped them on the table, grabbing a steno pad and a pen from the neighboring drawer. Pulling out her recorder, she was ready to get down to business. She dragged her finger down index page after index page, and opened the books wide. She read and gathered information, speaking into her recorder in case she lost the paper that she'd made the notes on. The pages flipped, the light on the machine blinking as her pen moved, filling the spaced lines of the paper.

*Streptococcus equi*: a common respiratory disease that caused fever, nasal discharge, and swelling of the throat. Treatable if caught early, but highly transmittable; the bacteria worked fast, spreading through the contact of shared water and feeding bins.

Kelly flinched. Commonly known as *Strangles,* if untreated the infection inflated the lymph nodes of the horse's throat until choking the animal. The pictures illustrated near fatal cases: horses with eyes swollen shut, open sores... Her eyes stayed glued to the photos as her handwriting veered off the paper.

"Knock, knock." Pippa stood in the door, her face lined with exhaustion.

"How is he?" Kelly asked, not bothering with preamble.

"Comfortable. Doctor Althea will be in first thing tomorrow to run tests. We thought you'd left. Are you okay for a ride home?"

Kelly looked at the clock, almost midnight. She'd been reading for over three hours.

"Yeah," Kelly said. The books' content caught Pippa's notice as Kelly closed the volumes one-by-one, stacking them into a haphazard pile.

Kelly gathered her things from her locker, tucking her recorder into her purse. The calm that lingered made her uneasy. A fake peace, it reminded her of that universal superstition, the one that if everyone remained still enough, their problems would freeze or vanish. That a lack of action would stop the circumstantial line of dominoes mid-fall.

She shook off the thought, casting away her doubts.

Wishful thinking may be naïve but it beat fearing the worst. And the facts remained the same—they wouldn't know what they were up against until Keegan saw the doctor.

Less than a day ago Kelly had cared for a recovering horse. Had laughed like she had no worries in the world. Been kissed until she saw stars.

*How quickly things change.*

Kelly looped her bag onto her shoulder and glanced up at Pippa, the woman's neutral smile shielding her from the heavy reality. "See you tomorrow?"

"First thing."

"Goodnight, Kel."

"Night, Pip."

The drive took no time at all, Kelly's brain outside of its case, floating around her head like the rings of Saturn. Mounting the stairs to her apartment, she flipped out her key, ready to get some sleep—

*Oh—*

Her heart beat triple time as the door swayed open, the metal face of the locks bent and damaged. Her breath turned into a ball in her throat as a tableau of chaos was revealed with an eerie creak of the door's hinges. Clothes and broken dishware littered the floor of her apartment, the closet and kitchen cupboards ripped apart, shoes and cups thrown down in haste. Heaps of her belongings lay scattered like confetti, furniture turned over and kicked until broken.

Kelly jumped. The door drifted, the limp, over-painted wood having no current function but to sway in the breeze from the hallway. She tiptoed through the shards, the pungent smell of spilled perfume melding with the sound of broken vanity glass crunching underneath her feet; the areas of the room blended together in a collage of busted pieces.

*Why? Why would someone do this?*

What could a robber possibly get from her? She had nothing of value—

*Oh no. No.*

Panicked, Kelly rushed over to the closet. Blocked by the lump of particleboard that used to be her dresser, she pushed the mass out of the way, the space a hollow with a rail as what had hung there previously was now cast about the room. Running her hand over the high shelf, the plane was empty, bare as if someone had brushed it clean.

Kelly dropped down onto her haunches to scour the ground. Through mixed debris of mirror and glass her eyes locked in on the small ring box lying on its side. Grabbing first, a stab of pain had her yanking her hand back, scarlet blood welling up in a line on her palm. She plucked a ragged shard of mirror out of her gashed flesh, her skin stinging as she made a fist. A trickle of red ran down her wrist, spotting the floor.

*Great.*

Next to the last of the unpacked boxes lay a ring of packing tape.

She crossed the room, grabbing the tape along with a neighboring roll of uncoiled paper towels. Ripping off several sheets, she applied pressure to the cut, wheeling the tape around the pad, ripping the adhesive with her teeth to seal the makeshift bandage in place. She returned to the closet and crouched down, utilizing her left hand to pick up the ring box.

She said a silent prayer as she popped the lid, the sight of her signet college ring nestled inside spurring tears.

They hadn't taken it.

Slipping the solid gold onto her finger, she clasped her good and bad hands around the empty case, the union both a shield and sign of thanks.

After a beat, she looked around and frowned. Her earrings and wristwatch lay visible in the rubble, the robber appearing to have left all of her jewelry.

The class ring alone was worth five hundred dollars.

Tilting her head, Kelly took a quick inventory. All of her clothes were there, socks tossed around where the dresser used to be. Her tube TV sat in smashed lump. She got to her feet, measuring the pattern of the wreckage. Some objects were destroyed with no thought, others rummaged through then busted, all in no discernible order.

*Strange.*

Not mauled or taken. Reviewed and then cast aside.

The blue envelope of the recent card from her mother stood out from the mosaic of destruction, its thick paper ripped. Leaning down Kelly flipped the card open—the support check that had been inside missing. Her eyes combed the areas of the room where she'd kept cash, a warning flare going off in her chest.

Glancing at her bed, she saw that the headboard lay splintered. The mattress sagged on its side, flipped over and stripped of its sheets, coils peeking out from a series of vertical cuts made with a—knife. The pad of her thumb ran over the smooth back-line of her ring, tucked in the crevice of her finger.

*Who would pass over gold and electronics to rip up my bed?*

The answer struck her as ominous.

This wasn't about money. They were looking for something.

She walked over to the kitchen to where the refrigerator door stood cracked open. She placed her hand in the cavern, pressing her good palm against the plastic container of milk.

*Still cold.*

Fear ignited in her chest, fueling her panic as she glanced back at the shambles that used to be her living space.

All this happened less than an hour ago. If she hadn't stayed late at Hammond's—

*What if the robbers come back?*

Neurons fired, jetting adrenaline through her as she set to scavenging. Dumping out an unpacked box, mundane items lay forgotten as Kelly threw in whatever she could salvage. One armful transported her clothes, another her shoes, scooping up remaining jewelry as she went, books—anything that would make the trip. A lone plastic cup rolled to a stop against an isolated torn-up sneaker.

She grabbed the box to leave when a flicker of red made her stop and turn, her eyes narrowing in on the kitchen counter. Sitting on a mound of tossed dirt, Kelly's sapling tomato plant lay uprooted, its fragile brown legs reaching.

*Hold on.*

In a flash of movement she put the box down and rushed over, lifting the little pot from its discarded position in the sink. Not crushed, it appeared to have been hit by a wayward plate, knocking the fledgling plant on its side. With pawing hands Kelly cupped up the dirt, the white of her padded hand turning brown as she replanted it with quick, gentle movements. Compressing the soil, she tucked the pot to her chest.

A glint of metal from the countertop caught her eye. She pulled her saucepan out of the debris by its handle before restarting her departure, tossing the pot atop the boxed heap.

Heart racing, she took a final look around. The spread of broken pieces had once been her plan. Her dream. The fleeting acknowledgment that she'd sifted through everything she owned in less than five minutes burned. The remnants of her good intentions charred to ash.

Did she really think she could pull this off? Moving away from home, from safety?

Blind ambition and foolish optimism did not win her anything other than failure.

*Time to go home.*

With one heave she lifted the carton holding her life, the stairs blowing past her in a fog. The parking lot outside was desolate, the dark quiet more menace than calm. Kelly glanced around as she secured the cardboard square in the back of the Jeep with shaking hands, careful as she picked up her plant and settled it into the console tray Kelly had sat between the front seats. The tiny green orb bobbing in the cup holder.

The brute didn't give her any grief on the start-up, even though she was still learning the gears. The car paid no heed to speed limits either, running them back to Hammond's fast, a loyal steed galloping them home.

*Home.* The definition sparked as the night outside passed in a blur.

As many times Kelly had made the jaunt to the farm, she knew this time would be different; a farewell. She strived to preserve the images to memory, the trees, the hills and fences of the back roads she took to get to Hammond's. The red barns and mailboxes that read names like *Mitchell, Brown,* and *Moore.* She wanted to take stock of the details, but the illuminated stretch of road ahead was all she could comprehend, as well as the place that waited at the end of it.

Memories flashed of what she'd be missing: Sophie's laugh, Hank's smile, Pippa's wise nod, Keegan's snort...Blue eyes paired with a touch that sent shivers through her.

She'd already leaned on all of them too much, stayed too long.

The lines of the road went blurry as Kelly hit the gas, her hand stinging as she gripped the steering wheel, bringing the end on faster.

The weathered sign for Hammond's rolled into view, the bumpy driveway like a homecoming. Pulling into the front parking spot, Kelly killed the engine, fumbling to pocket her keys with her left hand. She sat back and looked out the windshield, the aged red metal creating a rustic picture frame around the scene. The vintage yellow shingles on the farm house cut through the night, carving bright lines around the darkened windows, the household inside sound asleep.

Kelly vowed to send a letter of explanation to Sophie. There was no sense waking them, or calling, her drama wasn't worth all the fuss.

Her head went heavy as her mind went to Aidan—Kelly didn't have his telephone number. He'd never offered it and she'd never asked. What a way to underscore how uncommitted they were to one another.

She struggled to hold in the tears, and prayed that one day she'd look back and see him as a passing summer fascination. As a crush. Another one of her pie-in-the-sky, idealistic dreams crashing down.

Aidan would no doubt get over her quickly, if he had to at all. What interest did he have in her? He needed her for his case—that was it. It'd be days before he even noticed she was gone.

The cool night breeze soothed her cheeks as Kelly gathered up her plant and took the deep step out of the Jeep. Curling her arm around the red pot, she felt a strange solace in holding the thing. Two fragile things finding shelter in one another.

Shutting the car door with as little noise possible, she paused. With its dark roll of paddocks in the distance, full of barns and bales, Hammond's beauty was something she'd never forget. She hugged her pot and commanded her feet forward, toward her goodbye.

The main barn stood empty as she approached, lines of yellow marked with the word *caution* forming a neon net over the entrance. It being the first night of Keegan's illness, there must not have been enough last-minute volunteers to watch him. The gaps in coverage no doubt would be remedied within twenty-four hours, with Pippa and the staff taking shifts.

Bathing her shoes in the pan of disinfectant sitting out front, Kelly ducked the plastic ropes and walked over to the one occupied stall.

The heavy breathing hit Kelly's ears first, the strained pull and push of air worse than her first encounter with him, back when Keegan had been starved and scared. She peered through the upper rails, throat catching at the sight. Her horse stood hunched over, nose distended and glossy, eyes melded shut in congested sleep.

*Say goodbye. Say goodbye and leave.*

The thoughts pushed to the forefront, but Kelly's feet ignored the command. She watched him, tracing the lines of Keegan's face, his fur. She mentally relived its softness.

How his eyes lit up when she brought Keegan his mush, how proud he got when she praised him... So different now with his head hung low, his face drawn as if trapped in troubled dreams.

Her hand reached out mindlessly, falling short of contact by feet, limited by the bars.

In his sleep Keegan stirred, his brow ironing out, muzzle floating toward her open palm as if he sensed her presence.

Kelly's vision went watery again, and she didn't dare stop it.

How could she walk away, leaving Keegan sick and alone?

"I'm...sorry." The words choked off as she flipped herself around, pressing her back against the wall of the stall, listening.

Keegan inhaled a constricted pant, his exhale a plea: *Please don't go.*

Choices flared in Kelly's head, her body sliding down to the ground. Her plant flopped down next to her as she sat facing the open barn door, the inky black sky highlighted by the glowing moon in the distance. She was surprised that her breath didn't cloud the ambient air as her skin became gooseflesh; unable to breathe as the thoughts punched through her.

Why had she been brought there? Given a good place and good company, only for it all to be ripped away?

She cupped her bandaged hand, remembering Aidan's touch.

Would she ever know warmth like that again?

The rugged wall she'd slumped against picked at her worn clothes, the rasp of the rough wood and planks seeming to push at her to stand up—to *get up*.

She didn't move as the white glow of the car repair shop flashed in her memory for some reason. It was as if her soul were in for service, up on the lift for repair or dismantlement. Which one, she had no clue.

When she'd been rejected from school, she'd shaken her fist at the sky—at life.

Had her fury brought on this punishment? Her brazenness?

Keegan's stuttered breaths came through the wall behind her, tearing her apart. Tilting her head up toward Keegan's window, her face crumbled, eyes filling up.

She had no solution. No answers. No way out.

If she started driving now, she'd reach the New York state line by noon. She could contact her mom, confess all that had happened.

Pulling her knees up, Kelly let the tears stream down her face. She pivoted her head, wiping them away on the dirty knee of her jeans as the torrent continued.

Laying her head down she cried and waited. And cried some more.

*No solution.*

After a time she propped her chin up. Through the lines of the caution tape, her eyes settled on the fields beyond, the cool night air giving her a gauge of the time: past midnight, early morning—somewhere around three a.m. She focused on the place where the sun was to emerge as a sudden irrational fear struck her.

What if the dawn abandoned its duty, the constant light refusing to rise?

The celestial cycles were a given, expected. Reliable.

But nothing in life could be taken for granted— Health, prosperity. And she had to be there for when things got better.

*Things will get better...*

A distant star twinkled as if winking.

With a final surge of energy, Kelly fumbled to her feet, grabbing her plant. The adrenaline of her earlier ordeal had burned away, leaving nothing but stark exhaustion. Keegan came into view through the metal slats, his shape fuzzy through Kelly's swollen vision. Placing her palm on the door of his stall, Kelly laid her forehead on the back of her hand, the stance a vow.

"I'm not leaving you," she whispered. "I'm staying as long as you need me to." She knocked her head once against the palm, cementing the promise.

Still lost in dreams, Keegan lifted his head and let out a contorted sigh.

Kelly turned, listing for the door, her limbs like sandbags. Nearly falling, she stooped under the quarantine tape, cleansing her boots and charging forward with no destination in mind, her world a haze.

*Need a place...to stop.*

She staggered to the break room, gratitude tackling her as the door to the area opened; the yawn that burst from her throat a form of celebration. It was surreal that she'd been there just hours before, the environs like a parallel world that she knew to be friendly. It was fortunate that Pippa, with all the drama surrounding Keegan, must've forgotten to lock up. The clock ticked loudly on the wall as Kelly secured the door, coasting over to the large oak table. She dropped her plant on the flat expanse, stretching out on the long sitting bench tucked underneath. It'd be a hard bed, one she

had to center her weight on, but a refuge
nonetheless.

She just needed a few hours of rest, then
she'd figure out what to do.

Resting her hands on her chest, the dreams
came as a welcome reprieve to her leaden
worries, her mind discharging her fears, one-by-
one, as if releasing balloons by their strings.

*A solution will come in the morning*, she
thought as her mind dimmed.

The sun *will* rise, and bring with it her
answers.

# CHAPTER 14

Someone waited for Aidan, calling his name.

Aidan squinted, unable to see through the dark smoke. The vapor stung his eyes, clogged his throat. The source of the hazy barrier began tiny, a flame no larger than a dinner candle. In a blink it grew, expanding into a raging bonfire that sucked all the oxygen from the air. The more he pushed through the thickness, the more the person—the woman, faded into the murk. He fumbled, gasping.

He had to reach the woman. She needed his help—

His eyes peeled wide as an electronic bleating yanked him from the dreamscape.

Propping his torso up, he wiped his face with the heel of his palm, noting the time on his alarm clock with one eye. Snatching his cell off the nightstand, he glimpsed at the name on the digital display and cursed. Flopping to his side, he accepted the call with a grunt. "Something had better be on fire, Eric."

"I need you to come to Kelly's apartment." The guy's voice came across darker than usual.

"What's going on?" Aidan sat up, instantly awake.

"Someone broke in last night."

"Is she okay?"

The pause stretched out. Aidan hadn't known the guy long, but Eric only got quiet when he preferred to talk face to face. Or when the news was bad. "The address is—"

"I'll be there in ten." Aidan hung up, phone still in hand as he stuffed his arms and head through the appropriate holes of the first t-shirt he came across. Throwing on enough to avoid citation for indecent exposure, he raced over to the apartment complex, the drive an exercise in torture.

Why hadn't Eric mentioned Kelly's whereabouts?

A slew of reasons bashed around his brain, making him abuse the gas pedal as he hit the highway. From the girl's police file, she lived in a bad area.

If she wasn't huddled up in a police blanket waiting, he'd—

Squad cars crowded the parking lot. Taking the complex stairs at a jog, Aidan recognized guys from the force coming and going, one even paused to give him a questioning look.

*Yeah, an arson cop at a crime scene, cause for a double-take.*

Unless something really was on fire.

There were two apartments on the top floor, Aidan gravitating toward the one that held the party of blue uniforms. Glaring at the useless door as he passed, the lock busted open, he immediately searched for Kelly. Officers milled about, bagging items, taking pictures. He picked

Eric out of the pack, standing over near the closet.

*What used to be the closet... Holy—*

Aidan stopped to take in the whole scene. He'd seen robberies before, drug raids, but this seemed different. The girl's pad was a small space with few things, so he could scan the debris easily. House wares, mirrors, toiletries...a twin-sized bed with nominal bedding that lay in shreds. What little she owned had more mass after it'd been grated and thrown to the wind. He toed at a discarded sock on the floor, the thing frayed. It was all trash now.

Staring at all the mangled and broken, dread flicked in Aidan's gut.

He took a step forward and a loud crunch under his boot had him lifting his foot, revealing a smashed picture frame. The image of Kelly stared up at him, tucked in next to a pretty older woman with dark hair—her mother, the lady's smiling face obscured behind the fractured glass.

"Hey." Eric spotted him and hurried over.

"Where is she?"

"We don't know. I got the call around four a.m., the place was like this when we arrived."

Agitation turned to anger as Aidan ran through all the possible scenarios: Kelly could have been out, or with any luck, at Hammond's.

Or she could have been in bed, completely unaware as the burglar kicked the door in and—

Aidan focused on her bed, fixated by the rips. "Those slashes were made with a serrated knife."

"I know," Eric said.

He held off images of Kelly being taken off-guard, of a fight.

"Any sign of a struggle?"

Anger burned through Aidan's veins as he surveyed the damage, his attention instantly tripping over the spot where Eric had come from. A pair of officers analyzed something on the floor, taking photographs and swabbing for samples. Through the gap of their legs Aidan saw it—a dot of crimson on the floor.

Eric stepped in front of him, his face grave. "We don't know if it's hers."

Spots popped up in Aidan's vision, the sensation that he couldn't breathe taking over. Like in his dream, oxygen eluded him. Maintaining his trademark calm surface, Eric stepped over to the nearest corner, a subtle motion of his hand warning Aidan to keep his voice down. Aidan followed, anchoring his palms against his body so they wouldn't punch anything.

"This wasn't a normal B&E," Aidan breathed.

"What makes you think that?"

"A thief would time it, be in and out within minutes. Not hang out and cut shit up."

"Half the complex tenants have records. They see a young girl living alone, may have thought she had money stowed somewhere. Hell, even the guy next door is a suspect," Eric said, exhaling a long breath.

Aidan glanced past him, running his eyes over the room. The mess gave no clues, but something about the path of destruction struck him as unusual.

"Most of her clothes are missing along with other personal belongings. My guess is that she came home after it happened, got spooked and ran," Eric spoke, his voice calm. "Where would she go?"

The fact that Aidan knew Kelly better than Eric woke him up, cleared the smoke.

*Where would she go?*

"She wouldn't leave without seeing her horse. I'll head over to Hammond's—"

If she was there, Keegan was getting carrots the next time Aidan saw him, a whole bucket full.

"Call me if you find her," Eric called after Aidan as he eyed the other cops, a hint that he couldn't come along.

Energy channeled through Aidan like coal shoveled into the pit of a locomotive as he hit the stairs. He surveyed the exterior of the scene as he got into his truck. There were no indicators of further altercation in the parking lot, no more blood. A coil wound tighter in his chest as he headed out, calling the farm from the road in order to keep his mind off the worst case scenarios, away from the *what-ifs.*

When he hung up, the worry in Sophie's voice made him wish he'd waited to alert them. Aidan could hear Hank rustling around in the background, gearing up to search the property. The sounds pushed Aidan to drive faster.

She had to be there. If she were hurt, bleeding, Eric would have caught up to her by now, unless—*How did I let this happen?* The girl was under his watch.

A pricking pain struck him in his shoulder as the sign to the farm appeared over the hill.

Speeding down the rocky driveway, he pulled to abrupt stop behind Kelly's Jeep, but the hunk of red metal and big wheels didn't soothe him, rather egged him forward. For this nightmare to be over he needed to see her—to *hold* her.

He jumped out and peered through the Jeep's windows. A huge box dominated the trunk, affirming Eric's suspicions that she'd packed up and bolted. He placed his hand on the hood.

*Cold.* Parked there for a while.

"Aidan!" Sophie emerged from the front porch of the house, her clothes as disheveled as his, an old farm shirt thrown on over battered jeans.

"Have you seen her?" he called, lowering his voice as she ran up.

"No. Hank and Pippa have checked all the barns and are checking the paddocks now," she said breathlessly.

"Where's Keegan?"

Sophie's brow furrowed in confusion, as if they'd already checked on him. "He's in the main barn, but—"

Aidan started forward with Sophie hot on his heels.

"Aidan, wait! You have to—"

He slowed his pace a bit out of respect, and turned the corner only to halt, the barrier of yellow tape he came in contact with stunning him immobile. The breadth of the barn stood empty except for the one stall on the end, its occupant barely moving.

"What the hell?"

"Keegan's in quarantine. You'll need to disinfect if you go in there," Sophie said, catching up.

"When did this happen?"

"Yesterday."

Jesus. Everything happened *yesterday*.

In the dirt on the floor Aidan spied footprints, women's sized boots.

*Kelly.*

The thought of her spurred him to duck the blockade, careful to keep his distance from the stall. He circled the perimeter, following the pattern. The prints marked steps up to the gate of the stall, then went smudged into a large shape as if she'd sat down. Craning his neck, Aidan looked in on the horse. Keegan stood still and unresponsive, weaker than before.

Healthy bowels aside, it sucked that the animal had survived starvation only to go through the misery of sickness.

As if hearing the thought, Keegan leaned his head forward, the action afflicted, and followed by a wheezy cough. With Keegan unable to give Aidan any of his usual snark, the bug must be bad. Despite the swollen nose and the thin body, Aidan saw past the shadow. Underneath it all, the horse had mettle.

"Feel better, boy," Aidan murmured.

Retraining his eyes on the floor, Aidan picked back up on the trail, the tracks reemerging toward the exit, the pattern swerving.

*She staggered out. Is she hurt?*

There were no fresh spatters of blood, but the boot marks cut off as the barn floor met the cedar chips of the common area. Aidan followed the prints like a bloodhound, measuring the vicinity, rushing through Sophie's direction of how to clean his shoes.

Kelly wouldn't have made it far...

His eyes bounced around the closest stopping areas: an open, fenced-in training arena, a small shed for the feeding buckets, and—the *break room*.

Sophie kept in step as Aidan bolted for the door. Grasping the handle, the thing didn't turn. Locked. Cupping his eyes he stared in through the dirty square of glass, seeing nothing but obscured shapes.

"You have a key to this, Soph?"

If she produced it fast enough, he wouldn't take the knob off.

"You think she's in there?" Sophie moved as she talked, whipping out a weighty key ring, opening the door in time to let Aidan barrel in. "We lock the room at night..."

They peered around, finding everything still and serene.

Desolate as the first day he'd come back to Hammond's, a strange buzz lit off in Aidan's head. Instinct flaring, he felt *close*.

At first glance all seemed normal, every item in its place—a flash of red made him hone in on the table. A small plant pot sat stationed like a beacon on the far side of the ancient oak slab. Kelly's voice rang in his head, a flashback from days before, a spork clutched in her hand:

*It's good for cultivating the dirt... I have saplings—in small pots.*

Aidan rounded the table, holding his breath.

Like an angel in repose, Kelly lay tucked under the table's lip, arms folded across her chest, an improvised bandage smeared with dirt wrapped around her right hand, the mitt rising and falling with her gentle breath.

*Here and safe.*

Aidan wanted to scoop her up into his arms and kiss her. Holding back the impulse, he dropped down, resting his hip next to hers on the bench.

"Oh, thank heaven!" Sophie emerged behind him, hand over her heart. "Dear Lord, is she bleeding?" she asked, noticing the bandage.

Aidan performed a visual inspection, the dark spot of the wound appearing clotted.

"Physically, no." Emotionally, he'd bet she was pretty shaken up.

Deep in slumber, all of the lines of age and worry in Kelly's face went lax, revealing soft skin dusted with dirt, with streaks of clean channeling through the brown on her cheeks.

She'd been crying. And she'd spent the night on a hard bench.

Overriding his medical protocol, Aidan's body shook with the urge to take some form of action, to gather her up and carry her somewhere secure. Instead he reached out, smoothly placing two fingers to her throat, checking her pulse.

Jolted by the touch, Kelly's eyes whipped open. Alarmed, she jerked upward, her forehead clipping the side of the table, an audible *thunk* resounding off the walls. The rear of her head took a second hit as she fell back down on the bench, her face wincing at the blow.

*Crap.* He'd meant to wake her first—

Kelly slapped her bandaged hand to the whacked head spot and winced again. Groaning in pain, she retracted the wounded paw to her chest and went still.

*Great. Real smooth, Wright. Knock the girl out.*

He put his hands where she could see them, as if she were a horse he'd startled.

"Easy there." Aidan stationed his face in her line of vision and caught her disoriented gaze. She locked in on to him, pupils dilating. A good sign. "Sorry."

Behind them voices converged, bringing Sophie's head around. "That's Hank." In a flash she went out to talk to him, leaving Aidan and Kelly alone.

Kelly's head lolled on the bench. Her breathing slowed as her pretty eyes stared up at him, preoccupied as she kept her arm slung across her chest.

No concussion that he could tell, but he wanted to evaluate that hand—

"Good morning. Are you seeing three of me?" On instinct he slowly moved his palm to her forehead, assessing the knot she'd just self-administered. Without thinking he brushed her bangs back from her face, the locks flipping back into place, the forelock of brown-red softer than he'd imagined.

"No," she confirmed, her eyelids going heavy as he stroked, as if she found the touch soothing. The expression made him want to spend his life petting her.

"Is your hand bleeding?" he asked.

"I don't think so. It's a cut...from broken glass."

With a deep inhale she sat up, pulling her head away and steadying herself next to him on the bench, as if testing her balance. Purple-blue smudges brushed under her eyes, her face twisting as she got to her feet, staring down at the bulky mitt on her right palm.

*Still standing.*

"Let's change that bandage." Aidan stood and led her over to the sink, admittedly trying to hold on to her a little longer.

Running over the girl's options in his head, Aidan knew this ordeal didn't end after she got cleaned up. Kelly needed a place to stay. The crazy idea of letting her room with him popped to the fore, but the implications of that—his involvement with her case, his attraction to her—all vetoed the option quickly. The image of her at his place satisfied the protective instinct growling inside him. If only he could watch over her.

*Besides, where else could she go?*

Kelly waited as Aidan started the water. Rummaging through the cabinets, he pulled down the first aid kit, cracking it open and picking out a large sterile bandage, antiseptic, and an alcohol swab. With agile hands he turned her palm over, peeling off the packing tape. The paper towel came off in fragments as it'd adhered to her cut, revealing a lot of red centered by a line of bright burgundy. No fragments of glass left, though; that was good.

Aidan frowned as Kelly concealed a flinch, wishing he were better at being gentle. Hanging tough, the girl maintained a neutral face as he coaxed her raw hand under the lukewarm stream.

"This happened at your apartment?" he asked. Rinsing the area, he rested her hand in his, ripping an alcohol towelette from its sterile packet with his teeth.

"Someone—" She sucked in a breath.

He dabbed the square over the cut with swift movements, talking to help distract her from the sting. "Do you have any idea who'd want to rob you?"

"I don't know. I came home and...they'd already left," she said, observing him.

Aidan stood in awe of her composure. Any other girl he knew would be crying, shaking, hysterical after what she'd gone through.

"Eric—uh, Officer Carson is the one who called me. He's at your place now."

She looked up at him, the soft green and brown of her stare distracting. Aidan forced himself to concentrate, stripping the large bandage free of its plastic wrap and covering the newly cleansed cut with the synthetic skin. He pressed down over the edges, running the pads of his fingers over and over the side seams, the contact sending warmth up his arms. He hoped it'd heal well, leaving no marks on her perfect skin.

Feeling eyes on him, Aidan lifted his gaze, catching the full brunt of her stare. Lids heavy, her lips parted. Heat flared like it had when they'd kissed in the car. The memory of his mouth on hers made him stir, *react*.

She frowned as he released his hold, her amped-up expression returning as Aidan placed a palm on each side of her neck. A trail of goose bumps led from her shoulders to her cheeks, the sight utterly beautiful.

*How far down do those go?* The image of her stomach covered in the texture aroused him as he planned all the ways he could warm her...

Leaning in toward each other, they started to breathe in tandem, syncing to one another. He felt the heat of her body, of her mouth. She shivered.

"Are you cold?" he whispered, his lips an inch from hers.

"No—"

The squeak of the break room's rusty door sprang them apart, Kelly stepping back and turning in the direction of the sound while Aidan kept his shoulder to the newcomers; his reaction to Kelly visible to anyone paying attention. Finding a guise in reassembling the first aid kit, he returned to the sink as Hank rushed up to hug Kelly.

"You scared us," Hank murmured into the girl's shoulder, the old man catching Aidan's eye on the turnaround. Aidan had the decency to flush at little as Hank shot him a knowing glare.

Father to a forty-year-old daughter and grand-poppa to a ten-year-old named Millie, Hank had the guarding-the-roost glower down pat.

*Probably owns a shotgun, too*, Aidan mentally added, wondering if he should put the first aid kit away just yet.

Letting Kelly go, Hank stepped back, Sophie appearing at his side.

"I'm sorry to scare you—" Kelly started.

Sophie picked up Kelly's good hand, the motherly gesture cutting her off.

"Hank and I had a discussion. We don't know all of what happened last night, but with what you've done for us here and with your school— Well, before you make any decisions about going back to New York, we have something we'd like to show you."

With a gentle tug Sophie ushered Kelly out the door. Hank speared Aidan with a final glare of authority before walking out after the women. Needing some distraction of his own, Aidan pulled out his phone, thinking that a case update would help throw some cold water on the happy going on in his pants.

Eric picked up on the first ring and Aidan did all the talking: *girl shaken but safe, not sure what her plans are now.*

A little frog crept into Aidan's voice as he laid out his idea; he'd stick around until Kelly stated what she wanted to do, the choice to stay or leave up to her.

Aidan hung up and had to chuckle at the way Eric showed his concern. The guy operated in quiet like he had the copyright on self-possession. The crazy part was how Aidan could measure the level of the cop's apprehension by the beats of silence that punctuated the few words he spoke. The aptitude struck Aidan as strange, personal. What a friend would know.

*Damn, what a day.*

High potency sexual letdown chased with the comrade revelation, and all before breakfast. Good to see that his life had a little spark left in it after all.

The phone check-in had provided Aidan with a few minutes to get himself situated, although not fully recovered, his limbs still tingling. The throbbing underneath his belt kicked as he tried to banish thoughts of Kelly's mouth, which he knew firsthand was petal soft.

The vision was counterproductive to toning down his trouser salute. Aidan ran through a cerebral photo book of judgmental mothers-in-law, polar bear plunges, and shotgun weddings. Then he sauntered toward the house like a cowboy fresh from a ride.

It'd been a while since he'd gotten blue balls over something as chaste as a kiss, but the best cure was to keep his thoughts away from the girl. Which was more than a challenge.

Approaching the house, he heard the low hum of voices coming from the small storage building out back. He followed the sounds to the top floor extension Sophie and Hank had added on when their daughter was in college. Iron steps gripped the side of the two-story, leading up to a windowed door decorated with dusty, yellow gingham curtains. A second level loft that Aidan's dad had lent a hand to construct, Sophie used the unit as a separate penthouse for visitors, an overnight room for those coming from far distances to adopt the horses. Aidan had forgotten about it.

A broad smile spread across his face as he took the steps two at a time.

Peeking in the open door, he watched Kelly wander the large square of space, her gaze one of awe. The walls were industrial mauve save for one painted in eye-searing magenta pink. The dated, pop-culture motif was crowned with a New Kids on the Block poster tacked to its surface, the warped rectangle of paper texturized with a crusty layer of dust.

Sophie watched Kelly's reaction, saying nothing as Hank gave her the nickel tour.

A kitchenette like the one in the break room lined the far wall, the counter dead-ending in a small sink with an overhead cabinet. It was neighbored by a small microwave and a defrosted mini-fridge with its power cord dangling out like a cat's tail. A hardwood floor paved a path to a small door anchoring the opposite corner, where a powder room with a stall shower peeked out through the frame, the layout forming a compact living space.

Sophie and Hank were offering Kelly their daughter's old room.

"It needs work, but you're welcome to any of the cleaning supplies downstairs. We may have some leftover paint in the shed."

Flabbergasted, the girl simply nodded.

"So, is it a deal?" Hank asked, stepping within hand-shaking distance.

Kelly's eyes darted to Sophie, astonishment saturating the hazel green. "I'll pay you back for the rent, every single penny. I *promise*. I'll bus tables if I have to."

Sophie's smile lit up the room. "Honey, if you're offering, there's a horse farm out back that could use a hard worker like you," she said, throwing a hiker's thumb toward the window.

Kelly crossed the room in a flash, hugging Sophie so tight Aidan swore the woman buckled from the force.

Sophie rubbed her hand down Kelly's back and looked to Hank over the girl's shoulder. "We'll sort out the details tomorrow. Right now this young lady needs some sleep."

Aidan followed the group out, stopping near the Jeep as Hank escorted Kelly over to the main house. Sophie stayed with Aidan.

"Julie's old room," Aidan said softly, the words all gratitude. "That's generous of you."

Wisdom flashed in Sophie's brown eyes as she glanced over her shoulder, her profile regal. "She's one of our herd, Aidan."

The truth of her statement resounded, but before Aidan could muster a reply Sophie trudged past him, her voice a combo of sweet as honey crossed with authoritative as hell. "Hank's got his eye on you."

Aidan paused, the implication registering. The open expanse of grass around them stretched the distance from the house's covered porch to Hammond's welcome sign. Usually an area of tranquility, the space suddenly made Aidan feel like a stag exposed in a shooting field.

Sophie stopped halfway up the lawn, a bright grin popping up on her face before she continued up the green hill, her gait stilted. "He'll get over it. Come on up to the house. There's a twin bed in the guest bedroom that we need to move into the loft. Your back is thirty years younger than mine."

# CHAPTER 15

Kelly sat back on her heels, her hand swiping the paintbrush over the last spot of eye popping color. Rising to her feet, she looked over the work—the wall was toned down from teenybopper pink to professional white, and she was proud that she managed to paint the whole thing single-handedly.

Calling the job done, she looked herself over, the old t-shirt she had on taking the brunt of the paint spatters, sparing her baggy jeans. She dropped the brush into a neighboring cup of water and made a fist with her right hand. The cut hardly bothered her anymore, the gash healed for the most part, but she kept the bandage on for reasons other than keeping it clean. The recollection of Aidan's face heated her skin every time she looked at it.

She blew out a breath.

The intensity that radiated anytime he got within feet of her was hard to ignore. Not that she wanted to. Everything about him made her feel like taking a risk.

*Like having a summer fling with a hot guy.*

The hot guy in question a detective investigating her for drug dealing.

A great idea. *Not.*

Kelly did a visual check that the windows were cracked for ventilation. The dry summer air blew through the screened-in squares, the humidity lower in the early morning, providing the right conditions for the paint to dry. She stepped into the bathroom and shrugged out of her sweaty shirt, kicked out of the underwear she'd slept in, and headed for the shower with the hopes that some cool water would help her take her mind off a certain sexy arson detective.

Stepping under the spray, she peeled the adhesive bandage away from her palm, exposing a healthy pink line.

Almost back to normal. But she'd replace the dressing anyway because Sophie had asked her to take Moe out for some training this afternoon. Reins were rough on the hands even without the previous injury, and it'd be her first time in the saddle since she'd come to Hammond's. With Moe's consistent temperament and Kelly's history of lessons, she figured that the return to riding shouldn't be hard, but she wanted to be up to the task.

She lathered up her hair with her good hand as the bubbles made rivulets down her neck, the river of suds bringing back the memory of Aidan's strong fingers. She turned the knob further toward cold, but the contrast in temperature merely enhanced the sensation. The feel of him, the weight of his hands combined with the gentle rasp of his touch.

She remembered looking up and catching the erotic expression on his face.

With a wicked shift of thought she imagined them in bed together, him making that same face as he—she turned the dial all the way to blue, the cold making her quiver as she batted the image away.

There was no doubt that Aidan knew how to please a woman sexually, and it'd been a while since she'd seen any of that action. Kelly tried not to envision all his conquests, the lines of women whom he'd bedded in his life, which had to be a lot. No woman worth her estrogen would turn down those piercing blue eyes and hard body. But men like Aidan never stayed in one place, with one woman. Behind his fiery blue eyes lay a past of burning embers; she could see it. Sense it.

To get involved with him meant she'd eventually join the ranks of the loved and left.

Rushing with the conditioner, Kelly distracted herself by scrubbing the bar of soap over the dots of paint that speckled her arms. She scoured off all the flakes, rinsed clean, and shut off the water without ceremony.

Toweling off, she wrapped herself up and stepped out into her new apartment.

The sight made her smile.

Sophie had a twin bed and nightstand brought over from the house, the solid wood of the footboard peeking out from underneath an opaque plastic tarp that protected it from the paint. The closet gaped around the remainder of her clothes, and the kitchen more than held all the amenities; the place was everything she could want and more.

Sophie's kindness knew no bounds.

Kelly's head turned to a full paper bag sitting in the corner. Topping off her parade of luck, Sophie had dropped a paper sack off the night before, saying that there were riding clothes inside. Opening up the brown wrapper with a crinkle, Kelly pulled out two pairs of jeans with tags still attached, the price sticker ripped away; several short-sleeve shirts bearing the farm's emblem along with socks and underwear. She slumped down on her plastic covered bed, holding the denim as if it were silk.

*It's all too much—*

Her thought cut off as her foot knocked a large parcel lying on the floor. Glancing past her pile of a care package, she noticed the long, flat shoe box. A note taped to the lid read, *Try these on and let me know if they fit,* written in Sophie's pretty handwriting.

"She didn't..." Kelly murmured, gasping as she flipped open the lid, a pair of brown leather riding boots cushioned inside. "She *did.*"

Running a fingertip over the supple leather, Kelly gingerly lifted the first boot out, her new jeans draped over her arm.

*Like Christmas in July.*

And then and there Kelly vowed to pay Sophie back for everything. Every cent.

However much work Sophie wanted done on the farm, Kelly would do it and more.

Pulling in a breath, she yanked off the tags and got dressed, pausing to note how well the jeans fit, sliding up her legs and hugging her waist. She was built small, like her mother, limbs on the average side, but with muscle. In school the boys overlooked her athletic physique in lieu of bustier prospects, and the overpriced, fashionable clothes always trended toward curves.

Kelly pivoted in front of the mirror, the denim looking simple but stylish.

She opted to save the fresh shirts for another day, and dipped into the abundant closet space to pull on her old, cotton button-up. She caught a glimpse of herself in the full-length mirror bolted to the closet door, and the reflected glamour shot was complete.

Wow. *Feminine.* She grinned.

Was this what Aidan saw when he looked at her?

Kelly shook away the thought, staving off the heat that came with thoughts of him. Her eyes drifted over the freshly painted wall, the glowing kitchen, the open boot box on the floor...

Sophie had given her so much: a second chance to get a handle on school, a place to live, to work, and new clothes. Out of respect for the farm's rules and Sophie's property, Kelly was going to be on her best behavior, which meant nothing promiscuous.

Recommitted to the task at hand, Kelly vowed to pull her weight at the farm and work out her school issues. Whatever impulsive feelings she was having for Aidan, Kelly couldn't take advantage of the kindness that she'd been offered. Until she was back on her feet and living by her own means again she had to be responsible.

*No flings, no carelessness...regardless of how tempting Aidan comes across.*

It shouldn't be that hard, she reasoned. She'd stuck to her plan this far. She could make it through one crazy summer.

Her mind drifted back to the day she'd watched from a distance as students went about their lives, admiring how fun it must be to have a *real* life, a *real* summer. A time that carried with it no inhibitions. A three-month stretch where you could follow your urges: drive fast, run around in the sun-warmed air, laugh with friends...make love under the stars.

What if this was *her* time and she was missing it?

Pulling the stuffing out of the first leather boot, she sunk her heel in, her foot and calf encased perfectly in the dark brown leather.

*Incredible*, Kelly thought as she stepped into the other and stood up.

With a final look-over in the mirror, she felt like a real horsewoman in the functional clothes and quality footwear. She locked the apartment up tight and bounced down the metal steps, the sun heating the sky like an oven preparing for its midday bake. Returning the tarp and paint can to the supply barn, Kelly crossed the main paddock, the sunshine kissing the barns and grass with east-hanging gold.

Pausing at the mouth of the main barn, she wanted desperately to see Keegan but needed to keep her distance when working with other horses the same day. She sent him healing thoughts on the warm breeze that came up and tousled her hair, then continued on to the adjacent barn. The compact space was full with horses, a track of stalls lining both sides. Awake and curious, long noses poked out to say good morning as Kelly veered to the left, stopping at the second to last gate.

Light from the outside sprinkled the horse's warm brown coat with flecks of yellow glitter, and the mare lifted her head in greeting, the expression serene as a lady's portrait.

"Morning, Moe." Kelly smiled as she entered the stall, the body language between them that of good friends. "What do you say to a snack and a ride? Sound good?"

The horse nuzzled Kelly's palm, snuffling up her arm before pulling back expectantly.

"Apple first, work later?"

Moe gently sniffed the air then exhaled as if disappointed.

The mare was not searching for signs of food, but of Keegan. Kelly stroked her nose. Moe's eyes closed lazily at the touch as Kelly layered on some extra attention. "Sorry, babe. I haven't seen him today. I miss him, too."

*Everyone is missing a man today, it seems.*

"Maybe a girls' day out will be a nice distraction."

Kelly moved up to the front of the barn to separate a flake of hay, the loose bits catching on her clothes as she walked the scratchy armful back to the stall. She laid the thatch in Moe's bowl, and the mare started in on the food with her usual grace, lipping a small amount up into her mouth to chew slowly, like a noblewoman sitting at the breakfast table. After nursing Keegan, Kelly found solace in watching horses eat, a content spectator until the hectic patter of footfalls brought her attention out to the barn's aisle.

"Kelly!" Drea's face filled the space between the gate's metal bars, her voice breathless.

"Hey, Epona. What's up?"

"The doctor's here to see Keegan."

Kelly's face fell. "Keegan doesn't have a vet appointment today."

Moe stopped, ears bent forward as if trying to get in on the conversation. Kelly didn't ask questions. With the need to see for herself, she exited the stall and dashed out of the barn, Drea hot on her heels.

"Pippa said that it's a checkup, that his new sponsor wanted him to be seen right away—" Drea's words got cut off, the girl nearly walking into Kelly's back as she stopped dead in her tracks.

"Keegan's *sponsor*?" Kelly felt her heart beat in a sudden staccato rhythm.

Drea's brow furrowed in confusion. "Pippa said the papers were signed yesterday. He—the guy's in there with the doctor now. He's tall—and *cute*."

The girl blushed as Kelly felt her own cheeks turn to dry ice.

*Keegan has a sponsor? Someone funding his care until he gets adopted.*

*Crap.* She had to introduce herself. But as what?

She didn't own the horse, she just—

Kelly mindlessly brushed at her hair, trying to smooth it out enough to be presentable as she ran into straggles of hay. Glancing down, her cool, new outfit suddenly fell short of the mark.

She wished she owned something more formal, a blouse and a pair of dress slacks. Drea veered off to the break room, their paths forking as Kelly reached the door of the main barn, where the sound of two male voices carried.

*No fear.*

Shucking her insecurities, Kelly rounded the corner, the verbal exchange growing louder as Doctor Althea emerged from the cavern of the barn.

"I'd like to stop by tomorrow to follow up," the vet said as he turned to face—

Kelly's eyes flared in astonishment.

"Anything you need, Doc," Aidan replied as his eyes whipped over to Kelly. Flicking down her body like wildfire, his expression went from casual to explosive. His gaze shot up to lock with hers before turning back to the vet. "Just bill me, okay."

Aidan's body turned, clad in his arson uniform, the navy blue cotton shirt stretched over his broad chest paired with dark pants. Feet squared her direction, the man looked incredible. "I'm due in at work, but Kelly knows Keegan better than any of us. I'd like you to share your findings with her."

Catching what Aidan had said Kelly flipped her attention to the vet, her face dumbstruck.

"Okay," Dr. Althea affirmed, turning to her as if ready to give a full consultation. "The swabs we've taken look good and his temperature is back to normal."

Kelly popped out of her stupor as she realized what was happening.

*A doctor is standing here, answering questions about Keegan.*

A million inquiries sprang into her mind as she tried to narrow the flare down to the most relevant.

"Will he heal after this?" she blurted.

"Yes, he's past the worst of it, the swelling and the fever. The disease spreads fast, and while many racehorses are inoculated for influenza, tetanus, and rabies, the vaccine for Strangles is controversial. In some horses it can cause adverse reactions; abscesses and swelling of the legs. If Keegan has the lineage that Aidan suggests, my guess is that his previous owners didn't want to risk hurting their investment."

Kelly let the answers sink in, unable to view Keegan as a ticket to be bet on.

*Raised to race and win.*

Her heart did the murmur thing again, stealing her breath.

"Well, I'm going over to the house to show Sophie the test results. If this last one comes back clean, Keegan will recover just fine." The doctor's hand met Aidan's in a strong grip, and then gave Kelly a final wave before turning toward the house. The moment the doctor disappeared into the distance, Kelly felt Aidan's hot blue stare go over her again, settling on her face.

Admiration along with something else boiled in her veins.

"New clothes?" he asked, cocking an eyebrow.

"You. *You* sponsored Keegan."

A rare grin spread Aidan lips, the expression making Kelly's nerve endings spontaneously combust. He didn't reply, just studied her, a look of amusement lighting up his handsome features.

Kelly's mind mulled over the gift. Aidan had given Keegan what he needed: veterinary care, extra aid for special food, medicine. For the second time in one week he'd pulled her back from the brink.

*But why would a man with no interest in racehorses sponsor one?*

"Why?" The word exploded from Kelly's lips. She had to know.

His smile faded then, his features intense. "I wanted to help."

"I thought you didn't like him."

"I like him. I mean, he poops a lot." Aidan grinned, the expression turning sober as Kelly shot him a *not kidding* look. "I think it's what Sophie says: Keegan and I are too alike. We compete for attention." His eyes moved up to her hair.

A pang of guilt gripped her heart.

*If he's trying to make amends for what happened with school...*

"Aidan, you don't have to make anything up to—"

Before she could finish Aidan stepped in close, Kelly's skin igniting at the proximity. She held in a breath as he lifted his hand to her hair. There was a gentle tug followed by the lowering his upturned palm to her level of sight. Frail as an eyelash, a little string of green lay on his outstretched fingertips; bright in the morning sun, twitching in the wind.

"Make a wish."

The request was simple and unexpected. Intimate.

And it must have been the fragrant summer air, the heat radiating between them that left Kelly eager to humor him. She lifted her eyes to his. Heat coursed through her as she leaned forward, pursed her lips, and blew. The thread took flight, riding the invisible gust that floated it away like the soft pappus of a dandelion.

Her wish made, carried away on the wind, Aidan smoothed Kelly's ruffled hair back into place. He pulled back his hand, surveying her with burning eyes.

"If I'm not here, let me know what the doc says, okay?" His voice sounded two octaves lower than before, a rumble of tone that put butterflies low in Kelly's stomach.

*No answer and no apology.*

With sudden clarity Kelly understood how Aidan operated. He did what he wanted when he wanted, and didn't explain himself to anyone.

"I will." She looked at his lips. He was so close, right there.

How easy it'd be to get up on her tiptoes and—

"I have to go to work," he said, his voice deep. "I'll be back later." Aidan stepped back, his gait measured before he turned and walked away.

The man's attractiveness ranged somewhere between irresistible and overwhelming, but Kelly had made a promise. No summer flings. Especially not with Aidan.

Kelly stared after him in awe.

*Keegan's sponsor.*

In a daze, she lifted a hand to her hair, feeling the spot where he'd touched her.

*Make a wish?* All of her wishes had already come true.

Her eyes lingered over the empty space where he'd stood.

*All with the exception of one.*

# CHAPTER 16

"You're doing great!" Sophie called as Kelly and Moe trotted past.

Kelly's mind noted the praise but reverted back to the task at hand: keeping her shoulders, hips, and heels in line as she rolled with the bump of being in the saddle again. Sophie watched from the other side of the fence, her hands perched on the slats that bordered the training arena, her eyes evaluating.

It'd been a long time, but Kelly's previous riding lessons came back to her as she put Moe through the movements, the mare as genteel in the ring as she was in the stall.

"Good!" Sophie called out as Kelly controlled the gait, speeding up and slowing down on the second trip around. "Can you canter?"

Bringing Moe to a halt Kelly took a beat to collect herself. Then, recalling the cues, she maneuvered them into a trot, the post switching into a moving canter. With the squeeze of her calves, Kelly felt elation at the perfect transition. Her body moved with the undulation easily, the motion a natural bump and bounce that accompanied speed—her and Moe running together. They circled the arena and Kelly turned them around, demonstrating the change to her outside leg, their double-back as smooth as the first. Horse and rider finished the sequence like performers on a stage, pulling up to a graceful stop at the center of the ring, ready for a bow.

The late day sun illuminated Sophie's face, the warm brown of her eyes like molten chocolate as she clapped her hands in low applause. "Excellent!"

Kelly couldn't stop her smile as she dismounted and led Moe over to the fence.

"That was *good*, Kelly," Sophie said, beaming.

"I had a good partner," Kelly replied, lifting a hand to stroke Moe's cheek. The mare stood quietly despite all the exertion, the soft click of the bit rolling in her mouth.

"True," Sophie added, giving Moe an appreciative smile. "But you exhibited the control out there. A solid seat and clear commands. If we start you out with the greens, then move you through the ranks of the yellows, you might be the one to test him out in the saddle when he's ready."

Kelly's head popped up, heart revving. There was only one horse that Sophie didn't bother to call by name around her. "Really?"

Sophie knew how much she wanted to be the one to work with Keegan, but Kelly didn't want to push. A former racehorse, his rehabilitation would be tricky. Plus, there was his physical condition to consider. According to the doctor Keegan was responding well to the antibiotics, ready to rejoin the herd when his blood tests came back clean, but Keegan's body had been weak before he even caught the virus. To be on the safe side his recovery would require careful observation. Whoever got tapped to take him on had to be the right choice, had to be experienced with monitoring the signals of immune response and respiration.

Something Kelly had had firsthand involvement with during her time at Hammond's.

The lines of Sophie's face went taut, the expression she made whenever she had to make a heavy administrative decision. Kelly straightened, a page ready to be knighted.

"Practice more with other mounts. If you can show me more of what I saw today with a yellow, then we'll assign you and Pippa to Keegan."

Kelly had had few reasons to jump up and down as of late, and although Moe would stand still through a hurricane, she quelled the urge to squeal with glee. Instead she went with a cordial nod, putting her hand to her chest in acceptance.

Sophie picked up on her latent joy anyway, a grin pulling at her lips. "We have weeks to go yet, so let's plan on an hour session each day. I can't sit in on all of them, but I'll check in with you. Go ahead and cool Moe down."

Kelly felt a spark shoot off like a firecracker in her chest, the warmth spiraling out to her entire body as Sophie met her at the gate.

With deft fingers Kelly unbuckled Moe's leather bridle, looping the strappy headdress over her shoulder and replacing it with the green vinyl halter hanging on the fence post.

She released the girth of the saddle with equal ease, arms filling with the heft of rawhide and padding. Bracing the weight with poise, Kelly waved off Sophie's offer of help as she trudged to the tack room, passing a peg wall covered floor to ceiling in lead ropes.

The scent of leather and saddle soap hit her nose as she entered the tack area, aromas that for some reason made her think of achievement and effort. She welcomed the robust perfume, proud to know that she'd be in that room every day for the next three weeks.

She settled the saddle's winged flaps over one of the metal dowels protruding from the wall, hung the bridle up, and stepped back.

One of those saddles would crown Keegan's back, and *soon*.

Glowing at the thought, Kelly bounced back down the corridor, stopping in front of the stretch of leads. The farm budgeted money for supplies with care; things like new leads came along periodically as needed, when an existing rope snapped or became too frayed.

The hooks held a bulk of sisal tails, all varying lengths; each rope's strength contingent upon that of the horse. They were arranged in no particular order, and Kelly scanned the myriad, her eyes tripping over a flash of bright red. With a slow hand she pulled out the strand of scarlet, the pop of shiny color making it stand out from its worn, muted crowd. The fancy new lead lay thin and lightweight in her palm, the deep crimson a stark contrast to her skin.

*Pretty, but not strong enough for a horse of Moe's size.*

Perfect for one of the miniature horses that Kelly had heard were coming to stay at Hammond's next week, which was probably why it was purchased. She hung it back up at the front of the rack and grabbed its mid-weight neighbor. She filled a grooming tray at the other end of the hall, and brought Moe to the side of the mare paddock.

The baked ground threw off the day's heat, the last rays of the sun pushing through the thin cotton that stretched over Kelly's back. Lines of gold painted the horizon a gradient of glorious orange, purple, and indigo.

Moe relished the shade as Kelly administered the grooming, picking out the mare's hooves and preparing a bucket of bath water. Kelly ran the sponge over Moe's back, following the saturation with a sweat scraper. A medieval looking thing, the teardrop shaped band of teethed metal was a small version of a log man's saw when fully extended.

Everyone did a double take when learning how to use it for the first time, a prop straight out of a magician's arsenal, its purpose to squeegee off excess water rather than perpetrate illusions of sawing a horse in half.

As if a sign that Kelly was using the instrument right, Moe let out a contented sigh, the sluice of water combined with the cool air giving the mare comfort, her whistle of air sounding like a *thank you*.

"You did a *good job* today," Kelly murmured, finishing with the scraper, and unhooking the horse from her grooming station to release her into the mare paddock. Kelly watched Moe trot gracefully down the channel to join the mare herd in the fields before she turned to gather her supplies. She dumped the water bucket and carried her now jumbled grooming tray back to the tack room. In the fresh dark of the setting sun, Kelly switched on the lights. The shadows deepened the space as a gentle wind funneled through the crevices of the walls and bins, adding to the feeling of seclusion.

It was the time of day when the volunteer shifts changed, and with no one in sight, a person almost expected to see a tumbleweed roll by. The sudden quiet had to be what made Kelly rush to dissemble the tray, glancing around; the dark corridor that led outside holding her focus. She shook her head, trying to clear it, not sure what was giving her the jitters.

She stooped down and gave her shoulders a roll to loosen them.

Being at the farm twenty-four-seven had conditioned her to the presence of people. School, too. Even company of the non-human variety; spiders didn't scare her and neither did mice, raccoons, or any other dog-sized animal.

*Horse-sized, either, for that matter.* But the absence of them must have her on edge.

Dropping the curry comb into its holding tub, she carried the last item in the bin—Moe's lead—over to the wall. The area's overhead light was a spotlight on her, and for some reason, an unwelcome one. The illumination made it easy to be seen from the outside, while her vision was blinded.

Kelly shook her head again, the rattling not enough to stave off the paranoia.

Why was she so tense?

She pinned her eyes to the back wall, reason taking over.

*This must be post-robbery stress.*

Or maybe the heat of the practice session had taken more energy than she realized. She rubbed her palm against her arm, and the tremble that resulted smacked of an adrenaline response.

*Strange.*

She had to be overreacting. She hadn't had any coffee. Had eaten a full, healthy lunch.

*Just time to call it a day*, she thought, shucking the sensation.

Looping the metal clip of Moe's lead onto the closest hook, Kelly turned away, ready to go when something stopped her.

The peg wall stood as before, thick with leads, lines of faded colors: cream, black, green, purple....

She sifted through with her hand, sending the mass swinging. No red.

*The red lead is...gone.*

The still air went eerie as she swiveled her head, finding the common paddock outside the same. Vacant, empty. Her heartbeat picked up double-time as her eyes darted to the door's opening, then back to the leads. She was the only person in the room.

*The only one outside with Moe.*

There was no one around when she came back in.

Her racing heart invaded her ears.

The lead had been here just moments before. The texture thin, unbreakable.

*Red. Like blood.*

She jumped as a noise sounded from outside the door, a slight crunch like weight on woodchips. Kelly's hands whipped to her sides, balling into involuntary fists.

"Hello?" she called, her voice not the one she knew, now tinny and warped. "*Hello?*" she called again and waited.

No answer.

The wind picked up again, gusting through the hall, brushing a sliver of her bangs from her face, blowing the safe smell of leather away in a single blast.

She felt exposed. Alone. Vulnerable.

Why was she reacting like this? As if she were...in danger.

Every neuron in her brain screamed that she had to get back to the loft, back to her room—

Instinct taking over Kelly bolted through the door, not stopping to turn to see if her actions made her justified or a coward. Her boots revolved like a machine beneath her as she booked through the common paddock, racing past the farm house, making the hair-pin turn around the corner to the metal steps that ascended to the door of the loft.

The echo of her boots pounding against the metal steps were an alarm bell in her ears, everything telling her to flee, to—*Go! Run!*

With a flip of keys, she stabbed into the lock and unbolted the door. Knob in hand she paused for one second, using the height of the loft's platform to scan the paddock like a watchtower. The tack room stood obscured by the storage building's side wall, but Kelly could see the rectangle of light cast on the ground, the shape of the tack room door glowing. Her breath became a lead ball in her throat as in the square of yellow a silhouette emerged, the shape cut out in an outline of shadow. A figure with a line like a tail dangling at their side. Someone was there with her...with the lead rope.

Oh, *God*.

Hands shaking, Kelly lost hold of her keys, the mass of metal falling and hitting the steel platform with a loud clank, the sound reverberating. Retrieving them with a dip and snatch, she rechecked what she'd hoped was her imagination.

Looking back, the projected square of light was solid, the figure gone. A second passed, and then the room went...dark.

Heart thundering in her chest, Kelly twisted the knob and stumbled into the loft. Relocking the door in a panic, she scanned the bathroom, her closet.

Alone, fear pulsated through her as she located her cell phone, ticking out messages to Pippa and Sophie with unsteady fingers while she threw anxious glances about the room, ready to call the police—

She had no way to reach Aidan, she realized with a curse.

Why hadn't she asked for his number after the robbery?

*And could this be related? Did the robber somehow come for—?*

Gripping the phone, she tried to calm down.

This could be nothing, a volunteer that hadn't heard her call out to them. Had to be.

She tiptoed to the kitchen and peered out the window, the scope of the farm revealed in a spread of murky contrast and shadow. The view of the tack room showed no movement, and no noise other than her startled breathing.

All she had to do was wait for Sophie to text her back. Then she'd get Aidan's cell phone num—

Kelly's eyes went wide, body whipping around as the faint sound of metal rang out, the footfalls climbing the stairs growing heavy. Someone coming up to the loft.

*Too heavy to be Sophie. Not Pippa or Hank.*

Panic tackled Kelly hard and fast, the steady *tamp-tamp-tamp* getting louder, closer.

*The person outside the tack room...*

Kelly slid her stiff body alongside the kitchen counter. Reaching a silent hand out, she wrapped quivering fingers around the handle of the only blunt object she owned. The saucepan let out a mild scrape as she dragged it from the grate of the dish drainer and crept through the darkness.

The sound of footsteps stopped in front of the door, a looming figure paused on the other side, his face hidden through the curtained glass. A man, blocking her exit.

Kelly held the pan in her hard grasp, pushing down her terror as she laid her free hand on the lock.

On a one-count, she threw open the latch and *swung*.

Aidan peered in through the curtained window, scanning the dark apartment. Something seemed odd. Kelly was supposed to be there. He raised his hand to knock and fell forward.

*What the—?*

It took a split second to realize that he'd stepped into an onslaught; the knife, gun, *something*—coming at him from the shadows. His defense training flaring, he blocked an upward strike, a metallic sound reverberating at the deflection. Forearms braced, he took the impact as he grabbed his attacker's wrists, grunts echoing as Aidan wrestled the assailant inside. The blackness that engulfed them didn't help, further concealing the weapon, the person's face, their build.

*Not good.*

Locked together in a violent dance, Aidan felt the attacker using all their strength, pushing, kicking at him. In blind retaliation Aidan shook the guy, throwing him off balance, the motion so fast and jarring it sounded like the crackle of a raging fire. He cast the body away, holding tight to the attacker's wrists. The realization hit, the assailant's weight was too easy to toss, the person light, slender.

*Not a man.*

Aidan slowed as the dimensions he held in his palms registered—small wrists. He flipped the pad of his thumb down where it met with soft skin, the resonant drumroll of a thundering pulse kicking. He loosened his grip.

"Kelly?"

The reply came as a trembling female body slumped into him. He peeled the weapon out of her hand and carried her with him as he turned on the light. Adrenaline still surging he got a glimpse of her armament of choice. A cooking pan.

*Creative.*

"*Jesus*, I could of hurt you! What the hell—"

He felt his eyes flare and narrow as she pushed off from him and rushed to shut the door, locking it with conviction. Aidan's eyes tracked her as she crossed back to the kitchen to examine the window, the way she moved different than normal, springing and recoiling like a frightened animal.

He wanted an excuse to gather her up again, the impulse surprising him. He was used to riling people up not calming them down. "What's wrong?"

"Nothing." The word came unsteadily from her lips.

She finally turned, and he hated how terrified she looked. She moved again, tucking her hands into her arms to quell the shakes.

"*Nothing*," he repeated, not buying the universal blow-off line one bit. He waved the pan at her. "If this were cast iron I'd be unconscious."

He followed her to the kitchen, catching her flinch as he set the pan on the counter. He stepped back, letting her breathe. *Something scared her, and bad.*

Moving slower than he'd ever had in his life, Aidan gently lifted her chin with his finger, her green eyes lined with fear. "Kelly, what happened?"

The heat of their contact lasted only a second before she pulled away, eyes roving as her body inched toward him.

The words tumbled from her lips. "I was in the tack room. I thought—I thought I saw a red lead... But one minute it was there, the next it was gone. I didn't move it. There was a shadow, someone...someone else in there."

Aidan felt his forehead do the furrow landslide.

"It sounds crazy—" She pegged him with her direct stare. "I-I swear, I didn't move it." She pivoted into the counter and felt her head like she might have a fever. "I'm losing my mind."

Aidan thought about what had happened at her apartment, paranoia as a post-traumatic response. Up until now she hadn't exhibited any signs of stress.

*Would symptoms have taken this long to show?*

She stared at the floor, let out a shuddered breath.

*Maybe. The move could be a factor, too.*

Plus they were out in the woods. Aidan had grown up in a rural area; weird noises came out of the barn all the time, creaky walls and roof. The creepy ambiance could have been the barn cat, a raccoon, any number of animals trying to get into the horse feed. But a missing lead?

He looked down into her eyes, searching the orbs of soft hazel.

And why was she acting like he didn't believe her?

He thought back to how she'd reamed him over getting kicked out of school. The girl was truthful to a fault.

"I'll check it out. Stay here." He turned, the low sound of her objection stopping him halfway to the door. He popped his chin over his shoulder. Kelly's shoulders went lax under the weight of his stare, as if realizing it was futile to tell him not to go. She conceded, but her expression said *be careful,* a sentiment Aidan would normally resent.

*Normally, but not now.*

With a nod he walked out into the early night air, the lock clicking into place behind him. As he rounded the front of the building, Aidan saw Kelly's face covering him from her turret of a window. The realization came as a surprise. The way she watched him didn't bog him down; it gave him resolve. Her concern didn't coddle him; it backed him.

Like a... companion.

He took the walk to the barn in stride, staying hyperaware of his surroundings. The tack room came into view, the place quiet, deserted. A feeling of unease struck him at the threshold and he could see why Kelly had gotten antsy. Something felt off. Unsettled.

The correct word pinged in his head: *Disturbed.*

Aidan looked over the wall, lifting one lead and then another.

None of them red.

He checked the barn, the surrounding area, the place uninhabited. He stepped into the foyer of the main barn and Keegan snorted hello from his quarantine stall, recognizing him.

Searching the shadows, Aidan found nothing but empty space. No people or movement of the non-equine sort.

*Something's not right,* his instinct niggled, refusing to go away.

He stood in the open main area, the sweet summer air adding to the sense of vastness.

In a sudden inclination, he felt revealed, as if he could be seen from the outside...

In a blink his hand went to his hip, unsnapping the leather strap that secured his firearm.

"Aidan?"

Aidan retracted his hand and turned to where the voice had come from, Pippa emerging at the opposite end of the barn. She approached him carefully, Jason behind her.

"Hi. I didn't expect you today."

"Yeah." The thickness in Aidan's voice had him clearing his throat. "Yes, I'm just looking in on my man here." Aidan eyed Keegan, the horse eying him back as if calling him out on the lie.

Pippa smiled. "Jason and I are on the evening shift. You're welcome to stay and visit. We're getting Keegan's dinner ready."

"Great." Aidan glanced around again, his apprehension dissipating. "Will you guys be here all night?"

"Until one a.m. Then the graveyard shift will relieve us." She tilted her head. "Is something wrong?"

Aidan forced a smile, pulling out his cell phone while Jason ignored him, setting up for their stint. Pippa let the lack of an answer slide, moving to help prepare Keegan's food. Typing fast, Aidan sent the text, a minute passing before Eric's response came back with a beep of affirmation.

Aidan called Pippa over, keeping his voice low. "Officer Carson's going to stop by later to check in on you, that cool?"

"Sure," Pippa said, brow creasing with concern. "Aidan, is everything okay?"

"Just a routine follow up." Aidan tried to amp up the reassurance in his voice to make it more convincing. He gave up on smiling long ago, the show of teeth only making him look combative.

The woman's face eased. "Whatever you need. I'll let Sophie know."

"Thanks, Pippa."

Aidan trekked back to the loft, knocking carefully and holding up his hands in parody when Kelly opened the door. "I'm un-panned."

She didn't laugh as she let him in, soberly returning to the sanctuary of her kitchen.

"Pippa and Jason are with Keegan. I went in the tack room. I didn't see a red lead," he said.

Kelly stared at the saucepan on the counter as if she'd planned on never sleeping again.

Aidan frowned. "Kelly, I believe you."

"Sure you do." Her face was sad, her once bright laughter an echo in Aidan's memory.

*Maybe a little teasing will bring back her spirit.*

"I assume you don't cook with that," Aidan said, tugging at the handle of the saucepan.

"I've got a microwave," she replied, self-reliance steeling her voice.

He dared to put his hand on her arm, stroking her skin with his thumb. She was soft. Warm. *Trouble.*

She stared up at him with green eyes, her worry a lead weight in his chest.

"Come on," Aidan said, taking her hand, leading her to the door before she could say no. "Text Sophie in the car, tell her you're with me tonight."

# CHAPTER 17

Aidan owed Eric big time.

He had the blue boy to thank for the plastic tubs stacked in his fridge, the gourmet contents better than any delivery Aidan had ever ordered.

Kelly sat across from Aidan at his kitchen table, devouring the leftovers Eric had sent with Aidan the day before—the heavenly smelling turkey complete with fluffy clouds of mashed potatoes. The stuff melted in your mouth, the meat seasoned with something extra, popping with onion and some kind of almonds. One of the cop's many take-home samplers, the spread was a nice offset to Aidan's piss-poor culinary skills.

And Aidan didn't voice his knowledge that Eric was the one behind all the grub showing up at work. He figured that what his partner liked to do in his spare time was his own business. Besides, airing a man's creative talents wasn't something you did down at the station. Aidan was sure that the other officers were aware of Eric's clandestine pastime, having benefited from it on potluck Fridays, but they stayed hush about it out of respect for the guy.

A flash of Eric's ascetic glare came to mind.

*Or out of intimidation,* Aidan quickly amended. *Probably both.*

After getting a text update that Eric agreed to patrol the farm, Aidan felt so indebted to the uniform, he'd gladly take the man's Bobby Flay moonlighting to the grave.

Kelly picked that moment to turn the spoon over in her mouth, seeming to relish her last bite of the potatoes, a murmur of pleasure emanating from her throat.

Before the end Eric was going to cough up that mashed potatoes recipe.

*The way the guy pummels spuds doesn't have to remain a trade secret.*

"Good?" he asked.

"Um-hmm." She nodded, lying her spoon down on the spotless plate. "Thank you, I feel much—better."

"I'm glad." Aidan studied her, the mask of apprehension she'd worn had faded away on the drive over, her stiff body unfurling after an hour of settling in at his place. His bachelor pad had never had that affect on a girl in the past, but he was glad that Kelly felt comfortable.

Her pretty face tilted to appraise her surroundings, her curiosity evident. "How long have you lived here?"

"Four years. My parents live a few blocks down. They knew the previous owners. Gave me a heads up when the folks looked to sell."

His living room stood out under the strong ceiling lights: crisp carpet, solid walls. The house was in great shape when he'd bought it, with an updated roof and appliances, central heat and air. He pretty much just brought in the furniture and called it his. Aidan took in the wood-framed photos hanging on the wall with fresh eyes, the lone feminine area his mother's doing.

Simple touches, he realized. Nothing too girly. His diploma from college, awards; memories preserved and put on display. A place deep inside him liked the praise. For all the time he'd lived there he never really wondered what other people thought of it, but suddenly, with Kelly there, he wanted an impartial opinion. "You like it?"

"It's very *you*," she said, smiling. She twisted in her chair, the beams of light above them setting off the sparks of red in her hair. While she studied the simple décor, Aidan studied her. In a sudden shift she flipped her attention back to him, her face falling as she caught him staring.

He pulled his eyes away.

*The girl's already had one creepy encounter tonight. Let's not make it two.*

"Sorry—" Aidan felt the stupid urge to explain himself, but she cut him off.

"It's not my mother's," she said.

"What?"

"My hair color, it's not...hers."

Aidan frowned, watching the girl stare at the tabletop as if she were humbled by the fact. She'd responded that way before when he'd drawn attention to it. "I know."

Her face popped up, perplexed.

"I saw a picture, in your apartment."

"Oh." She nodded, her hand absently smoothing at her ponytail, an insecure movement.

Her hair color made her self-conscious. Why, Aidan had no idea. The red with her eyes and that body made her a knock-out.

"You get it from your dad, then?" he asked. Kelly gave another nod of admission, her expression solemn.

"I think so. I never met him. He didn't...stick around after I was born. May I?" She stood up, her body language asking permission to wander around.

"Go ahead," Aidan said, gauging her. It was a wonder how any man could abandon his kid. Especially with how cool Kelly turned out, hard working. Kind.

*Beautiful.* He forced himself to collect the dirty dishes and take them to the sink. The mindless chore of rinsing wasn't enough to distract him, his attention returning to her at the first opportunity. He found her edging the room as if she were browsing an art museum: leaning in to examine the details of each of the photographs hanging on the wall, popping up on her toes to catch the ones hung high.

Watching, Aidan couldn't help but measure the long lines of her body; she was built like a true horsewoman, with lean limbs drawn downward, sinewy muscle around her thighs, her calves. The girl was lithe, graceful. Gorgeous.

"Who's this?" The question came out subdued, respectful as she pointed.

Dropping the dishtowel on the counter, Aidan walked over, taking his place behind her. He faced the aged five-by-seven snapshot as his twenty-two-year-old self stared back at him, smiling; his arm locked playfully around the neck of his best friend. The two stood up straight in academy uniforms, blue mats blanketing the expanse of the gym around them.

"My partner, Paul." Aidan heard the sadness infiltrate his voice.

She murmured something like *sorry*, touching the pads of her fingers to the glass briefly before pulling back respectfully.

It didn't surprise Aidan that word had gotten around to her about what had happened.

"Is it true? That you...you were shot?" Her question was tentative as her eyes locked on his. She was driven by her need to know things, and for the first time Aidan didn't feel anger at the subject. He awaited the familiar jab of pain that came with the mention of Paul, but this time it didn't come. It was a surprise he could be so candid with her.

Something about Kelly gave him...hope.

He stared into his friend's face, a young officer. A good man.

"We were tracking a pro group of drug traffickers, the Dove Ring. Paul had called for backup." Adan flinched slightly at the memory. "He'd arrived on the scene first, intercepted the dealers before—I got there too late."

The air in his lungs burned at the confession. Time—*seconds*, had stolen his friend away.

*If I'd been ONE minute faster...*

"It should have been me."

Paul's face smiled at him from behind the glass, a soul lost.

"The Dove group, they're the ones you think were at the bonfire? The criminals you're trying to catch?" Kelly's voice tugged Aidan away from his grief, her eyes full of concern. The expression made his chest ache.

"Yeah," he grumbled, and turned away. Like devils, the people who'd murdered his partner had come back, had been at the field party. And Aidan was expected to stay cool while more cops risked their lives while banning him from the investigation. Aidan thought of Eric, of how many times the uniform had already put himself close to the same danger.

His chin went up, fingers flexing.

*We have the bad guys on the run.*

"I'm sorry," Kelly said softly, gaining his focus.

"We're going to catch them," he said, stepping back. Kelly withdrew and he realized how forcefully he'd said the words. He felt keyed up, restless.

He turned back to the picture, his eyes loitering on Paul's face, their arms locked together in playful battle. Aidan's lips stretched into an unexpected grin. "Paul could always kick my ass in hand-to-hand."

Kelly smiled and stepped in closer, as if encouraging Aidan's change in mood.

"He could've taught you a thing or two," Aidan jibbed, eyeing her.

"Like what?" She threw him a challenging look, half questioning, half goading.

"Like don't use a pan. You never want to get within arm's length of an attacker, especially as petite as you are." He took her hand gently, held it up. "You want to stay out of striking distance."

Using the length of her arm as an example, he extended it to measure the distance between them. "If you have to hit back, you want to use the densest muscles you have. Utilize your body weight. Step back and *kick*." He dipped down and tapped her thigh, the sensation of firm skin under the denim making his hand tingle. "Put all the force you can into it."

A foot apart, heat shot through their connected palms, the buzz going straight to Aidan's head. They were too close.

Aidan paused when he caught Kelly's eyes appraising him, watching him with admiration.

Before he could blink, she went up on her tiptoes, putting her mouth on his and dropping a sweet, lingering kiss on his lips. The link broke as she fell away, her height preventing her from maintaining the connection.

Heat coursed over Aidan's skin like wildfire. The chemistry they had the kind that left bed sheets sweaty and tangled.

*Bad analogy*, he thought as his body responded.

Stunned, Aidan dipped his chin, searching for some excuse to write it off; some valid cause for him to not pick her up and continue what she'd started. His eyes locked in on her, and what he saw ignited his cravings and incinerated all his senses. There were no demure signs of childish affection in her face. No, standing in front of him wasn't some naïve girl unaware of her actions. A woman stared up at from under heavy eyelids, the expression holding one universal meaning.

*Holy crap.*

His whole body stiffened, his lower half responding without any further invitation, his brain trying to rein in his body's primal instincts.

He moved back, Kelly closing the gap no sooner than he'd created it, confusing him.

"Kelly." Her name left his mouth with too much bass.

Her fingertips went to his mouth, silencing him.

"You can say no if you want. We barely know each other. I, I just—" She stroked his bottom lip, the sensation driving him insane. "My whole life I've never seized the moment. You're a good man." She cupped his face. "One night, Aidan. That's all I want. Just one carefree night."

Aidan felt the air in his body leave in a rush, all the oxygen in the room evacuating the building like a three-eleven. A beautiful, smart woman was offering herself up to him, no strings attached.

*Not just any woman,* Kelly.

A smoldering lit off in his chest as the final lifelines of reason ignited one by one, sending him up in flames.

*One night.*

His mind got trumped as he lifted a hand to her hair, freeing the tie of her ponytail. With one long sensuous pull, the strands fell over his arm like silk, her eyes closing in erotic response, egging him on. He ran his fingers through the length, letting it drop over her shoulders, the sight of it setting off fireworks in him, a wildfire in his veins. Tangling his hands, the locks flashed crimson as he paused to look at the passion in her face. Her eyes open, confirming what awaited him.

"You are beautiful, just as you are— amazing," he whispered, cupping her head, touching her hair. "But we shouldn't..."

"Aidan, I'm sure. This is what I want..."

He stopped, looking into her eyes. His stare asking again, *Are you sure?*

"Positive," she said, reading his mind. She stared up at him with total consent, the look setting fire to his objections.

He moved in for a kiss, every connection they'd experienced before paling in comparison to now as she met his invasion with sweet reply. Free to delve, he deepened the contact, exploring her, experiencing her. His blood exploded, his body revving, the heat and pressure a volcano in his belly as her hands traveled over his chest, his shoulders, then headed south to pull at the belt of his jeans. He stilled her hands with his, the issue of protection suddenly wafting through his clouded brain.

"I'm on the pill, if you're clean." She punctuated the statement with peppered kisses up his throat, making it damn near impossible for him to think.

*Clean? Yes.*

He'd been tested the year prior, hadn't had any partners since, but wanted to be careful with her. She was more than a one night stand.

"I am, but hold on—" Few times in his life had Aidan ever moved so fast. He left her suspended in time as he bolted for the bathroom. He tore into the medicine cabinet and dug around, whipping out the line of foil squares with relief. With a check of the stamp on them, the expiration date cut it close but just came in under, which was pathetic but a victory nonetheless.

On his return he both hoped and feared that the respite would have cooled her down, but found her eyes lit up with desire at the sight of him.

Her stare darted to the condoms, and back up to his face as she reeled him down into another kiss, sweeter than before. She popped free the fly of his jeans and then her own, denim hitting the floor in tandem.

*Oh man.*

His jaw made no sound as it fell open, the length of her flawless legs making his tongue loll like a dog, her shirt barely covering the slender lines of perfect flesh. The mental image of having those legs wrapped around him in a minute had his body pulsating under the confines of his boxer-briefs. She put her hands on his shirt, and Aidan took vicarious pleasure in watching her undress him, ready to return the favor. With his teeth.

At the last button he stopped her hand, giving her one last chance to change her mind.

He caught her gaze. *No turning back now.*

Kelly reached for him without hesitation, touching his most intimate part, stroking, caressing. She kissed him, doubling the sexual intoxication.

All common sense dissipated like smoke from a fire as Aidan lost himself in their kiss, a soft tearing sound emanating as together they descended to the floor. Her chest lay bare to him at last as Aidan peeled away her bra, lavishing attention on her breasts.

Both of them touched and kissed until they neared the verge. Aidan pushed himself up on his muscled arms and tore into a condom, sheathing himself in a quick motion. As he braced himself in the cradle between her legs, the heat of where they would soon be joined was a siren song against which he was powerless.

He wanted her. Wanted to be good enough for her...

He looked at Kelly one last time before he entered, her face ardent. He slid in and they both gasped, his thick arms shaking as he began move, the glorious friction making his brain coil and spin. The momentum encompassed them together as she moaned and gripped his shoulders. Repositioning himself, he tilted her body to better advantage, sending waves of gratification through him, making him lose control.

"Feel good?" he asked in her ear, slowing his pace to ensure that she fully shared his pleasure. Her response came in the form of a passionate kiss followed by the arch of her leg, the gazelle limb angling up and wrapping around him, her heel coming to rest on his ass.

The action sent him reeling to the edge, his hand whipping around to grip her thigh, the feel of her all around him, *in* him, sending him up in a blaze. With a ragged exhale Aidan sank in, their two bodies melting together, not an inch separating them.

"Kelly," he breathed. "I'm...close..."

Without words she rolled her hips as he burrowed deep and fell back, the motion revolving, intensifying, a piston going between them. A maelstrom taking over, Aidan thought of slowing down and glanced down at Kelly's face. She hung the edge; the sight of her awaiting the apex with pleading eyes that destroyed all his reserve. The image burned in his brain he grasped her legs, pivoting and moving and working, pushing them to climax.

With a muted cry he both watched and felt her release, the hold detonating his own as he forced his eyes to stay open, to witness her peak, her satisfaction compounding his own.

He collapsed, careful not to crush her, his face nuzzling her hair spread across the floor. He listened as her breathing slowed, proud that it took her a while to come down. Minutes passed before he stirred, his arms burning from the workout of holding himself up.

Kelly lay still under him as he went to pull himself out, spent and satisfied.

She vised him with her legs. Aidan froze.

"Wait," she murmured, breathless.

*Too rough?*

"I'm sorry." He held his lower half still while he brushed sweaty bangs away from her face.

Her immediate smile came as a relief. "It's been a while for me. Are you okay?"

"Yes." She sighed. "Yes, I'm lingering. Don't go yet." He felt her fingers make languid circles over his lower back, sending flickers up his spine.

If she kept it up it wouldn't be long before he was ready to go again.

He pushed back her hair to reveal red-tinged cheeks, her smile glorious.

With a replete exhale she knocked her head down onto the hard living room floor, a repeat of the break room bench. Aidan winced, throwing out his palm to buffer the blow. Her laugh bounced off the walls, joyful and self-effacing, like sunlight.

"We got carried away," he said, chuckling with her, their bodies a tangle of limbs laying in a circle of hastily discarded clothing.

The sounds trailed off as he slipped free of her carefully. Motionless, she lay staring at the indention on his shoulder, the spot raised and dark. Aidan glanced at the blemished circle of magenta skin. The mark had never been pretty, the skin mottled like crepe paper. The bullet had luckily gone straight through, but it left a gaping hole, in more than just his body.

He tied off the condom as her intense eyes measured the scar, her hands stopping his before he could move to cover it. Wordlessly she placed her free hand to her mouth, kissed the pads of her fingers and placed them to the marred flesh.

Stunned, Aidan covered her hand with his, their warmth combining to solder the injury, the burn not hurting but healing.

*She understood.* And something in that simple revelation stoked something in him.

He'd been alone with his grief for so long.

He brought her hand to his lips, kissing her palm before tucking it around her torso. He ducked to the side, scooping her up in his arms, her tiny form as light as he suspected, her feet dangling.

"What are you doing?" she asked, her voice muffled by a soft yawn.

"We're not spending the night on the floor."

She offered no further protest, just peered around as Aidan carried her down the hall and into his bedroom. He left the light off, entering without fear of tripping over anything. His career had drilled tidiness into him over the years; the only areas that fell outside the realm of order were his bed and his closet. And if he'd gotten notice she was coming over, he might have straightened those up, too.

He set her down for less than a second to pull back the disheveled covers. As he deposited her on the side opposite him, the thought that she belonged there shot through his brain.

Kelly sunk into the fresh pillow, her free hair spread out on the cotton case as she watched him with an expression that was *her*—generous, giving.

He brushed his hand against her cheek and pulled himself away, wanting to let her rest.

After taking his place beside her, the night passed, except that even with his eyes closed

Aidan didn't reach REM. His consciousness peaked, the numbers on the alarm clock progressing as if on fast-forward.

Sometime before dawn, Kelly rolled over wanting more of him.

Aidan let her take the lead their second time, the experience bringing a kind of pleasure he'd rarely known before. She wrapped her legs around him, the curtain of her hair covering both their faces as she lavished deep kisses on him, the new morning light illuminating her like...an angel.

Aidan came awake a while later to the window curtains glowing a pale blue, the clock declaring it to be a little after six a.m. The flutter behind Kelly's lids told him that she'd finally nodded off. Aidan refrained from disturbing her although her soft skin beckoned to him. In one spry movement he slipped from the bed and padded to the bathroom to clean up after the night's activities. Toothbrush pocketed in his cheek, Aidan peeked out to check on her.

*Still asleep.*

With a rinse and an underwear pit-stop, he back-tracked to the living room, plucking up the heaps of clothes, and cursing when he reached for Kelly's shirt. The ripping noise replayed in his head, reminding him why the frayed strip of fabric in his hands no longer classified as wearable. The old thing hadn't been that strong to start with, and boy had he put it to the test. The scraps held a future as dust rags.

*Shit.*

Aidan evaluated the damage, holding the sad pieces of cloth together, trying to remember if he even owned a needle and thread. The image of the cotton covered in Frankenstein stitches had him throwing the thing over his arm in defeat.

He'd find something for her to go home in. Hank's ire awaited him anyway.

He ambled back to the room to find Kelly blinking at him from beneath the covers and Aidan couldn't stop his smile.

"G'Morning."

"Good Morning." She sat up, swathed in a sheet, her hair mussed up.

The sexiest thing Aidan had ever laid eyes on.

His libido had come awake like a broiler oven after its long hiatus. And wearing nothing but his underwear, Aidan opted to check his dresser for her replacement shirt before his morning inclinations started to show. He crouched down, burrowing through the drawers in search of—yes!

A family friend had passed on a new lightweight, blue plaid button down. The color looked good on him, but was way too small. Add in an accidental trip through the dryer on high heat and the thing had shrunk to Barbie-sized.

Which would still dwarf her, but it worked.

He swiveled around, Kelly's attention flipping up from his ass. The Cheshire-Cat grin that spread across his face made his cheeks hurt.

"Caught you," he teased, catching her ogle.

Her blush had him covertly adjusting himself again, a frown staining her expression as her eyes traveled to the shirt. She clutched the sheet closer to her chest, looking stricken.

"Hey, I'm sorry about this—" Aidan held up the remnants of her old shirt, feeling like a letch.

*What kind of man mauls the clothes off a woman's body, no matter how pre-torn?*

"It's okay." She held out her hand for the ripped fabric. "I'll...get going."

*Whoa.* She thought he was kicking her out?

The words: *One, Night,* and *Stand* pinged through his brain and he nearly dropped everything, stumbling to keep her in the room.

"Kelly, I'm not telling you to leave." His tone made her halt with one lean leg kicked out from underneath the bedding. "Hey, come here."

He waggled his finger as she slowly rose to her knees on the bed, the pose making her look like a goddess, an award he didn't deserve. Aidan meet her at the edge of the mattress, their bodies parallel as she gazed up at him. He held up the wad of useless material and frowned. "I owe you a new shirt."

"Oh." She bit her lip. "You don't have to—" As she realized that the alternative was to return to Hammond's topless, she paused. "Thanks."

"Let's see if this fits." He motioned to the replacement, pegging his eyes to her face while she dropped the sheet, his peripheral vision clearly detecting her perfect-handful breasts, the display even more stunning in the light of day.

She pulled the sleeves over her arms as the unbuttoned halves dangled open, illustrating a flawless valley of smooth, tan skin. The shirt's plaid pattern of white, yellow, and blue was a compliment to the red in her hair, and her smile at the gift warmed Aidan from the inside out.

"This is nicer than my old one. Thank you," she breathed, petting the fabric.

The smile she hit him with knocked down all restraint as Aidan tried to keep his distance. Kelly picked up on the combustion and laid her hands on his chest, propping herself up to give him a kiss. On autopilot Aidan's hands dipped under the shirt to hold her, his brain shutting down as the meeting of their lips set his brain aflame. Kissing turned into caressing, as Aidan ran his hands down Kelly's waist. He stopped, holding his palms up in surrender.

"You want to go again?" he asked impishly against her lips, his body more than willing.

"Again," Kelly murmured back, her fingertips roaming as Aidan kissed her deep, his hands still in the air. She glanced suspiciously at his pose.

"You take the shirt off this time," he said playfully. "I don't want to be a serial shirt ripper."

Kelly let out a radiant chuckle and let the plaid cotton slip from her shoulders.

# CHAPTER 18

"I'll get Jason to help unload," Pippa called as she hopped out of the Jeep.

Kelly backed the car up to the feed barn and seized the opportunity to get out and stretch. The sun hung at high noon, the supply store trip taking up the morning hours. Kelly opened up the brute's trunk where the bags of horse feed waited to be moved, and meandered over to the main barn to check in on Keegan. On the last visit Dr. Althea had confirmed that the horse was days away from being given a clean bill of health, cleared to return to the gelding field. Keegan had been more responsive too, less congested, and exhibited a better appetite. Kelly could tell that he longed for Moe's company by the way he constantly nosed at the adjacent stall.

Kelly patted her back pocket to feel for her audio recorder, keeping the device close to monitor Keegan's breathing. The comparison of his respiratory patterns during the last few visits all sounded the same, which was good. She listened carefully; if any symptoms crept back up she wanted to catch them at the onset.

As she crossed the main paddock, her hand traveled over the soft plaid of the shirt she wore. *Aidan's shirt.*

She felt limber, desirable under the plain cotton, having worn the button-down practically every day for the two weeks since he'd given it to her. A private smile pulled at her lips at the memory of their nights together. The material was a reminder of his touch, which struck her as silly as they were hardly ever apart. She stayed at his house almost every night, the pair returning to the farm before dawn, the rumor mill well aware of their involvement.

She stroked the sleeve, shaking off the idea of it being her boyfriend's. Her heart constricted at the amendment, the fact on repeat in her brain: Aidan wasn't her boyfriend.

*He was a lover, a guardian, her friend. Nothing more.*

A smart woman wouldn't speculate about love, while her brain climbed over the caution tape that bordered the zone of relationship status without a second thought. It was a place she rarely ventured, and knew led to heartache. She just couldn't resist.

*You're either an item or an arrangement,* she reminded herself.

Their relationship was likely an amusement that served both people, and would eventually end. The ache squeezed again, the truth stinging.

When she was with Aidan, it didn't feel like a fling. When they were together the span of distance and space disappeared as if they were one, dining together, talking— *other* things. He shared his thoughts with her without hesitation, and his body any time she asked. An unspoken agreement, by staying together they both were set free. And somewhere in the words and moments and pleasure something had sparked.

Aidan's honesty and fearlessness had brought Kelly to *trust* him.

*In such a short time?*

Reality jumped in the middle of Kelly's reasoning, her reverie spreading like fire over spilled kerosene. There could be no commitment between them. Aidan would invite her over to his place each night; she would accept.

*No strings.*

She steeled herself to the consequences. She could do it, stay for the impulse, the mutual pleasure.

Aidan was more to her than a summer fling, but she had no right to expect more. She'd promised not to become attached. He gave her what she asked for, and in return she owed him autonomy, the ability to walk away. Her heart answered with another twinge, a palpitation that punched in her chest.

*This will hurt when it ends. Like hellfire.*

She smoothed her hand down the shirt-sleeve again, vowing to live in the moment.

*For whatever short time that lasts.*

As she turned the corner Kelly's feet squeaked to a halt. As if he'd manifested from her dreams, Aidan stood at the corner stall, a bag of baby carrots in hand.

"Hey there." The gorgeous bass of his voice sent flutters through her stomach, the short sleeve t-shirt he had on a second skin that stretched around his thick arms, one of the many parts of him she knew intimately well.

"The doc just left. The last test came back negative, our friend here is cleared." He grinned, holding up a bright orange nugget to Keegan, the horse making an instant appearance at the presentation of the treat.

Catching sight of Kelly, Keegan picked up Aidan's offering and shuffled to her side of the gate, seconding the warm *hello*. Kelly's heart picked up double-time at the tableau: Keegan's anticipation and Aidan unwavering blue gaze.

*My men, side by side.*

She closed her eyes.

*Not mine.*

"What's wrong?" The concern in Aidan voice pulled her back to the present.

"Nothing. You're sneaking him contraband," Kelly joked, watching Keegan's jaw move like the wheel of a locomotive, all crunch and gobble, his eyelids low as if savoring the taste.

Aidan leaned against the frame of the stall's open top half. "He earned it today. Have you seen the size of the swabs they use on his nose?"

Keegan stopped mid-chew, ears doing an insta-flip forward like, *Where? Not again.*

Aidan reached out to pet him with a broad hand, the animal easing back into his munching.

"Doc Althea said carrots are okay, it gives him some calories." Aidan laid another piece out on his flat palm, Keegan at the ready, leaning in and lipping the food up into his mouth. The horse looked out at Aidan then over to Kelly, his expression an all-encompassing, *I like this guy.*

"Those were the doctor's exact words?"

"Well..." Aidan hedged, his hand stilled in the bag.

"Uh-huh." *Busted.* "Keegan's colon is looking better, but too much glucose isn't good. Let's stick to alfalfa until his GI track—" Kelly eyed the inch of vegetable Aidan tried to covertly tuck into his palm.

He shot her a devilish smile, the one that got him what he wanted.

"You listen well," Kelly ribbed, snagging the bag and pilfering the hidden carrot with a flash of her hand. She let out a laugh at Aidan's face, his pseudo-shock at the speed of her reflexes, the challenge lighting him up.

"I was listening."

"Riiight." Kelly held up the carrot as evidence.

"Intestines, a lifetime of gruel—I heard you." In a blink he bent down snapped up the carrot with his teeth, giving Kelly a bulging chipmunk cheek grin as he grabbed her hips and drew her close. Body against body, Aidan chewed the carrot as if he were starving and looking like he wanted her next.

*Irresistible man.*

Mesmerized by the close proximity to his blazing blue eyes, Kelly felt something fuzzy nudge its way between them.

Keegan's muzzle appeared, the horse's expression one of slight annoyance:

*Excuse me, PEOPLE. You're eating my food and bringing your hormones into my stall.*

"I think we're standing too close to him." Kelly laughed, Aidan not surrendering his grip on her waist. With a spry turn Keegan darted to the opening to the stall next door.

"He's been looking for Moe." Aidan patted the rails, stepping back. "It's okay, boy, we'll go." Sentiment morphed into competition as he held an open palm out to Kelly for the carrot bag.

Kelly let out another giggle, stashing the thing behind her back with a loud crinkle.

Aidan's glare went mischievous.

*Uh-oh.*

She took measured steps backward. "The first rule of working with large animals—" she started as he remained eerily still. "No sudden move—"

Aidan pounced and Kelly squealed, both of them bolting for the exit. Laughter tumbled from her lungs as she didn't make it to the door before a pair of strong arms caught her, a loose hold she could easily break but didn't want to. Aidan barked a chuckle in her ear as she tickled him and ducked free, making a scampered leap for the main paddock.

Kelly stopped short.

She'd seen Officer Carson gloomy before, but the guy's natural gravity was amped up to that of a black hole. He stood deathly still in the center of the paddock, his uniform a deep blue cloud in the middle of the broad sunlight. The officer's dark eyes fell on her, full of grim resolve, and the hairs on the back of Kelly's neck stood on end.

*What happened?*

She felt Aidan body's sidle up against her back, his firm chest a wall of reinforcement behind her.

"Hey, Eric, what's up?"

Kelly watched the men exchange glances, a visual back-and-forth, Aidan's face confused.

The officer's voice went dour. "I got a phone call after you left this morning. I need to talk to you both."

"They found *what* in my car?" Kelly stammered.

Aidan inched closer to Kelly's chair, in case she fell out of the thing.

"Two kilos of cocaine, wrapped in plastic and strapped to the inside of the gas tank. One of the packs got nicked and started to leak. It got into the fuel line," Eric answered without hesitation. "Which explains your engine trouble."

Aidan watched the cop move slowly about the break room, the guy's face squinting as he stopped in front of the window then returned to his pacing.

Evidently the news didn't sit well with him, either.

"The dealership didn't know what was causing the problem until they opened the car up to repair it a few days ago. We confiscated the entire load this morning."

*So that's how the drugs got smuggled in undetected.*

Aidan utilized the moment of quiet to put the puzzle pieces together. If the Dove group snuck the shipment in using stolen cars, they'd could extract it using their hired gorillas, divide it up, and then perform one night of heavy distribution.

Profit big then go another round.

*Too damn easy.*

Aidan watched Kelly's mouth make a small O, shock and disbelief setting a gray pallor in place of all the radiant joy she'd shown earlier.

She looked pale, too pale.

"Two kilos of *cocaine?*" She repeated the words as if she wished they were just air. "The Honda wasn't driving well, it was getting up in age. The mechanic had found something in the tank. I didn't, I didn't think it was..." She put a hand to her throat, the pose reminding him of Sophie.

"We ruled you out as a suspect. A person doesn't simply trade in seventy thousand dollars' worth of Blow for a, uh—used car." Eric shifted the comment to cordial, as if Kelly's ex-grad of a Jeep might come barreling in to kick his ass if he said anything derogatory.

The uniform pegged Aidan with a level stare before flipping his intense brown eyes down to where Kelly sat at the head of the table. "The night of the party, when you got sick. Did you have your car keys on you the entire time?"

Aidan's lips flattened out, his hand making a fist that came down silently against the back of Kelly's chair.

*That's how they pulled it off.*

The girl's eyes widened, the facts clicking together. "Rebecca had my purse. I got it back a few days later." Kelly leaned forward, hand on her forehead as if testing for a fever, or insanity.

"They planted the drugs in her car while she was passed out?" Aidan asked, the question a growl.

"When she was *supposed* to be passed out. Copied her key and lifted her address from her license. Maybe planned on just stealing the car later. Clean, no one the wiser," Eric added.

Kelly's brow crumpled.

Aidan felt his eyes narrow, the picture fitting the MO. Kelly's odd sickness that night, the Dove crew uncharacteristically out in the open after years of staying underground. It made sense, all of it. They needed Kelly as a scapegoat, they just didn't bargain on the girl keeping the goods.

Or Aidan showing up.

Eric's tone softened as he addressed her. "You don't drink often, right?"

Kelly shook her head, her back stiff.

"And a few sips of wine made you nauseous?" Aidan added, picking up on the line of questioning.

"You think they tried to poison me?" Kelly retorted.

Aidan's chest knotted at the thought of Kelly lying on the grass, skin ashen...

"The vomiting, the blackouts—I think someone put a mickey in your drink to sedate you," Eric answered. "You eat like a bird. I think your system rejected it, made you sick instead."

"And they couldn't risk her seeing them take the car," Aidan deduced, steering the conversation back to between the two cops.

"They'd need enough time to deposit the shipment before the missing car raised suspicions. After I got the first report, I checked into a few of the previous Dove cases. There were odd details, missing possessions reported by students, assumed stolen. If that's how they've been getting past us, they may have used other cars and objects to smuggle in the drugs." Eric leaned a hip against the table. "With Kelly, they couldn't reclaim the Honda right away. And the break-in at her apartment occurred a few days after she traded the car in. It's plausible, the burglar broke in but didn't steal anything of value—"

"A check," Kelly cut in, commanding all attention. "The robber took a check... with my mother's address on it...oh, *no*."

Aidan frowned as the temperature in the room dropped. Kelly looked up at him, beautiful eyes stricken with fear.

"I'll make some calls. We'll ask New York State police to put a watch on your family," Eric said.

"We have to assume that they're trailing her." Aidan's mind flashed to the tack room, the missing lead.

"An entire cocaine shipment, gone." Eric cocked an eyebrow. "Payment is due to their supplier, the cronies that did the auto work... They're *desperate* by now."

With a scrape of her chair Kelly stood up, stopping all conversation, a sudden fury replacing anguish on her face. "Why? *Why* did they pick me?"

Eric dipped his chin at Aidan: a hand off. As if heartbreaking honesty was Aidan's area of expertise. Aidan shot Eric a look. *Thanks, buddy.*

"New girl in town, no friends." Aidan felt his chest turn to concrete as the explanation came out, blunt but true. "You were easy to corner, easy to isolate."

Kelly's expression went numb, unseeing. In that moment Aidan wished he knew how to comfort, wished he could be anything but a rigid, damaged excuse of a man who happened to have a badge.

"Does Sophie know?" Kelly's voice fell to a whisper.

"I can tell her—" Aidan started.

"*No.*" The word burst from her lips, stunning the room silent for the second time. "No, I need to do it. This, this mess. *This...*" She looked around, eyes wide.

In a blink she turned, exploding out of the room.

"I got her." Aidan held a hand up to Eric, catching the door before it closed. She hadn't gotten far, idling at the fence to the riding ring. She gripped the wooden slats, a myriad of feelings playing across her face. Her eyes on the fields, she didn't look away when Aidan stepped beside her.

"This isn't your fault," he spoke first.

"You sure?" she questioned, her voice monotone, the beautiful smile she'd shown him earlier missing, banished. The crazy fear that he may never see the carefree expression again cut at him, but he couldn't remove her pain. She was a victim, taking the responsibility with shame.

Eric's concerned face peered out at them from the break room window.

"*Kelly.*"

"You said it yourself. A girl from another state, found drunk at a college party. The drugs were in my car, why don't we just go back into the break room and let Eric arrest me."

Aidan felt his hackles rise but refused to engage. He could see her intention clear as day; she wanted to foot the blame, to veer the trouble away from her family and the farm.

Noble as it was he couldn't give it to her. "Because you didn't do it."

She let out a frustrated puff of air, pushing against the fence as if she wanted to shake it, to bend the wood with her bare hands. "You thought I was guilty when we first met, thought I was in with the dealers. What happened, Aidan? All that change when we started sleeping together?"

Aidan felt his blood heat. Fresh out of other options, she chose to antagonize, to push his buttons. She was scrapping for a fight. He wouldn't indulge her. "Stop it, Kelly."

"Why? I could've done it. A little extra school money. A roll in the hay with the detective on the case, to throw him off the trail."

The profile of Rachel Lancaster burned through Aidan's brain. The remorseless expression she wore as she murdered Paul without a second thought, of Josh Moreland's mutilated body. The line of people who'd been set up and mowed down by these selfish, immoral people.

*How many more will they harm? How many more?*

Aidan's brain fired out the words before he could stop it.

"You want to know why? Because criminals are *callus*. They don't retain relationships. They torture to maintain dominance, kill for amusement, and accuse others of their sins because they *don't think they're wrong*." Aidan leaned down, eyes level with hers. "You're no criminal, Kelly. And you can't take the fall for this. *They used you*. Don't give them more than that!"

Her head snapped up, the gold flecks of her hazel eyes glowing like embers. "I brought *drugs* onto this farm, Aidan! Onto Sophie's property! We're still fighting a legal battle to keep Keegan. Do have *any* idea what would happen if word of this leaked?!" She swung her arms out at the paddocks, illustrating like an enraged Vanna White.

"You didn't know."

"Decades of rescue work, Aidan! Shut down because of a *stupid*, naïve—" She whirled around, punching her hand into the nearest post, the force and the object colliding to break even with a dull thud. Pulling back she shook out her knuckles, the outburst seeming to do more damage to her than the inanimate wood.

Kelly curled into herself, eyes blinking rapid fire. Sensing the eruption was over, Aidan approached slowly. Taking her whacked hand, he unfurled her fingers gently, rubbed her skin. Her knuckles had started to swell, would probably bruise. An outward contusion, small compared to the injury done inside. He sandwiched her palm between his, holding, soothing. With a sniffle she closed her eyes.

"Kelly, don't do this. Don't let them win."

Her stare flipped up to his, devoid of hope, the look stabbed at him.

"They know where my mother lives." She croaked the words.

"We'll protect her, and you."

She shook her head, unshed tears glistening like stars visible in the daylight.

"They don't know that we have the shipment, Kelly. They think it's still in the Honda. We can catch them. We can stop this."

"So, I'm the bait." Tears fell as she stared aimlessly out at the hills of grass.

Aidan felt his heart sink. What he wouldn't give to take her away, remove her from all of it.

"I don't like any of this. They used you the night of the party and they're trying to use you now. I want *them* arrested. I want them sitting in a courtroom, facing the people they abused, and then I want them behind bars for the rest of their lives. With your help, Kelly."

His own voice echoed in his ears, the tone strange. It reminded him of something, a word. When he'd asked Sophie, *please.*

Kelly stared at him, silent.

Deep in the recesses of his head he knew the request was too much. A volcano of images blurred: Kelly, her mother, Sophie, Hank, Pippa, Eric... The culmination burned, the risk was—too much.

Kelly shook her head. Her eyes glassy, she tugged her hand free.

"I know you're scared."

"I can't stay, Aidan. I'm a danger to the farm."

"If you leave now it'll be harder to patrol. The dealers know you're here, it's safer to stay. We'll get cops to monitor the perimeter. The Dove group comes close, and we'll *finish* this."

*Finish them.*

A stillness fell over her, and like a soldier about to go into battle, Aidan watched her back slowly straighten, her head lift with steeled reserve.

"Okay." With a shaky breath she nodded, placing her palm on his shoulder, over his scar, the warmth of her touch a healing tingle.

"I wish I were brave like you," she whispered.

Incomprehension stunned him. The girl moved to another state alone to follow her dreams, worked her way up to every accomplishment, put others needs before her own. She handled wild horses and untamed arson detectives with steadfast optimism. And now, with little hesitation, she'd agreed to take on one of the largest drug rings on the east coast.

Aidan covered her hand with his, squeezed.

His gaze unwavering he replied, "You're the bravest woman I've ever met."

# CHAPTER 19

Kelly tapped her fingers against the counter, ready to go crazy.

With an indiscernible turn of his head, Eric eyeballed the movement, then returned his heavy stare back to the door. The knobbed plank of wood was caught in the war of their two intentions: she wanted to walk out of the thing, while it was the officer's duty to keep her safe behind it.

Beyond the man's resigned expression Kelly figured the cop didn't like the babysitting any more than she did, except composure came naturally to him, not her.

Bringing the finger drumroll to a stop, she made another loop around the kitchen, the movement not appearing to faze Eric, she had done it so much in the last few days. The bright square of living space that had once been her haven for food and rest was now a cramped pen from which she couldn't escape.

Kelly repeated the terms and conditions in her head: the police were assigned to do patrols. One to guard her mother in New York, another for the farm where she'd sworn to stay inside, out of public view.

Day one of the arrangement had been bearable. By day three she'd caught up on every TV drama in existence. Day five the pacing had started. Day six the revolving door of different officers that'd shown up got narrowed down to Eric during the day and Aidan at night. With visitors like Sophie and Pippa stopping by to keep her in touch with the farm, the time with Aidan and the updates on Keegan were the only things keeping Kelly sane.

*Keegan.* The horse had been cleared to go back to the gelding field two days ago, but the staff was holding him until Kelly could see him. She missed him, the farm—hell, even her chores were a welcome reprieve from all the inactivity, the stagnancy a waste of good energy.

Kelly huffed out a breath, lips reverberating.

"You want to see what's on cable?" Eric offered.

*If the man were any more placid he'd be using telepathy to communicate.*

"No thanks. The movies are all the same, and if I see one more reality show my brain won't recover."

Eric snorted a laugh, the two settling back into their puddle of quiet.

Familiar footsteps sounded up the stairs, making Kelly jump while Eric maintained his casual nonchalance. Nothing short of a nuclear blast could shake the guy's calm.

Aidan emerged in the doorway as Kelly sat at attention, eyeing the open sunlight behind him with unbridled desire.

"Hey, I need you check something with me," he said to Eric, voice serious.

"Sure. Let me call for a replacement." Without question Eric grabbed the two-way radio Velcro-ed on his shoulder, calling in another officer to relieve him. The first proof Kelly'd seen that the cop was dying to leave, too.

"What's up?" Kelly piped up, jockeying for her own voucher of freedom.

"It's probably nothing. Pippa noticed a car parked on one of the off roads as she came in. It's sitting a half-mile away. Could just be a motorist, but I'm not taking any chances. I have two squad cars coming as back up."

Interpreting the squawk coming from his radio, Eric frowned. "Another officer can be here in ten. You want to wait?"

"Can't I stay here alone?"

Both men looked at her, the joint inspection a soundless *no way.*

"I can guard myself," she objected. Turning to Aidan, she had a better chance at winning the visual game of chicken with him than with Eric, the cop's glare capable of boring holes through concrete. "I'll lock the door. I won't open it for anyone."

Disapproval lay clear on Eric's face, but behind the censure Kelly could see something deeper looming. Worry.

"Officer on his way," Eric said, tossing a look of caution at Aidan.

"Could it be them, the dealers?" Kelly questioned. Eric pegged her with his stare, as if warning her not to egg Aidan on.

Her heart thumped in her chest. It'd been a week with no news.

*Is this the Dove group's move?*

Frowning, Kelly didn't want them to go out alone, either of them. Better to leave her to hold down the fort than leave Aidan scouting without help. She hated the idea of them out there while the whole situation was at a standstill. Like waiting for the pivotal move in a card game, the end of which potentially fast and fatal.

"Pippa described a new model BMW, parked facing outward on the Miller's farm driveway. I've never seen anything but pickup trucks out on that road, and it backs up to Hammond's west paddocks. I want to check it out."

Eric released a breath and pointed at Kelly. "The officer's name is Moore. You don't open the door until he shows a badge, got it?"

Kelly nodded obediently, trailing the men to the door. Eric glanced away as Kelly kissed Aidan goodbye and secured the door behind them. She watched through the window, sending silent prayers of safety with them as the two disappeared into the parking lot.

Ten minutes dragged by, feeling like an hour.

Everyone had a job except her. Aidan was out in the field with Eric, while Keegan was stuck in his stall. Kelly's restlessness turned into empathy. The doctor had said the horse didn't need to be cooped up, and with a quick turn loose, he could be out in the grazing paddock.

One visit and she could...

Kelly heard her foot tapping the floor before she felt it. The minutes ticked by, tormenting her, the image of Keegan isolated in the barn making her fidget worse.

No one would notice a fast run to the barn.

She'd text Sophie afterward to tell her that she'd let Keegan out. The idea had her on her feet, her hand on the door. She stopped, guilt crippling her plan.

*No.* No leaving, no jeopardizing the work the police were doing to protect her.

The impatience made her hands tremble, an internal fight as to whether the jaunt was really all about Keegan.

She had to do something and sitting there taking up space didn't count.

In a final trump of mental negotiation, she noted the time and grabbed her recorder off the counter.

*Five minutes.*

Her apprehension blew away as she booked down the metal steps, the warm air and sun rejuvenating her in a solar rush. She dismissed the temptation to stop and lift her face toward the radiance, instead she made a beeline to the tack room, yanking free the closest lead and heading for the barn.

The shafts of light from the main barn's roof cast beams on the floor as she entered, the space undisturbed but for the soft sound of breathing coming from the corner stall. Kelly poked her head into the space, eager for a glimpse of her guy.

More beautiful than any horse she'd ever seen, Keegan raised his head, blinking as if he couldn't believe she was real.

"Hey, did you forget about me?" Kelly reached out and Keegan immediately trotted over, filling her palm with his cheek, exhaling with a sigh. "I missed you, too," she murmured, giving his ear a scratch before sliding open the gate. Hanging on a wall nail was a sweat scrapper, apparently left out by a volunteer. Keegan must have had a bath. The evidence that he'd been looked after in her absence eased Kelly's conscience a bit. She made a note to personally thank whoever had taken care of him.

She clicked on her recorder, the device hanging off the belt of her jeans, close to the horse's face, its red light glowing as it documented Keegan's respiration. Listening, Kelly didn't detect any congestion, although Keegan jumped a little at her approach, the coordination a good sign.

*Probably just overstimulation from all the medical poking and prodding.*

"Hey, it's okay." The relief she felt seeing him was a balm, although the horse's jitters seemed to get worse. Maybe he was just excited to see her. Wishing they had more time, Kelly clipped the lead rope to his halter, ready to take him out, when Keegan pulled back, yanking them both to a stop.

Had he gotten accustomed to being inside?

Two seconds out in the sunlight should cure him of that. Then she could come see him again later, after she came off house-arrest.

"Come on, boy. You ready to go?" She hoped the words would encourage, but he continued to dig in with his feet. Kelly paused to look him over. The horse's eyes went wide, nostrils flaring. "What's wrong, Keegan?"

"He doesn't like me." A deep male voice came from behind her.

Kelly spun around, her gasp caught in her throat.

The man had a medium build, tan, with a cold dark stare that registered her with complete disregard, watching her as if she weren't a person but an object standing in his way. Fear trickled down Kelly's body, chilling her as her eyes traveled down the man's arm, falling on the gun he had leveled at her chest.

Oh, God. *No.*

"Nobody likes me," the man continued, an arrogant smirk stretching over his twisted mouth.

Underneath the smooth expression Kelly could feel anger rolling off the man, a red aura of hatred.

*He must be the ring leader, the head guy Aidan had talked about.*

Kelly's heavy breaths echoed through the barn, birds launching from their perches in response as if sensing the danger. Keegan's trepidation was a hedge behind her, the horse snorting and pawing the ground with his hooves. She had to keep him calm, had to keep her wits.

*This is it. Game on.*

"I don't have much time, so we'll make this fast. *Where's the car?*" The question oozed contempt.

"I don't...know." She fought to keep the stammer out of her voice.

He smiled wider, unnaturally white teeth gleaming out of his rigid face.

Kelly's attention flipped to a square of silver flashing from the man's free hand, a lighter. She sucked in a breath as the rasp of flint conjured a small flame, ready to do damage. The wood that erected the structure around them screamed at her, every beam and balance flammable.

*Easy to destroy, to incinerate in a matter of minutes.*

Leaning to the side, he touched the glowing tongue to a string of hay, the glow moving in a blink, a wisp of gray smoke floating up into the air.

"Wait!" Kelly threw out a hand as the man closed the lighter with satisfaction.

"You *don't know*? You don't expect me to believe that, do you?" He kicked a foot at the base of the hay, the jostle inciting the growing flame.

"Why are you...?" Kelly stepped back. Keegan's flank hard at her shoulder, the horse breathed heavily, twitching as if ready to lunge, to kick. "Easy, boy." The words came out a whisper.

The man chuckled. "I'm giving your boyfriend a little homework. Cause of death takes a while to determine under normal conditions, but after a fire..." He pointed the muzzle of the gun at a box fan sitting in the corner. "Maybe a short created the spark. Oh, what a dreadful accident!" His tone turned mocking as he made an elaborate display of releasing the safety on the gun with a click.

Aidan's voice filled Kelly's head as she watched the villain live up to his profile.

*Callus. Kills for fun.*

With no preface she thought of Paul, the partner she'd never met.

*Did he die the same way, at the hands of these monsters?*

Aidan's face invaded her mind, her chest folding in. Paul's best friend. The one who loved him, grieved him.

Would Aidan grieve for her, too?

The sting in her heart answered. Their weeks together passed too quickly, and she'd never gotten a chance to...she never told him that she loved him.

*And now he'll never know.*

Kelly stared at the drug lord holding the weapon, his heartless eyes appraising. A steadiness came over her, a steel that filled her shoulders, expanded her chest. If she was going to die, she'd do so on her terms. The bastard didn't own her, had no claim to the people he'd killed, hurt, affected. She'd be damned if she'd let the rat take her out so effortlessly. No, she was going make him work for it, make him earn every breath he'd steal. He was nothing but a *thief*, a criminal, and she owed him as much mercy as he'd shown his victims.

"Let's try this again." His expression fell into one of complete malice. "Where's the car?"

"It's gone," Kelly answered defiantly.

He aimed the gun at her heart. The smoke darkened, wafting around them in a thick mist.

"Tell me where it is!"

"You *shoot* me and—"

With a flick of his hand the man shifted aim to Keegan.

Kelly's blood went cold. She shuffled to the side. There was too much of Keegan to protect, the agitated horse too big to shield with her body. She threw her arms out to corral him, her palm hitting the wall, running into—metal?

"How noble." The man's focus stayed on the horse, waiting for Kelly to falter, to waver enough for him to get a clear shot. Keegan coughed from the smoke, stilling him as the bale of hay continued to smolder, flames starting to flare.

"Tell me what I want to know and I'll let the horse go."

*Liar.* Kelly narrowed her eyes.

He was going to shoot her without remorse, and leave her and Keegan to burn. The horse swayed behind her. With a firm grip on Keegan's lead, Kelly's right hand wrapped around the plastic handle, the metal sweat scrapper secured in her grip, hidden behind the lip of the wall. A small weapon, but better than nothing. Behind the man hay ignited with a pop, the spark jumping to the next bale in the stack.

*No time.*

She felt Keegan dip behind her, the sway a signal that his hind legs were in position. Kelly breathed in, aware that the intake of murky air could be her last.

*Get ready, boy.*

"The car is here," Kelly nodded in surrender, goading the man to come close. "It's—"

The man stepped forward, and she swung with all her might, the metal teeth of the scrapper dragging macabre lines down his face.

The boom of the gun deafened in the confined space, firing at the ceiling.

In the clamor Kelly leapt away, whirling to slap Keegan on the rump, the startled horse rearing back on his hind legs, making both humans take cover. The recorder hit the floor along with the gun, the plastic skidding out of sight as the animal galloped from the barn. The man shouted, pawing at the claw-like, inflamed streaks dripping down his damaged cheek, unchecked rage twisting his features.

Kelly's ears rang with the echo of the gun as she lay in the dirt, lungs choking on the thick air. Dizzy, she peered around. The man was nowhere to be seen.

She scoured the ground.

*The gun—where's the gun? Forget it—Get up, get UP! RUN!*

Arms outstretched, a wet drop hit the skin of her arm and Kelly froze. The red dot both immobilized and marked her for dead. She rolled over in slow motion.

The man loomed above her like an angel of death, spite branded on his marred face.

Light beamed through the open barn door behind him, the hope of rescue laid just outside of her reach. Hatred morphed into pure evil on the man's face, his blood-streaked skin the mark of an executioner.

He'd take pleasure in killing her now, he'd draw it out.

Kelly stiffened, bracing for her fate, her final wish being that Aidan's eyes would be the last image she'd see on this earth. His smiling face.

The man craned forward as terror turned Kelly's body to ice.

No, there'd be no peace in the end.

She cringed as the man wound back his fist, the air whistling as his hand thrust forward.

Striking like a cobra, the morbid impact of knuckles hitting skin resounded.

Kelly felt a burst of pain, disorientation; a fleeting consciousness before her vision tilted, and the world went dark.

"Damn it!"

Eric watched as profanity popped and crackled out of Aidan like a stoked fire. The detective pivoted around and kicked the tire of the deserted BMW, his frustration radiating.

Eric gave the man some space, accustomed to the flare ups.

None of the venting was bad, just noisy. *Boom, Bam, Shit!*

Aidan huffed a bit, paced. Blew his stack some more and then came back down. The guy's way of dealing. His process.

Eric wondered if any of the other guys at the station knew that about him.

Eric remembered when he'd gotten the full debrief, back before he'd first approached the detective. According to the rumors, Aidan Wright was impulsive, a hot head. And the arson cop's scarred past and crappy people skills got him slapped him with a bad reputation fast.

*Reckless, explosive, doesn't play well with others.*

The labels were proven, but did anyone bother to get to know his other traits?

*Loyal. Fearless.*

"Damn it, Eric, say something. What am I not seeing?" Aidan commanded.

*Cocky.*

Eric walked over.

"You're seeing an abandoned car. I see it, too." Bare interior with license plates belonging to a nearby resident. Not reported stolen. The expensive model of car stood out, not the brand name of choice for a local farmer or minimum-wage teenager, leaving only the possibility of a trespasser.

The timing and position made Eric nervous, too.

*Suspicious.*

Eric surveyed the area for the tenth time, the stony expanse an overgrown common ground set amongst a stretch of wild grass and trees. Well concealed, it was a good place to camp...or hide.

*A strange car showing up near the farm. Not good.*

Eric's intuition was on high alert, and his gut had never failed him. He didn't dare underestimate the resolve of the Dove group. After years of working the beat he'd come across his fair share of smarmy, but the lower rungs of street corner drug dealers paled compared the upper ranks. The pro-level of drug lords were their own special brand of sinister. Unlike the rookies, one shot didn't stop them. Like water snakes, one attacked while another waited in the wings.

*You needed two rounds to take them out.*

Hand on his gun, Eric scanned the trees, the slight sway made by the wind putting him on edge. His attention rotated back to Aidan.

He watched the guy's eyes squint to find more, his profile determined. Undaunted.

He had to admit that Aidan did fit all of the negative descriptors to the tee, but then again Eric never bought into the stereotypes. Arrogance to one person was courage to another. It was all based on who did the looking. And no one else factored in the fact that the guy had been through hell. They just wrote off the loss of his partner as a career-ending injury. A tragic pitfall of the job.

Beyond the macho shithead exterior, Eric and Aidan had that in common. They both knew what loss felt like.

*With lucid clarity,* Eric mused, his father's dark hair and eyes filling his mind like a glassy pool of water, the snapshot suspended in time. The old man never changed, never aged.

Eric drowned out the image, mentally slapping ripples in it until the memory faded away.

*Same sorrow, different causes.*

Eric had been assigned to watch Aidan, to keep him in play and on the level, but along the way Eric had fallen head-long into the mission, too. The Dove group needed to be apprehended for more than just public safety. Kelly was a good girl, and Josh Moreland still a kid. One life shaken, the other destroyed at the hands of Marcus De Silva. The drug lord needed to be taken down, for no other reason than the justice it'd give his victims.

Eric glanced at Aidan.

And the solace it'd give his...friend.

Tantrum subsiding, Eric watched Aidan take a steadying breath, his gaze flipping over to the swath of trees that bordered the farm. Following his line of vision, Eric saw Sophie's pale yellow house peek out from the branches of foliage. They were close, Hammond's barns within walking distance.

With no sign of the vehicle's owner, the cold engine indicated that the thing had been stationed there for a while. And none of that evidence was enough to warrant a search. Which left them two choices: stay and look or head back to Kelly.

The two law men went quiet, thoughts syncing between them. The mindreading seemed to have formed during their short association, but Eric attributed it to the job. Police work was teamwork, always.

"Let's go. I don't want her left alone," Aidan announced.

Eric nodded, going along with the detective's call, knowing that the guy had more than a professional reason for wanting to get back to the farm. Aidan hadn't come out and admitted that Kelly was his girlfriend, but seeing the two together said it all. While Eric didn't readily condone fraternization with a witness, he couldn't argue with Aidan's feelings for the girl.

Eric had made an exception, a rare one given the circumstances, because Aidan deserved happiness. He saw that the girl kindled something in the Aidan, a joy that had been beaten down and dormant. She'd brought the guy back to life.

*Amazing the effect love had on a man.*

Not that Eric was an expert on the subject. Love was a rocky road he'd been dragged over one too many times.

The literal sound of rubber on gravel brought both their heads around as a squad car rolled down the dirt road, and trundled to a stop in front of them, a uniform popping out the driver's side.

"Moore," Eric greeted, inspecting the passenger seat through the car's windshield.

Empty. "Where's Kelly?"

"That's what I'm here to ask you. The loft was vacant. I checked the parking lot and the surrounding barns. Did you bring her with you?"

"No." Aidan barked the word, stepping up shoulder to shoulder with Eric. He opened his mouth just as birds erupted from the trees, the sound of a gunshot stunning them all silent.

The three cops twisted the direction of the farm, the gray-blue cloud rising from the barn making them scramble into action.

Aidan took off at a dead run as Moore tore at his radio, speaking rapid-fire. "Moore calling in a ten-forty-seven. Shots fired at twenty-four-ten Sundown Road. Requesting ten-thirty for possible ten-ten. Use caution."

Eric ran for his squad car and stopped short. A small movement hit his peripheral vision. His head swiveled the direction of the trees, the foliage swaying to more than just wind.

His inner radar wailed. *Someone's in the woods.*

Moore stood behind the open car door, waiting. Eric signaled him to halt.

The leaves moved in a line, branches snapping as a flash of a body, bigger than a deer, ran through the green.

*Getting away.*

Moore got back on the radio. "Ten-forty-seven, half-mile west. Possible ten-fifty-nine. Carson and Moore in pursuit."

Eric spared a glance toward the growing cloud over Hammond's before he bolted down the trail, legs pumping, propelling him as fast as he could move; Moore right behind him.

Eric knew that the movement could be nothing, a startled animal.

*Or a suspect fleeing the scene.*

If wrong, Aidan could be running head-first into an attack without backup.

*If this is the wrong call—*

Oxygen sawed through Eric's lungs, his intuition rolling over him like an undertow, the thoughts reeling.

*Snakes. Pairs. One strikes, one waits.*

Moore stayed close behind him, stepping up as Eric's reinforcement. There were only three of them on the scene, leaving Aidan the odd man out.

*And running straight into a gunfight.*

The flutter of leaves proved they were gaining on the one who'd fled.

Heart in his throat, Eric ran harder, a mental plea rotating in step with his pounding stride: *Please let Kelly Monroe be alive.*

# CHAPTER 20

Aidan hit the farm's common paddock like a madman, tumbling to a stop at the front gate, his lungs burning.

The door to the house flew open as people filed out: Hank, Sophie, and Pippa emerging, all gaping at the scene unfolding in front of them. Smoke poured from the main barn, the progression fast; flames ready to poke through the rafters at any minute.

"Was that a gunshot?" Sophie's face went alight with fear as she caught sight of the burning barn. *"Oh my God!"*

A loud whiny had everyone turning. A large shape caught Aidan's attention, pacing the open area through the haze. Aidan recognized Keegan, lead rope dangling, the horse pawing the dirt in a frenzy.

"What the hell is going on?" Sophie went for Keegan at the same time as Aidan, the horse prancing in agitation, lashing the ground with the rope. Keegan's eyes peeled wide as they approached, whinnying and thrusting his head back. Aidan grabbed the animal's lead, unable to calm him down.

"Get the staff and volunteers inside. Direct police reinforcements to the barn. Go, *now!*" Aidan commanded as he handed the horse off, the sound of Sophie's pleas for him to wait lost in the heartbeat that filled his ears. Unholstering his gun, Aidan aimed the weapon at the ground as he took measured steps toward the mouth of the main barn, readying himself for the worst.

*Kelly could be...*

His eyes watered as smoke clouds billowed out from the top of the door. He sidled up, took a deep breath and rounded the corner. Heat slapped into him, the smell burning his nostrils, invading his lungs. Flames licked up the left wall as the tower of hay bales glowed, sucking all the clean air out of the space. Spreading fast, the flames would eat up the wood within minutes.

*No time to wait for backup.*

Gun leveled, Aidan searched the ground for shapes, his vision blurring as he saw—

*No, NO!*

All reason rushed out of him at the sight. Kelly's limp body lay unmoving, still and quiet as Marc De Silva retrieved a gun from the ground, his demeanor calm. Victorious.

She was...gone.

*Son of a—*

In an explosion of rage Aidan vaulted, colliding with De Silva's craned body like a freight train, pinning the villain to a stall door. Dual clunks of metal hit the ground as Aidan grasped the bastard's shirt and threw him against the hard wall again, and again, the guy's back a battering ram against the creaking wood.

A glow of red and gold illuminated the room as flames climbed the far wall, catching and igniting the cross beams, fumes tumbling out of the windows and doors. Aidan sucked in the dirty air, the biological imperative of breathing taking a back seat to his anger.

He had the bastard in his grasp, the scoundrel in charge of it all.

Aidan threw the first punch, catching De Silva's chin in an uppercut. He relished the grunt of pain that came out of the drug lord, the groan a long awaited justice. His knuckles wet, it dawned on Aidan that the guy's face was already strewn with blood, serrated lines dribbling crimson as if he'd been mauled by a lion.

*Kelly fought back.*

The fact made him shake, his hands quivering with fury.

*She fought back and lost...*

Aidan slammed De Silva again as his throat burned, squeezing the last drop out of the transient oxygen that fed his blood. He intended to get his licks in with every last ounce of his energy, whatever he had left.

Aidan palmed De Silva's throat, ready to squeeze. He paused. As if standing outside himself, Aidan watched like a spectator, his brain and heart at war. The devil in his hands deserved no protocol, no due diligence.

De Silva had burned, killed. Fueled the addictions of thousands of college kids.

A loud pop emanated overhead, a girder corroding above them, ready to snap.

De Silva slid down the stall's bars and Aidan hefted the rat back up, death anxiety and common sense expunged from his gray matter. He gripped the bastard's shirt, wishing it were his skin. Head rolling against the rails of the stall, De Silva's black eyes focused, his stare shifting to Kelly's body. Chest heaving, Aidan glanced at the ground. The visual stabbed him. Kelly's lean legs lay folded in a heap, arms limp at her sides. A line of blood trickled down her temple, her motionless cheek swollen, bruised.

*Too late.*

Aidan turned back and the villain smiled, venomous.

Hauling back, the crack of Aidan's fist as it made contact with De Silva's jaw ricocheted, the pain in his hand a numb afterthought as he swung again, pounding the bastard in the chin, the stomach, the repetition of *oofs!* sweet music to him. Aidan moved like a prizefighter, his vision gone red.

He didn't care if there was anything left of the thug to stand trial, he wanted Marc De Silva to *bleed.*

Aidan wound up for another hit when a forearm hurled forward, bone hitting bone as De Silva blocked. The counter that followed came out of nowhere, knocking Aidan in the jaw, throwing him backward.

Stumbling, Aidan's foot knocked something—
*Shit, his gun.*

His pistol knocked into De Silva's discarded Glock 19, the pieces knocking off each other like pool balls, sliding to a stop at their feet.

Aidan and the felon jumped at the same time, diving for the weapons, their bodies colliding, hitting the floor in fierce tandem. Arms locked in a death grip, Aidan dug in, the heat baking his skin as the fire traveled across the floor. Black clouds rippled across the ceiling as De Silva rolled, trying to break Aidan's grip.

The barn fumed, a consuming trail of flames slowing over the mats and regaining speed with the straw lining the stalls. Aidan kicked his head back, noting the proximity of the fire to the girl's lifeless body.

*Kelly.*

A blaze blew a line up the door of the stall next to them, the last of the air evaporating.

*No time.*

Aidan's upper body quivered from the force of the deadlock, De Silva glaring down at him with pure hatred. Aidan pivoted his head, the handle of his Baretta flashing, inches from his face.

If he could just free his hand and—

Something shifted in the distance.

Through the haze and dirt Kelly's head lolled. Her eyes closed, movement flickered underneath her eyelids, her nostrils widening.

*Breathing. She's breathing!*

De Silva's face went sinister, reanimating the struggle as he yanked his hand free and slapped it against Aidan's face, pushing the detective's chin back. Aidan's neck cracked, throat stretched to a breaking point as his free hand reached for his gun.

A gag rang out, Aidan's head slanted toward the sound. Kelly's back arched as coughs wracked her body. Flopping to her side, her eyes fluttered open, her dazed eyes locking in on Aidan's.

"Kelly—get out!" he croaked, his hand brushing the Beretta's muzzle, a sweeping motion beating him to the grab. De Silva bounded to the side and gripped the gun's handle, the criminal's eyes glowing with satisfaction in the flickering light. De Silva popped the safety and reared back. Aidan wrestled with the business end of the weapon, the barrel edged up, aligning point-blank with his forehead.

The memory of the drive in Kelly's Jeep came to him.

*The end of the road.*

Aidan stared down the barrel of his fate, waiting for the final *pop.*

A swoop of force interjected, a flash of brown, and a crack that knocked De Silva's hand away. *A foot?*

Aidan craned his head in astonishment to see Kelly's arms and legs forming a weak crab crawl; her booted feet bounding up and back like fists. Kicking. Fighting.

"*Little bitch!*" De Silva growled, reaching out in retaliation. He snagged Kelly's angle and dragged her toward him, her small form collapsing, making a line across the dirt.

*No you don't—*

Aidan wound his arm to punch. Kelly didn't retreat. She barreled forward, her face drawn with determination. There was no terror, no intimidation in her face, only courage as unwavering arms propelled her, her feet delivering steady hits.

A connection surged between them as Kelly raised her free leg and horse-kicked the bastard in the shoulder with all her might. De Silva's bloody face scowled in pain, relinquishing his hold on the gun, the blow flipping the villain around as Aidan nailed his stomach with a follow-up punch, the *one-two* leveling him.

The drug lord hit the ground in a lump, mouth opening and closing like a fish out of water as Aidan's eyes snapped to the ceiling. Wood planks compacted one by one with audible cracks, the flames closing in on them.

Aidan stood up, a whoosh of vertigo making him sway on his feet. The air gone, they needed to get out. The door was an open square to freedom, only steps away.

Aidan looked to Kelly, her legs splayed out on the ground as she crawled toward something on the floor, a hunk of plastic lying next to the tower of burning hay.

*Her recorder.*

"Kelly, *don't!*" Aidan shouted.

Playing possum, De Silva's skull swiveled on his spine as Aidan watched in horror. With military precision the drug lord spun to his feet and sprung forward. He seized Kelly by the hair, dragging her to her feet as if she were no more than a rag doll. Kelly thrashed to get free as the bastard pulled her backward, hunching her over the bank of nipping flames.

"De Silva!" Aidan bellowed.

The bastard made a show of nudging her, testing his limits. The murderer's ultimatum was clear, he planned to walk out alive.

*One push, that's all it'll take.*

Adrenaline threaded Aidan's pulse, Kelly's terrified stare meeting his, her fear illuminated in the firelight.

"Let her go—and we'll negotiate," Aidan said, voice booming.

The rat snorted. A tearing sound stilled them all as De Silva wrenched Kelly's nape, hair ripping as he navigated her over the undulating flame. "Not much to negotiate, you have the goods."

Bristling, Aidan held himself in check, body ready to jump as the ceiling rained sparks on them. Kelly winced and pushed back against the bastard's grip, the flames of the burning hay bales under her growing, leaping up as if trying to touch her.

"Stop!" Aidan broke down, reaching out a hand.

*Switch, take me instead.*

The murderer smiled and Aidan's game face returned full force, staring the bastard down. Kelly went still, eerily calm, her elbow covertly inching back, ready to strike.

Panic detonated in Aidan's chest.

*He'll throw her in—into the fire.*

Aidan's shoulders arched forward, his gaze locked on Kelly's as she mouthed something.

Two silent words: *Love. You.*

"Kelly!" Aidan shouted and lunged forward as the events exploded before his eyes.

Kelly hit De Silva in the gut; the two losing their balance together, both falling face-first into the inferno.

The wave of heat slammed into Kelly, the scorching sting hitting so fast she hoped the accompanying pain would pass as quickly. On instinct, her arms whipped up to block her face, an autonomic defense against the inevitable as the singe intensified; building to a final degree.

The throbbing at the back of her head eased, the relief accompanying the drop, the look on Aidan's face a horrible escort to oblivion. Behind her Kelly felt her captor's body push away, scrambling to save himself. In the scuffle there were screams, her own, and that of her jailor, then all went still. The world stopped.

The smell of burning flesh filled her nose as two strong arms wrapped around her, yanking her backward. A gasp of air lodged in her throat as the momentum cast her sideways, her legs staggering as she unconsciously followed the trail of fresh oxygen. The main paddock appeared in front of her like a dream, clusters of people running up as she gagged, dragging in the clean air. Sirens wailed as a parade of blue, white, and yellow colored uniforms filed out of rescue vehicles, Sophie leading the pack. Kelly's foggy head took in the circus of overstimulation.

She'd made it out. But how?

Kelly turned to gape at the scene she'd exited. Bolts of flame surged through the barn's roof, the walls deteriorating as flakes of ash peppered the air. A cloud of black poured out of the door.

Alarms flared in her head, a crazed jolt of energy lifting her dead feet as she realized who she'd left inside.

"Aid-Aidan!" Kelly struggled to scream, her stilted gait making her slip backward on the woodchips, her world rolling in reverse.

No, someone holding her back.

"Kelly, stop! Stop!" A familiar voice filled her ears. *Sophie.*

More forms appeared in Kelly's periphery, approaching the fire with equipment. The light of the blaze illuminated their stern faces, the water hoses, and ambulances.

They stood around motionless, a plan of rescue in place but not implemented.

*Go in! He's alive! He's ALIVE!*

"Let me go! Aidan! AIDAN!" Kelly shouted at the blaze, fighting to break free. Sophie didn't let up as the coughs dropped Kelly to her knees in the woman's hold. Her throat burning, Kelly took heaving breaths. "Aidan's—still—"

A male cry broke the air, stunning onlookers silent as a ball of fire stumbled from the barn. Kelly's heart stopped as a man, set ablaze like a movie stunt gone wrong, staggered across the paddock, shrieking in agony.

*"Aidan?"* The name left Kelly's lips in a petrified murmur.

Kelly battled to make out the fireball's face, the man's charred clothes making his form indistinguishable. Launching to her feet, she tried to yank away, to disentangle her limbs from Sophie's.

Then another shadow burst from the barn, a ghost holding some kind of heavy tarp in his hands, the material flapping as he jutted toward the human Roman candle. The crowd watched in rapt attention as Kelly went to her knees again.

Aidan tackled the man on fire, wrapping the square of material around him with one cast, patting the edges with rapid movements. The human flame hit the ground with a moan as Aidan sped around him, smothering sparks, snuffing out the fire.

"Good God." Kelly heard Sophie mutter as the medical teams converged.

Quivering on the ground with pain, De Silva lay covered, his hair burned away; patches of exposed muscles visible from the open places where the damp horse blanket cocooned him.

For that one moment, Kelly felt pity for the drug lord, mutilated and helpless. Her thoughts then turned to the boys at the bonfire. It was ironic justice that the man now knew what his victims had suffered.

Kelly's eyes shifted to Aidan. He weaved on his feet, his left arm tucked to his chest. Waving off the EMTs who approached, Aidan beckoned to two of the cops. He barked quick orders as the officers nodded and returned to the throng of first responders.

"Where's—?" Aidan turned, eyes wild as he honed in on Kelly.

Sophie's arms retracted as Aidan lurched forward. Kelly stood up and tripped into him, hugging him with all her might.

"You okay?" He clasped her face with one palm, rubbing his thumb gingerly over her bruised cheek.

"I'm fine. You're alive! Aidan!" she exclaimed, squeezing him hard. A small grunt came out of him and Kelly looked up, noticing that he was favoring one side of his body.

*He's hurt.*

She stepped back, evaluating him from head to toe, her eyes catching on the limb he had cradled to his side. He extended his hand, revealing the inflamed patch of magenta skin that covered his forearm.

"This man needs medical attention!" Kelly yelled, all but attacking a wandering paramedic. The EMT rushed over.

"It's nothing," Aidan fronted.

Kelly spared him the accusatory glare.

*He pulled me to safety. Put his arm through fire.*

"Sit," she demanded as the EMT pitched a treatment camp.

Quick with the burn ointment and bandages, the EMT utilized his supplies as Kelly stayed close to observe the damage. A first degree burn. Kelly trailed soft fingers down the underside of Aidan's wound, trying to stay out of the paramedic's way while still holding him.

She never wanted to leave Aidan again.

"If I'm getting fixed up, you are, too. Hold this —there." Aidan picked up an ice pack from the first aid kit, placing it one-handedly to

Kelly's bruised cheek. She balked at the cold, but she held the arctic square to her face while he held still for his bandages, the compromise unspoken. It seemed to ease Aidan to watch Kelly nurse her black eye, and a sudden wave of pride came over her.

She'd taken a punch, had stood up to a drug kingpin.

Kelly winced as the cold pack hit the hyper-sensitive area of her cheek.

She didn't intend on doing that ever again.

As the paramedic wound the gauze around Aidan's blistered skin, guilt, fresh and unwarranted rose behind Kelly's rib cage.

Her getting clobbered was nothing.

The night of the bonfire drifted back to her, the screams. As if reliving the nightmare, a holler of pain brought everyone's attention to the gurney in the middle of the paddock. Medics gathered around De Silva, a group of five EMTs carefully lifting the man's backboard onto the transport bed, the drug lord's face twisting in misery at every bump. Onlookers paused to grimace as the group trundled the criminal into the ambulance, taking off moments later with sirens blaring.

Aidan's eyes stayed on the vehicle until the lights of the police escort flickered out of sight. His gaze then returned to the smoldering barn. The firefighters had sprayed down the last of the blaze with water—the cindered roof caved in, the frame of the blackened building all that remained.

Kelly watched his profile in the dimming light; he looked numb.

"Aidan, you should have left me—" she started.

She got cut off as Aidan lifted her chin with his good hand. His lips met hers, a deep kiss ending the argument. When Kelly opened her eyes, Aidan smiled.

She thanked the sky. They'd made it out: Aidan, Keeg— *Keegan!*

Kelly's head swiveled around, glancing franticly between the uniformed bodies.

"He's in the mare shoot," Aidan said, reading her mind. He kept still while the EMT finished his dressing, nodding his head the direction of the paddock.

Discarding her ice pack without a second thought, Kelly rushed over. Keegan paced at the gate, the horse's round eyes glowing. A whinny erupted from him when he saw her as if he were outraged at having been penned up during all the action.

Relief spread through Kelly at the sight of him, her puff of laughter ringing.

Aidan and Keegan, alive and safe.

She was lucky. Damned lucky.

Keegan tucked his muzzle into her palm as she stroked his nose, the horse calming at her touch. She ran her fingers down the lines of his cheek.

"You listened when I needed you. You're such a *good boy,"* she praised, holding back her tears.

"He loves you."

Kelly turned. Sophie stood with Hank, her husband's supportive arm encircling her as they surveyed the damage. The barn stood extinguished as responders toured the charred

insides, retracting gear from the four
brittle walls.

"Sophie, I'm so sorry."

The glow that overtook her face disarmed
Kelly. Grasping her hand, Sophie pulled her into
a hug that warmed Kelly's soul.

"Everything I care about is right here,"
Sophie said softly. Aidan appeared over Kelly's
shoulder. Sophie stepped back, retaining her
hold on Kelly, the woman's solemn eyes trailing
over the barn's destruction. "We'll be all right.
We'll build again."

Kelly looked over to Aidan, his happy
expression evaporating, his attention drawn the
direction of the break room. Kelly stiffened,
following the line of his gaze.

A legion of police clustered around a
handcuffed woman being led straight toward
them. Officer Carson followed behind them, his
stern expression that of a warden on guard.
Every step the captive took forward was one of
defiance as her dark curls blew behind her in
the clouded air, her hard, red-brown eyes
securitizing her environs with contempt.

Aidan bristled as the caravan stopped in front
of them, Rebecca's ragged appearance
discernible on closer view, grass stained and
muddy as if she'd been dragged through the
jungle. Her red gaze shot daggers, the dark
circles under her eyes and the dirty clothes not
dulling the woman's obvious resentment.

Kelly felt her skin prickle. She'd stood alone
in a room with this woman.

*This deadly woman.*

Sophie took a stance next to them, her shoulders squared.

"I didn't want to throw this on you now," Eric said as he gauged Aidan. "But we caught her fleeing the scene. She parked the stolen car at the east woods, and this was inside." Eric held up a large, plastic evidence bag, a bright red lead rope coiled inside.

Kelly put her hand to her throat.

*The missing lead from the tack room.*

"Along with a handgun and serrated knife," Eric added. "We need an ID to book her." Eric focused on Aidan, closure written on the officer's face. Aidan's stare went detached, utterly neutral as the woman shot him a hateful look.

"Be sure to add murder to the list of charges. This is Rachel Lancaster."

Aidan turned to Kelly.

"Rebecca LaCorte," Kelly said in a whisper. The woman pegged her with a scowl.

"Officer Carson," Sophie said, stepping in front of Kelly, as if shielding her. "Please escort this felon off my property." The eye contact between the women flared, Rachel losing the stare-down as Sophie's glower went imperial.

"Yes, ma'am," Eric said with a nod to the others. "We have what we need. Thank you."

Kelly could swear that she'd caught the glint of Eric's smirk, the expression dissolving as quickly as it had appeared on the officer's face; a wave cresting and ebbing.

The cops led Rachel away as Aidan watched, motionless except for the rise and fall of his chest.

Eric turned to him, eyeing the fresh gauze on Aidan's arm. "I'm sorry I wasn't there to back you up."

"You followed procedure," Aidan said. "And I couldn't catch them both on my own." His gaze trailed over Rachel's retreating form before floating over to the clusters of police. A figure jutted through the crowd, the badge on the man's chest bigger than the others.

"Capt. Reeves," Eric said. "I'll run interference, give you a few minutes."

Aidan reached out and gripped the officer's arm. "Thank you, Eric. For everything."

The cop clasped Aidan's upper arm to avoid his injury, his sincere eyes smiling.

They released one another, and with a glance at Kelly, a nod to Sophie, Eric made a beeline for their boss.

Sophie heaved a loud sigh. "Well, I'm going to go call the insurance company." She laid a kiss on Aidan's cheek, his expression one of surprise. "Glad you're still here," she said, her eyes narrowing with authority. "And don't you *ever* scare me like that again."

With a gentle tug Hank led her away, the couple making a slow trail back to the house.

Behind them Keegan let out a snort, the sound directed at Aidan. A plea for attention. Aidan obliged him; the three of them standing together in comfortable silence. Kelly couldn't help but watch Aidan, mesmerized by his face.

He'd saved her life. He'd run into a burning building and faced down an armed criminal.

*My real life hero.*

"What are you thinking?" he asked.

"That you walked through fire for me," she said, her eyes starting to blink from more than the lingering smoke.

"So did you..." he countered, his forehead creased, as if he'd come to a conclusion about something. "And you didn't get burned." He let out a chuckle, adoration glinting in the blue flame of his eyes.

"What?" She tugged on his sleeve until he leaned down to meet her nose to nose. "What are *you* thinking?"

"That I love you, too. Fire Walker."

And he kissed her passionately before she could argue.

# CHAPTER 21

*One Year Later*

The newspaper lay in a flimsy pile on Aidan's kitchen counter, the monochrome image of Josh Moreland sitting on the witness stand of a court room staring up at him. The boy's disfigured mouth was open, frozen in mid-sentence, describing the events of the bonfire.

Kelly's recorder lay on the counter in the background, the audio proof that De Silva had been the one behind the Dove ring and the one who'd started the fire. The testimonies were three dimensional in Aidan's mind, as he'd been present when the photo was taken. The boy had sat down next to him after his turn on the stand, all of the victims present for the sentencing, ready to testify. Aidan was witness to both the crime and the fanfare of journalists jotting down notes and jumping to snap pictures. The flash of the cameras highlighted the marks on the boy's skin, the blemishes much less noticeable in person.

Josh had healed a lot since his accident. On the inside and out.

The thought made Aidan smile. Justice had taken a while, but it'd been served in the end.

Aidan glanced down. His arm lay at rest atop the paper, next to a steaming cup of coffee, his marred skin the same texture as Josh's.

*Identical scars*. Birth by fire.

Aidan scanned the rest of the article, his eyes locking onto an archive photo from the arraignment. Swathed in large patches of translucent white film, Marcus De Silva's unresponsive eyes stared off the page, his guilty plea barely a mumble. Rachel Lancaster's profession of guilt was given the next day, the judge's ruling swift and ironclad. Both criminals were sentenced to life in prison, along with the five men affiliated with the Dove group, all of them apprehended within weeks of their ringleaders' capture.

*All the ends tied up.*

While the victims involved were changed forever.

The deep rumble of an engine rattled the window behind him, winning the bid for Aidan's attention.

*She's here.*

Through the gossamer curtains, He watched Kelly's Jeep trundle down the driveway, its volcanic idle announcing her arrival.

Unexpected nerves shook him as he reached into the pocket of his pants, fingers wrapping around the little velvet box. He'd checked on the ring every five minutes since he'd picked the thing up the day before. He'd had it custom created with the local jeweler, and he needed to give the thing to her soon or risk losing it.

Aidan pushed the window's curtain out his way with his hand. Kelly's petite leg jutted out of the car, hopping her down to the ground. She bounced when she walked, enthusiasm in her gait as if her entire body was happy. Aidan knew that she liked to come in the back door so she could make her routine stop to see Keegan first, the horse waiting for her at the fence like a dog.

Aidan lost sight of her as she turned the corner of the house, and transferred his view to the window above the kitchen sink. Just in time to catch her surprise.

Two horses there to welcome her instead of one.

"Hi there, girl!"

Aidan heard Kelly's elated voice through the glass.

*Present number one—received.*

Aidan grinned as Kelly dished out the dual-handed attention first to Keegan and then Moe, both animals flipping their tails and snorting with excitement.

The his and hers equine scene was complete with the three-acre stretch of grass behind them, divided down the middle by a fence; the left side Keegan's paddock, the right, Moe's.

Aidan hadn't minded the loss of his back yard. The two multi-stall barns didn't take up that much yardage, and they were built using fire safe materials. Along with the covered hay cabinets, the whole setup anchored the outside structures nicely. A place Keegan readily claimed as his home.

Aidan didn't waste time in adopting Keegan after the barn fire. Once the legal dispute with the racetrack had settled in Hammond's favor, Aidan signed the papers and brought the horse home. Keegan had galloped around the field like a yearling that first day. A racehorse at heart, Aidan thought the guy would never run out of steam. In the weeks that followed, Keegan laid claim to the grass, acting like he'd been put out to pasture. As if Keegan were ready to be retired. Aidan had to admit, the lug had grown on him, attitude and all.

The horse belonged with him. And with Kelly.

And Keegan had mellowed even more after Sophie had brought Moe over the day before. The moment Moe was released into her paddock the equine couple kept close to one another despite the partition, the mare a sweet companion to Keegan's bold temperament. Aidan could see them sticking together.

Which brought on other decisions.

Keegan had been too sick to be gelded when he was at Hammond's, so in fact, Aidan had adopted a stallion. As the mates nuzzled each other over the fence Aidan envisioned a foal with Keegan's coloring and Moe's temperament.

*Wright Stables.* Had a nice ring to it.

He smiled at the thought and flipped his gaze to Kelly, her hair glowing burgundy in the morning sun.

*And maybe a rambunctious little boy with auburn hair.*

Aidan thumbed at the ring box.

Keegan stood at attention behind Kelly, the horse's big brown eyes illuminated, his head down low as she scratched between his ears. The male then stepped away to allow the attention to go to Moe.

*What a gentleman.* Aidan would have to tease him about that later.

Kelly gave them each a final pat and climbed the back stairs. Aidan jumped to meet her at the door.

"Hey there." She greeted him with a kiss, the room growing brighter simply because she was in it.

"Hey." Aidan looked her over. His girl looked better in jeans than any supermodel on a magazine cover. The nylon jacket that covered her shoulders had *UMBC Biology* stitched in red, black, and gold. The insignia of her new college. She'd been so thrilled to start the dual-degree program, earning both her masters and a PhD at the same time, the school accepting her despite what they'd seen in her file.

Which proved they had brains.

A brilliant student, his girl was destined to go far. She'd already wowed her professors, turning down three other out-of-state colleges to stay in Maryland.

Aidan told himself that she stayed for him. And Keegan.

Mostly him. And because she'd found the right school.

"You fostered Moe?" she questioned, bringing Aidan back to the main event.

"Not foster," he replied, hand going to his pocket.

He knew that the traditional thing would be to take Kelly out to a fancy dinner. Someplace formal with candles and ambiance, but he didn't want to propose in front of strangers. He had the feeling Kelly wouldn't want it that way either.

Kelly was worth the crystal and champagne, but Aidan wanted the moment to be for *her*. Just the two of them.

Aidan knew his girl—she liked the smell of dirt and leather, fresh air and horses.

"You mean...we're keeping her?" Kelly's face lit up.

"I signed the papers yesterday."

She jumped up into his arms, warming him from head to toe. Aidan held her close, letting her feet dangle.

"You happy?" he asked in her ear, bringing her nose to his.

"Very. Keegan is too." She smiled as the morning sun put a halo around her, his personal angel.

"It was supposed to be a surprise for later. You're home early—" The fact dawned on him. "Shit, the barn raising's today, isn't it?"

Kelly laughed, the sound like auditory beams of sunlight. "It's a ribbon cutting. For the Sophia L. Hammond indoor training ring." She patted his chest. "Already built. You don't even have to get sweaty."

"Darn, I like to get sweaty." He eyed her legs.

"I know you do," she said suggestively as she stepped over to the counter. The sun chose that minute to go behind a cloud, levity fading with the light as her eyes honed in on the newspaper.

"They sentenced them all," Aidan said, summarizing.

She turned back to him. "Are you okay?"

Concern flickered in her green stare, the same as when she'd stood in front of the flames, staring down her death. He glanced at the table, the drug lord's face gazing back at him.

Aidan recalled his testimony. The explanation of how he'd tried to get everyone out alive. It came down to one decision: De Silva or Kelly.

"That is in the past. Right now, I'm here with you," he said, leaning over to kiss her gently. When they parted, she ran her palm over his forearm and retained his hand, pulling him toward the door.

*Now or never.*

He tugged back, bringing her to a halt.

"Moe is one part of the gift. I have something else for you."

She turned to look up at him, puzzled.

"Kelly, I thought about this. It's been over a year and you...you spend every night over here and I...wanted...You can finish with school first, but I want us to—"

Crap, he was botching this already.

*Smooth, Wright. Real smooth.*

"—Keegan isn't the only one who needs company."

Kelly's eyes went wide as he fumbled to pull out the box, the edges catching on the material of his pocket, forcing him to yank the velvet block free.

"Aidan," she said his name on a gasp.

He froze.

Maybe she didn't want this. Was he asking too soon?

He looked into her eyes, the words forming, the truth coming out on its own.

"Kelly, I love you. You're—you're the woman I want to grow old with." He flipped the lid open, revealing the goods. "Marry me."

She gaped at the one-carat round diamond, and then at him.

"Yes," she whispered, breathless.

"Yes?" He hadn't realized that he'd stopped breathing too, his heart starting up a drumroll in his ears.

"Yes!" She jumped at him again, this time peppering his face with kisses.

Relishing the ambush, Aidan stopped her lips and deepened their connection, their hands roaming so much that Aidan had to make them stop to put the ring on her shaking left hand. The stone sparkled, the dainty gold band a perfect fit.

Kelly. His girl. His wife.

She brought their palms together, lacing their fingers as she beamed up at him.

"I am the luckiest girl who ever lived." She darted up on her tiptoes for another kiss, the soft contact of her mouth sending heat through Aidan's body. She paused to smile against his lips. "We can be a little late, you know."

Without further permission Aidan popped his fiancée off her feet, his plodding steps the swagger of a lucky man.

At that moment the sun reemerged full force, illuminating the house in golden victory as Aidan carried his heart down the hall to the bedroom, and into their bright future together.

# AUTHOR BIO

Shelley spent her early years living abroad which resulted in a love of philosophy as well as a big imagination. The joy of creating plots in her mind started early along with her love of nature.

An intermediate photographer and avid walker, Shelley exercises her mind with writing, her heart with pictures, and her body with the steady beat of her sneakers.

A late bloomer, she returned to school to earn a BA in English that has been since deemed her "First Born." Through her years of study she gained a deep appreciation for the writing process, able to view the page as an author, editor and reader. From classic literature to contemporary romance, she loves getting lost in a good story.

Shelley is a member of the Romance Writers of America as well as her RWA state chapter of the Maryland Romance Writers.